Readers love JOHN INMAN

Acting Up

"This was a quick fun read."

—Alpha Book Club

"…*Acting Up* turned out to be unexpectedly sweet and enjoyable…"

—Just Love: Queer Book Reviews

Ben and Shiloh

"Author John Inman has built a family, beginning with a fairy godfather in Arthur, and has just continued to add to the group with one fascinating person after another."

—The Novel Approach

"This book was so full of humor and love. It was like a fun adventure…"

—Gay Book Reviews

My Busboy

"Please read *My Busboy*. I mean this with all my heart."

—Joyfully Jay

"Both of these characters are so loveable and seeing them fall in love for the first time was wonderful."

—Scattered Thoughts and Rogue Words

By JOHN INMAN

Acting Up
Chasing the Swallows
A Hard Winter Rain
Head-on
Hobbled
Jasper's Mountain
Loving Hector
My Busboy
My Dragon, My Knight
Paulie
Payback
The Poodle Apocalypse
Scrudge & Barley, Inc.
Shy
Snow on the Roof (Dreamspinner Anthology)
Spirit
Sunset Lake
Two Pet Dicks

THE BELLADONNA ARMS
Serenading Stanley
Work in Progress
Coming Back
Ben and Shiloh

Published by DREAMSPINNER PRESS
www.dreamspinnerpress.com

MY DRAGON, MY KNIGHT
John Inman

DREAMSPINNER PRESS

Published by
DREAMSPINNER PRESS

5032 Capital Circle SW, Suite 2, PMB# 279, Tallahassee, FL 32305-7886 USA
www.dreamspinnerpress.com

This is a work of fiction. Names, characters, places, and incidents either are the product of author imagination or are used fictitiously, and any resemblance to actual persons, living or dead, business establishments, events, or locales is entirely coincidental.

My Dragon, My Knight
© 2017 John Inman.

Cover Art
© 2017 Reese Dante.
http://www.reesedante.com
Cover content is for illustrative purposes only and any person depicted on the cover is a model.

All rights reserved. This book is licensed to the original purchaser only. Duplication or distribution via any means is illegal and a violation of international copyright law, subject to criminal prosecution and upon conviction, fines, and/or imprisonment. Any eBook format cannot be legally loaned or given to others. No part of this book may be reproduced or transmitted in any form or by any means, electronic or mechanical, including photocopying, recording, or by any information storage and retrieval system, without the written permission of the Publisher, except where permitted by law. To request permission and all other inquiries, contact Dreamspinner Press, 5032 Capital Circle SW, Suite 2, PMB# 279, Tallahassee, FL 32305-7886, USA, or www.dreamspinnerpress.com.

ISBN: 978-1-63533-284-1
Digital ISBN: 978-1-63533-285-8
Library of Congress Control Number: 2016958592
Published March 2017
v. 1.0

Printed in the United States of America
∞
This paper meets the requirements of
ANSI/NISO Z39.48-1992 (Permanence of Paper).

For John B, as ever.

CHAPTER ONE

THE YOUNG guy Jay knew only as Danny sat at the horseshoe bar, slowly sipping his beer. Jay figured Danny *had* to sip it slowly since his jaw was so swollen. The old queen across the way kept eyeballing Danny like he was in the market for a piece of fresh meat, but good grief, Danny was forty years younger than him. As pathetic as Danny looked at that moment, it was still doubtful he would be okay being schmoozed by a drunken Methuselah.

It was not yet noon. The bar was deserted aside from Danny, the old horndog, and him, Jay Holtsclaw, the bartender-slash-owner of the establishment known to the gay community of San Diego as The Clubhouse. Jay was cutting limes at the other end of the bar, minding his own business. But like any good bartender, he was also a perceptive guy. When he saw Danny squirming under the determined stares of old Rafe the Drunk, he decided to intervene. He grabbed up his bag of limes and his cutting board and positioned himself smack in front of the boy to block the old guy's view. Once there, Jay proceeded to cut his limes as if nothing had happened. Danny watched him work, the kid's blue eyes darting around, seemingly fascinated by the glints of light coming off the razor-sharp knife as it sliced through the fruit. Jay thought he saw a gleam of appreciation spark in Danny's eyes for finding himself suddenly out of the line of fire of the old queen across the way.

Jay had seen Danny around occasionally, of course. Anyone as cute as Danny was bound to be noticed. He was usually on the arm of his lover, a slightly older guy. Not that old. Maybe in his early thirties compared to Danny's twenty-two or twenty-three. Actually Jay didn't know if the older guy was really Danny's lover or not, but since they were always together, he figured it was a safe bet. Jay didn't know the lover's name. Didn't think it was any of his business anyway.

"He's harmless," Jay said quietly, glancing over his shoulder at Rafe. "Don't let it upset you."

Danny jumped as if he'd been poked with a pin. "I—I know."

When Danny jumped, he also winced. Clearly that puffed-up jaw was hurting like a mother.

Jay tapped his own jaw, commiserating. "Accident?" Being a bartender, you learn a lot about human nature. When Danny said, "Fell off my bike like a dumbass," Jay knew immediately he was lying. He wasn't sure how he knew—he just knew.

"Yep," Jay said around a sympathetic chuckle, all the while appraising Danny wryly. "Only a dumbass would do something like that."

Danny didn't return the chuckle. He plucked a maraschino cherry out of the tray by the waiter's station, unmanned at the moment since the joint had just opened. Jay was amused when the kid stopped in midchew as if just realizing what he'd done, stealing the cherry right out from under the boss's nose.

"Oh, I'm sorry," he said, looking stricken. "I didn't think—"

Jay grinned. "Don't worry about it. Help yourself." With the kid's embarrassment laid to rest, Jay went back to slicing the limes. "Seriously, though, bikes are tricky things. You need to be more careful."

Danny took another sip of his draft. Jay suspected it was a nervous reaction more than thirst. Jay wasn't sure, but he also suspected young Danny, for all his good looks and youth, was actually sort of shy.

When Danny mumbled, "I will," it took all of Jay's self-control not to reach over with a napkin and wipe the beer foam off the kid's upper lip.

"Say," Jay said, only half joking. "Are you old enough to be in here?"

Danny cocked an eyebrow and went through the motions of starting a smile, which was truncated by a flash of pain when his sore jaw came into play. He good-naturedly reached into his back pocket, pulled out his wallet, and slapped his ID on the bar.

Jay wiped his hands on a towel and picked up the ID, twisting around until some light fell on it. The kid's name was Danny Sims. To Jay's surprise, the kid was actually younger than he originally thought, although still of legal age. He was just coming up on his twenty-second birthday. According to his driver's license, he was also five foot nine, had reddish-blond hair, blue eyes, and was cute enough that even the DMV couldn't take a bad picture of him. As if he wasn't photogenic enough, God had even sprinkled a few freckles across his nose.

Jay handed the ID back and recommenced cutting limes.

Old Rafe half fell off his barstool and stumbled off toward the bathroom in the back. Neither Jay nor Danny watched him go. The final insult for an aging queen.

Danny's eyes were still centered on the stupid limes. "You have big hands," he said quietly.

The statement surprised Jay, who stopped and stared at his hands for a minute as if suddenly realizing the kid was right. He *did* have big hands.

"Golly," he said, "I guess I do."

When he saw another flash of pain cross Danny's face, Jay reached over and plucked a bottle of aspirin off the bar. He shook a couple out and laid them in front of the boy.

"Thanks," Danny said, carefully poking the aspirin into his mouth before washing them down with another slug of beer.

"You didn't fall off your bike," Jay said conversationally. "Somebody whapped you. I can see four knuckle bruises on your jaw."

Danny stared down into his beer, his eyes sad. "I'd rather not talk about it."

"Okay, Danny. I didn't mean to be nosy."

Danny looked up. "How did you know my name?" Then he made a goofy face, sort of like a mental head slap. "Oh, you just saw my ID."

Jay shrugged. "There's that. But I've also seen you in here a few times. I'm good with names. Sometimes they just stick, whether I actually meet people or not. Once I hear them, I never forget them. Of course, then I turn around and forget to gas up the car and end up walking ten miles to get home."

Danny laughed, or tried to. It obviously hurt so badly, he squirmed his ass around on the barstool like he was sitting on tacks.

"Wait a minute," Jay said.

Turning away, he snatched up a clean towel from underneath the bar, scooped some crushed ice onto it, and wrapped it up in a tight little bundle before handing it over.

"Hold this to your jaw for a while. Maybe it'll help," Jay said. "It might even get the swelling down."

Danny's expression was somewhere between embarrassed and grateful, or quite possibly appalled, but he did as he was instructed.

"Thanks," he said softly, closing his eyes when the cold began seeping into his aching jaw. By the ensuing sigh of relief, Jay felt certain the ice was indeed helping. He was even surer of it when Danny added, "This feels good."

Jay went back to his limes.

Old Rafe returned and parked his ass back on his barstool. He was humming softly to himself. It took Jay a minute to recognize the theme song to *Mighty Mouse*, the old cartoon show that hadn't run on TV for fifty years. Poor Rafe had to get some new material.

Without being asked, Jay refilled Danny's glass at the Heineken tap, and when Danny tried to pay, Jay waved him off, saying, "It's on the house."

In the dim light Jay couldn't be sure, but he thought the kid blushed. Despite what he'd said earlier, he decided to go ahead and be nosy anyway.

"I see you in here sometimes with your friend. Is he the one who bopped you?"

Danny's blush went redder. A flash of irritation crossed his face, but Jay couldn't be sure if he was aggravated by the question or by the upcoming answer, if he should choose to express it. Which he finally did.

"Yeah," Danny said, trying to sip from his beer and keep the ice on his cheek at the same time. A tricky maneuver. "But it was my fault. I was being annoying."

His knife frozen in midair, Jay studied the boy in front of him. "Kid, just because you're annoying doesn't mean somebody has the right to do *that* to you. He could have broken your jaw. Or knocked your teeth out. The last thing you should be doing is making excuses for him."

Danny spun on the stool and eyed the pool table in the corner, obviously because he didn't know where else to look. His gaze ranged over the old Toulouse-Lautrec posters along the wall like he hadn't seen them a thousand times before. "I know," he said. "He didn't mean to hit me so hard. And he almost never hits me on my face. He just—"

"You mean he's hit you *before*?"

Danny jerked around like a fish on a hook. "No. That's not what I meant."

"It might not be what you meant, but it's certainly what you said."

MY DRAGON, MY KNIGHT

Danny kept his eyes down, studying his own fingertip as he drew patterns in the condensation on his glass. "Joshua's a good guy. He loves me a lot. He just gets—I don't know—excitable sometimes. He—he lashes out without thinking. He doesn't mean to. And like I said, I had it coming. I was being a pain in the ass."

Jay knew this was his cue to back off. You couldn't help some people. You just couldn't. But something about that innocent face in front of him, those pain-filled eyes, that blush of shame for something he shouldn't be ashamed of at all, made Jay mad. Against his own better judgment, he reached over and laid his hand on the boy's arm. Gently. Just to get his attention. The kid's skin was so soft and warm against the palm of his hand, Jay almost forgot what he was about to say, but he pulled himself together. This was important.

"Danny," he said, his voice little more than a hushed whisper since he didn't want old Rafe to overhear, "nobody has the right to hit you. Ever. If you love somebody, you don't do that. Hell, even if you *hate* somebody, you don't do that."

He pulled his hand away when he saw tears rise in Danny's eyes. "I'm sorry," Jay said hastily. "I didn't mean to make you cry. It's just that—well, shit, kid—you just can't let yourself be used for a punching bag."

Danny impatiently brushed away a tear as it etched a damp path down his cheek. "I know. It won't happen again. Honest. Thanks for—you know—caring." He sniffed. "And I'm not a kid."

Jay had to smile at that. From Jay's thirty-two-year-old perspective, a kid was exactly what Danny was. He also remembered what it was like to *be* twenty-one. You know it all at that age. At least you think you do. Unfortunately, Jay was certain young Danny had a whole lot of learning yet to do. And by the looks of him, he'd better learn it damn fast.

"Just don't let him hit you again," Jay said.

Danny gave him a businesslike nod. His face wasn't as red anymore. His tears were drying up. "I won't."

"Have some self-respect."

"I will."

"And if he *does* hit you again, let me know. I'll punch him into next week."

Just to make the kid—Danny—laugh, Jay struck a weight-lifter's pose, biceps flexed, chest expanded. He was no weight lifter by any stretch of the imagination, but he wasn't a wienie either. Jay stood six two and worked out on a regular basis. He felt a little surge of excitement when he thought he saw a flash of appreciation cross Danny's face.

Danny picked his ass up off the barstool and leaned over the bar, testing the firmness of Jay's bicep like he was squeezing fruit in the market. Jay had to admit he liked the way Danny's fingers lingered for a second. Or at least Jay imagined they did.

When Danny was finished, he plopped his ass back down on the barstool, returned the ice-filled towel to his jaw, and said with a wink (a wink more than likely being less painful than a smile), "My hero."

Jay winked back. "And don't you forget it." A smile threatened to brighten Danny's face, and Jay had just enough time to enjoy it before laughter rang out from the door leading onto the street. Three regulars came waltzing in, killing the moment. Reluctantly, Jay turned away to prep their drinks, without needing to ask what they wanted to order. He would've liked to have had a few more quiet moments with Danny, enough time to reiterate that he shouldn't let himself be pounded on by his asshole lover, but Jay supposed he had gotten his point across well enough.

He placed the three drinks on the bar farther down, grabbed up his limes and cutting board—giving Danny another wink when he did—and sauntered off to begin his day of bartending in earnest. Soon the place would be jumping.

It was perhaps thirty minutes later, while Jay was pretending to laugh at a joke he had heard a dozen times before from the same customer, when he looked up and saw Danny was gone.

He had left a dollar bill behind on the bar.

Jay cleaned up the bar where the kid had been sitting, and because it seemed like a good idea, he pressed his lips to the dollar bill before stuffing it in the tip jar.

Poor guy. Jay hoped he'd be all right.

DANNY SIMS unlocked the door of the downtown condo and held his breath, listening. Nothing. Then the tippy-tap of doggy toenails clattered down the hall. Jingles, coming to say hello.

The fact that Jingles, a small white terrier mix Danny had owned since high school, was running through the condo at all was enough to tell Danny that Joshua wasn't home. Joshua forbade Jingles to run inside, and Jingles was frightened enough of Danny's lover to stay on his best behavior, unless Joshua was gone. Then pretty much all bets were off.

Danny didn't blame Joshua. He had worked hard for the condo. It was in an expensive high-rise mere strides from the San Diego Bay, with a luscious view of the yachts moored to the docks down on the Embarcadero, and the Coronado Bridge farther off in the distance.

Joshua Stone and Danny Sims had been lovers for almost a year. Joshua's temper showed up about three months into the relationship. Now Danny, like Jingles, walked around on eggshells all the time. Still, Danny loved the guy. He could be sweet and romantic. He was generous. He could even be funny and sexy.

When he wasn't mad, that was. Or, God forbid, jealous.

Danny stooped to pet Jingles, shushing him to calm down. He didn't know where Joshua was, but he knew he wouldn't be gone long. It was both of their days off. Joshua had stormed out after punching Danny over an imagined slight. Something to do with the stupid guy down the hall whom Joshua thought Danny was infatuated with. Which he wasn't. But when Joshua got in one of those jealous rages, you couldn't tell him anything. So Danny had simply picked himself up off the floor and left, heading straight for the only place he knew where he could get some alone time. The bar up the street.

Danny had half expected Joshua to hunt him down, but he hadn't.

Grateful for a few moments alone, Danny fished a doggy treat from the bag in the kitchen cupboard and rewarded Jingles for being a good boy. Then he stood in the middle of his own kitchen like a trespasser, wondering where Joshua had gone and how mad he would be when he returned.

Danny headed for the bathroom down the hall and parked himself in front of the mirror over the sink to check out his injuries.

Jesus, he'd had no idea his jaw was *that* swollen. No wonder the bartender had been so concerned.

Danny ran some cold water over a washcloth and pressed the cool fabric to his fevered jaw.

At a sound behind him, he turned and saw Joshua standing in the doorway, watching him. Joshua held a bunch of flowers in his hand.

"I'm sorry, baby," Joshua said, holding out the flowers. Then he saw how swollen Danny's face was, and he dropped the flowers to the floor and rushed across the bathroom to gather Danny into his arms. He pulled Danny into an embrace, and Danny almost cried out when Joshua smashed his sore jaw against his chest.

"Oh Jesus, baby. I didn't mean to hit you that hard. Let me see."

He gently eased Danny to arm's length and gave Danny's jaw the once-over. When he laid his fingertips to it, Danny winced.

Danny was tearing up again. He hated himself for doing that.

Joshua stepped back. A flash of impatience crossed his face. "You're not going to cry, are you?"

Danny clenched the muscles in his jaw—which hurt like a motherfucker—and bit back the emotion welling up in him. "No," he said, determined. "I'm not going to fucking cry."

"Well, good. You don't want to be a baby about it. I said I was sorry, so let's just get past it." Joshua's eyes lit up. He stepped away and snatched the flowers off the floor, then presented them to Danny like a reward. "Look what I got you, baby. Yellow roses. Your favorite. By way of apology."

Danny took the flowers. He didn't have much choice. "Thanks."

Joshua gave an exaggerated pout. "Is that all I get? A measly thanks?"

He plucked the flowers from Danny's hand and dropped them on the counter, then pulled Danny into his arms again. He eased Danny around until they were both facing the mirror, and from there Danny watched as Joshua began stroking his hands up the inside of Danny's shirt, pushing the fabric high on Danny's shoulder so he could kiss his way down Danny's spine.

"Not here," Danny said, but Joshua ignored him.

He reached around and released Danny's belt buckle, then without any preamble, he pushed Danny's trousers down past his hips.

Danny sighed. *Goddammit, don't.* But he didn't say it out loud. What was the point?

"No underwear, I see," Joshua mumbled into Danny's skin while his strong hands slid down Danny's thighs, gently easing Danny's legs apart.

Anger swelled in Danny, but when Joshua laid his mouth to Danny's ass, desire welled up too. He couldn't deny it. As Joshua's hands foraged over his bare skin, he shuddered, and he gave an eager gasp when Joshua slid his tongue into the cleft of warm flesh and found Danny's hole. Danny grabbed the edge of the sink and stared at his own reflection. He saw shame there in his blue eyes. But he saw need too. He saw excitement.

He was hard now, hard and disgusted with himself for not fighting back. But Joshua's mouth felt so good, tasting him, exploring him.

When Joshua's hand slid around to grasp Danny's cock, Danny leaned farther over the sink and opened himself up to Joshua's attentions even more. He reached around and grabbed a fistful of Joshua's hair, steering his head to exactly where Danny wanted him to go.

Joshua chuckled and gave him what he wanted. For a moment.

The next thing Danny knew, Joshua rose up behind him, and Danny watched in the mirror as Joshua liberated himself from his clothes. Danny kicked his own trousers from his feet, freeing his legs completely.

Once again, Joshua bent and laid his mouth to Danny's opening, using his tongue to moisten it, to make Danny tremble, to make Danny once again reach around to grab Joshua's hair, steer his mouth, encourage that heavenly tongue. He pushed back with his ass, pleading for more. Always more.

Joshua stood and snatched up a bottle of lotion from the side of the sink. He filled his hand with the cream and slathered it over Danny's ass, then inserted a finger in Danny's anus, making Danny cry out with surprise and a sudden upwelling of lust.

As Danny watched in the mirror, Joshua smiled a heated smile. His eyes narrowed in that way they always did when he was turned-on. Danny reached down and grabbed his own cock to hold it away from the hard, cold surface of the sink. Trying not to stroke himself yet.

When Joshua nudged Danny's opening with the head of his stiff cock—teasing, threatening—Danny opened his legs wider. Unafraid now. Eager even. Eager for it to start. Eager to feel Joshua inside him. Eager to feel that fat cock delving deep.

"Yes," he muttered on a gasping breath. "Do it, Josh. Do it."

Joshua pressed his cock to Danny's hole, applying just enough pressure to make Danny tense in anticipation. Then Joshua reached around and cupped his free hand over Danny's throat, all the while staring at them both in the mirror.

Now Joshua's lips tortured Danny's ear as he whispered hungry words. "My baby likes this."

Danny nodded. "Oh, please. Get a condom. Fuck me."

"My baby's begging," Joshua breathed as his cock pushed inward, popped the anal ring, and began a long, slow slide into Danny's warm satin depths. "My baby's hungry. No time for a condom. We're together. We don't need a condom."

"Then fuck me," Danny whispered, knowing it was hopeless to argue, leaning forward over the sink now, his breath fogging the mirror in front of him. He hated himself for saying the words. He hated Joshua for what he was doing. But he wanted Joshua too. He wanted it all. He relished the filling, the sudden throbbing impalement. There was nothing in the world like it. Nothing.

"Fuck me," he said again, his voice a stranger's voice. His eyes stared back at him in the mirror. A stranger's eyes.

As Joshua's cock slid deep into Danny's ass in one long, determined glide, Danny cried out. There was pain in that cry now, but Danny's desire laid the pain to rest quickly enough. Joshua's eyes burned into his in the mirror while the probing cock that had so abruptly seared through him began to move. The look of dominance, the look of *victory*, that shone in Joshua's eyes was both frightening and exciting. At this particular moment in time, Danny liked being controlled. He liked that Joshua owned him. He liked being the spoils in this stupid power game they sometimes played.

He liked, too, that Joshua knew all the right buttons to push. He knew Danny's weaknesses. He knew Danny's needs. If only the fists didn't come out to play now and then. If only the real pain didn't sometimes intercede.

But Danny pushed that thought away. For now he had other priorities.

"Yes," Danny breathed, the uninjured side of his face pressed against the mirror now, his hot breath steaming the glass. Joshua bent over him, crowding him against the sharp, cold edges of the marble sink.

He pressed his mouth to the back of Danny's neck. Pumping. Pumping Danny with his cock.

Pumping too hard.

"That hurts," Danny gasped. "Slow down, Josh."

"Shut up. Tell me you love me," Joshua demanded. His cock never stopped moving. Never slowed. Not once. "Tell me you love me, Danny. Tell me you love my cock."

Danny tried to ignore the pain. He forced himself to relax, and the worst of it eased a little. He began to stroke his own dick then, but Joshua slapped his hand away.

"I'm going to come." He breathed hot breath over Danny's ear. "Without the condom maybe you can feel me come inside you, Danny. Let me do that. Then I'll take care of you. Right now just concentrate on me. Concentrate on my dick deep inside you."

So Danny pushed away his own desire and let himself be owned by that pummeling cock. In truth, he usually loved Josh's cock. He loved what it did to him. He loved how it made him feel. But not this time. Not this time.

"Tell me you love me," Joshua said again, his hands on Danny's hips, his driving cock stabbing its way through Danny like a pile driver, causing him to scrunch up his face in anguish. "Tell me! Tell me, goddammit!"

"I love you!" Danny bellowed, shame coursing through him. Shame and excitement.

In the next instant, Danny threw his head back against Joshua as his body betrayed him and spewed his come into the sink without Danny even touching himself. "Oh God!" he cried out. "Dammit!" There was no pleasure in his spilling. His mouth hung open, the pain of Josh's searing cock excruciating.

Joshua's cock never slowed. Even while Joshua reached around Danny, scooped the come up from the sink with his fingertips, and smeared it over Danny's mouth, smeared it *into* Danny's mouth, feeding it to him, watching him in the mirror as he did it. Smiling when Danny opened his mouth and allowed Joshua's come-soaked fingers in, sucked them clean, blinded by his own need to get it over with, to put a stop to that iron cock still tearing into him from behind.

Danny clutched Joshua's hip and pulled him closer, deeper, stuffing that driving cock ever farther inside himself. Biting back his anger. Biting back the pain. Joshua tensed against him, shuddering as his cock swelled inside Danny.

Good, Danny thought. *Finish it. Finish it.*

And as if obeying Danny's unspoken demand, with a great yell Joshua shot his unfettered seed deep in Danny's ass. He bucked and writhed and moaned with the explosion, taking Danny along with him.

Joshua pressed his sweat-soaked face between Danny's shoulder blades as his cock continued to move, slowly now, in and out, still making Danny gasp with every stroke. But his gasps were quieter now. His trembling eased. His thundering heart quieted. Slowly quieted. The pain diminished, thank God, as Joshua's cock began to shrink, began to soften inside him.

"My baby," Joshua mumbled into Danny's skin. "My baby."

When Joshua's wilting cock eased itself free from Danny's ass, sliding away completely, Danny all but collapsed over the sink. Sated. Sore. Well fucked and hating himself for it.

When Joshua stepped back, releasing Danny from his embrace, the pain in Danny's jaw returned, sweeping in out of nowhere. Mad to have been forgotten, maybe. Claiming its revenge for being ignored, even for a moment.

The anger Danny felt toward the man who caused that pain returned as well, all in a rush, but Danny swallowed down the anger, just as he had swallowed his own seed.

He squeezed his eyes shut and tried to push the anger away. Joshua was his lover. Joshua had done a lot for him. Danny owed him forgiveness, at least. Didn't he?

Joshua turned Danny away from the sink and tucked a finger under Danny's chin. Gently, for once, he raised Danny's face so their eyes met.

"Forgiven?" Joshua asked. His hair was fuck-mussed, and a shimmer of perspiration sparkled his forehead. His eyes were open, wide, earnest. But for all the sincerity shining in their chestnut depths, there was also the expectation that Danny would react the way Joshua wanted him to. The way Joshua *demanded*.

Joshua, after all, was in charge. He was always in charge.

Danny nodded, hating himself all over again. He stared at the upturned smile, not quite a smirk of superiority, that twisted Joshua's mouth, which only moments before had caressed Danny's skin with hungry kisses, whispered words of passion and want. Above all else, Danny tried to ignore that annoying spark of victory that lit Joshua's eyes.

He tried not to think about the meekness, the shame, that probably hazed his own. But the pain in his jaw overshadowed all of it. The memory of the blow came rushing back—the blow that hadn't just hurt Danny's jaw but had torn a hole in his heart as well. And now he'd been coerced into fucking without a condom, which he hated. Danny loved Joshua. He did. But he had to face the truth as well. The abuse was escalating.

Joshua pulled away then, almost as if nothing had transpired between them at all. Moving to the shower stall, he twisted the crank to warm the water. He stood there, his long, naked body elegant and trim, his cock softly swaying, shrunken now, not erect and pulsing with blood. But asleep. Resting.

Danny watched Joshua for a moment, then turned, picked up the roses from the counter, and still in only socks and a T-shirt, moved toward the door, easing past Joshua's bare body. Avoiding his touch for some reason. He needed to put the roses in a vase. Josh would be mad if he didn't.

Before stepping into the shower, Joshua clutched Danny's arm and stopped him at the door. Strong fingers dug into his flesh. "I smelled beer on your breath. We don't have any beer in the house. You must have gone to a bar."

"I—I did. I was upset."

Joshua glowered, all the while casually gliding his foreskin up and down with the fingertips of his other hand, cupping his balls, flexing his back.

"Don't do it again," he said. "Not unless I'm with you."

Danny hesitated, just for a second, before nodding. "All right."

Only then did Joshua step through the shower curtain and pull it closed behind him. He immediately began humming under the spray. Carefree as ever. The ruler of his kingdom.

Danny stood there, listening to the rush of the water. The screams he heard were only inside his head. Where they always were.

CHAPTER TWO

ON SUNDAY morning, Jay picked up the usual spray of blossoms from his florist. The florist, Arturo, was a happy young Mexican man with a knockout smile. He green-carded up from Tijuana every day to earn his living in the makeshift flower stand he set up in the space he rented adjacent to the liquor store on Redwood. Always friendly, always eager to please, he had the flowers ready for Jay, as he always did. Today they were irises, Jay's favorite.

Jay passed a few minutes with Arturo, using his limited Spanish, as *he* always did. Then he waved good-bye, wished the young Mexican man a happy day, told Arturo to give his best to his wife and their small boy, of whom Arturo was immensely proud and dragged pictures out for Jay's amusement more often than not. Climbing back in the car and carefully laying the flowers on the front seat beside him, immediately filling the car with their sweet scent, Jay then headed out to the cemetery.

Everything about Sunday mornings was a ritual for Jay. The flowers. Arturo. The trek on Highway 94 out to Holy Cross Cemetery. The slow, winding drive past the cemetery gate to a secluded spot on a hillside beneath a tall eucalyptus tree where Jay's lover now spent his lonely, silent days in a concrete box six feet underground.

The ache in Jay's heart as he stood there in the dewy grass contemplating the grave was a ritual too. The marker that lay flush to the ground with his once-lover's name etched into the marble was like a heartache carved in stone.

The flowers from the previous week were always gone when Jay arrived. Jay supposed the groundskeeper took them when he mowed. Jay would spend a few moments arranging the new flowers in the little cup provided at the side of the marker. Then he would brush the dust and cut grass from the stone to make it look pretty, after which he would stand at the foot of Simon's grave and let the ache take him.

For the last couple of months, his sore heart was accompanied by considerable guilt as well. The guilt came from the fact that the ache of grief he always felt, standing at the foot of his lover's grave, had lessened of late. That lessening of grief troubled Jay a lot.

A year had passed since the cerebral hemorrhage took Simon—a random, passing swipe of the Grim Reaper's scythe. Almost like a cruel prank. An afterthought. The old bastard in his flowing black robes asserting his authority, maybe. Flexing his muscles. Blithely destroying two lives on a whim.

The doctors told a different tale, of course. They said the flaw in Simon's brain stem must have always been present. A weakened arterial wall. Probably there since birth. The hemorrhage was bound to happen sooner or later, the doctors said. Impossible to predict. Highly difficult to prevent. Nothing more than an imperfection. A simple glitch in the machinery.

So at thirty years old, on a day following a romantic candlelit dinner and a night of lovemaking that would never be repeated, Simon simply stopped breathing as his brain pan filled with blood while he slept in Jay's arms—the act of death slipping in so quietly it did not even waken Simon from his slumbers.

There Jay would find him, cooling in his arms, hours later. Death had not even jarred the smile of contentment from Simon's face when it took him.

It jarred Jay, though. It jarred Jay to his very core. In fact, it had taken almost this complete year for Jay to recover. And now that he was recovering, now that the pain *had* begun to lessen, his grief had been replaced with guilt. The guilt he felt for beginning to forget. For beginning to heal.

Jay squeezed his eyes shut, thinking of that day now. Remembering Simon's cool hand, already freed from life, resting on Jay's chest. Simon's cool cheek, which would never again wear the blush of passion, lying immobile atop Jay's shoulder, where he had spoken gentle words before sleep took them both the night before. In the ensuing months, Jay had tortured himself trying to remember what those words had been. What Simon had said. But he could only remember the hushed way Simon spoke them. And the smile Jay had heard in Simon's voice when he uttered them as they lay there on their last night together, wrapped in each other's arms, the taste of their spilled juices still flavoring their lips. Their hearts still softly thundering down to peace after the exertions of love had ended.

Jay thought of that morning now as he stood by the grave and watched the sun begin to warm this other California morning surrounding him. The frantic CPR. The fumbled punching of 9-1-1 on the cell phone after scrambling around to find the phone among the flotsam on his nightstand. The averted glances from the EMTs when they realized immediately there was nothing they could do. Simon had already been dead for a couple of hours by then. All hope of resuscitation had been lost long ago. And perhaps there had been no hope for resuscitation anyway, even if the EMTs had been there the moment the artery burst.

It was a fait accompli. A done deal.

Just like Jay's broken heart was a done deal. Until lately.

While Jay still missed Simon, he also knew it was time now for him to move on. If not to find another lover, at least to seek out a little happiness for himself. It was time to stop being a monk and put the celibacy aside. In other words, it was time to rejoin the human fucking race. Whether he wanted to or not. After months of living it, Jay knew now that grief was a trap. You could lose yourself in it, let it swallow you whole. Cowering in a well of grief was nothing more than a safe way to hide from the world. A coward's way. He didn't want to be a coward anymore. He had loved Simon with all his heart, and Simon's death had wounded him deeply, but what good would it do for Jay to throw his life away because of it? It wouldn't bring Simon back. All it would do was create another corpse. This one still living, but a corpse nevertheless.

One corpse was more than enough in one household, thank you very much.

Jay sucked in a deep breath of morning air, squinted against the rising sun just now peeking over the trees on the hillside. He gazed out over the sea of tombstones surrounding him. The ocean of lost lives. Of silenced voices. His brain dredged through his memory banks and skittered across a panoply of faces, people he had known, people he had merely glimpsed in passing. People who meant something to him. People who meant nothing. People he'd seen in the bar. People he'd passed on the street. Row upon row of faces, many nameless, slid past inside his head. Then the skittering stopped, and his mind's eye settled on one face. One beautiful young face.

MY DRAGON, MY KNIGHT

It was the golden-haired boy from a week ago. The boy at the bar. The one with the swollen jaw. Danny.

The young man's countenance filled Jay's mind suddenly. The crisp blue eyes, dimmed with misery. The innocent spray of freckles across his nose. The way his sweet mouth was firmly set, afraid of the pain a smile might cause. The way his arm felt under Jay's hand. So soft. So pliant. So deliciously warm. The way the boy had tested the firmness of Jay's bicep with his cool fingertips.

Jay stood in that sea of tombstones and was surprised to feel another ache set in. A brand-new ache. Deep inside. Down in the space where Simon had once resided. Down in the space where Simon *still* resided from time to time, but not nearly often enough anymore.

Jay hoped the kid was all right. Simon's suffering had ended. Danny was still living his. Or had he and his lover made up? Had his lover begged Danny's forgiveness for what he'd done, and had Danny forgiven him if he did? Would it never happen again, or would Danny follow the trail of so many other troubled lovers and sink deeper beneath a pall of abuse that he found himself unable—or unwilling—to escape?

Jay gave his head a shake, trying to dislodge the flurry of thoughts that had come at him like an avalanche. What the hell was he worrying about Danny for? He had his own life to repair. His own happiness to salvage.

He bent down and plucked a dandelion from the acres of green grass surrounding him. The one yellow bloom, the one splash of color as far as the eye could see. Just like Danny was the one splash of color inside his head.

Jay walked slowly to the car, spinning the dandelion between his thumb and forefinger, enjoying the perfection of it. The color. He held it to his nose and inhaled the scent. It was just a weed, he had to remind himself. A beautiful weed.

Days later he would find the dandelion tucked inside his shirt pocket when he was prepping the shirt for the laundry. He would remember Simon when he did.

He would also remember Danny.

But on this particular Sunday morning, by the time Jay was halfway home, Danny was forgotten. Placed back on that shelf inside Jay's head where he would rest until the next time he made himself known.

The next time would come sooner than Jay expected.

DANNY SET aside the textbook for his bookkeeping class at City College, where he was in his first year of studying business management, attending night classes two days a week, slowly working his way toward an associate degree. It was a class Danny hated but one Joshua said would be worth its weight in gold if Danny ever wanted to get out of the Macy's store where he currently worked in the men's department selling overpriced socks. At least that's how Joshua described it.

Joshua was a CPA at a downtown firm and made good money. Danny suspected Joshua wondered more than once why he had fallen for someone like Danny, who barely eked out a living by the seat of his pants. Of course, Danny thought with a smirk, the seat of Danny's pants probably had a lot to do with Joshua's devotion. Lord knows, Joshua paid enough attention to it.

Danny stared down at Jingles, who was sitting on the floor by his desk, gazing up at him and trembling in anticipation. The terrier's white face and mottled gray-and-white coat was an explosion of cowlicks that stuck out in a hundred different directions, a gift from his confused bloodlines. Joshua called him a mutt. Danny called him unique. At the moment, Jingles was looking hopeful, and since he was holding the end of his leash, which he had retrieved from the front doorknob and dragged through the condo to Danny's side, it wasn't hard to figure out what Jingles was hopeful about.

Danny bent and made a kissy face, and Jingles leapt into his lap and gave him a swipe or two with his tongue. Then he jumped back down and took off running across the condo toward the front door, trailing the leash behind him, as if he thought maybe Danny was so slow as to need reminding *again* it was time to walk the damn dog.

Danny laughed, pulled on his sneakers, and grabbed the house keys before clipping the leash to Jingles's collar and heading out the door.

It was moments like this, when Joshua was at work and Danny and Jingles were on their own, that the dog came alive. When Joshua was home, Jingles lay on a pillow on the balcony more often than not, staring out at the city looking sad. Terriers are smart. They know when they are not wanted.

MY DRAGON, MY KNIGHT

When Joshua proclaimed his love for Danny almost a year ago and pleaded with him to share his life, he had asked Danny to find other arrangements for the dog. Danny had refused. It was one of the few times Danny had showed a little backbone, he thought, where Joshua was concerned. In the end, Josh had grudgingly acquiesced. But he had made no attempt since to get close to Jingles or even allow the dog to feel at home in the condo where Danny had brought him to live.

It was left up to Danny to fill the dog's life with as much love and happiness as he could squeeze in from time to time. The last thing Danny wanted was for Jingles to start getting bored and wreak his revenge on the carpet. Or the drapes. Or Joshua's expensive furniture. Danny suspected that with the proper motivation, Jingles could reduce Josh's two-thousand-dollar leather sofa to a pile of moist cow parts in no time at all.

It would also be the end of Jingles.

So Danny and the dog danced a wary dance, Danny keeping Joshua happy, Jingles maintaining a low profile, and both Danny and the dog wishing Joshua would just lighten the fuck up once in a while.

At least Joshua's temper had been under wraps lately. Ever since he almost broke Danny's jaw, Josh had been on his best behavior, for which Danny was more than grateful. Still, Danny knew, the threat was always there, and it was that lingering possibility of violence that kept Danny on pins and needles—even during the good times.

It was a wearying balance to try to maintain, and once in a while Danny needed to get away for a quiet drink. Today he thought he would share the experience with Jingles, if his favorite bartender had no objection.

The Clubhouse was only four blocks from the condo, and since it was barely noon, the bar would have just opened. Remembering the kindness Jay had shown him the last time he was there, Danny thought the bartender might not mind a little company while he prepared his bar for the day ahead.

Along the way, Jingles did his business, so they got that out of the way. With Jingles prancing at his feet, Danny stepped from the sunlight into the darkness of the bar, where he experienced an immediate feeling of déjà vu. For there at the horseshoe stood Jay, cutting fruit. Lemons this time. He was deftly slicing the peels into thin strips.

He looked up and smiled when Danny walked through the doorway. They were the only two people in the bar.

Danny took only one step inside and stopped, blinking the light from his eyes and adjusting to the dark. He liked the way Jay's eyes fell on him from across the room. The kind appraisal. The instant recognition. Jay remembered him. Danny knew it immediately, and any unease he might have felt before suddenly fell by the wayside.

"Mind if my dog and I join you?" he asked. Jay smiled, his teeth alabaster white in the glow of the black lights underneath the bar, while his hands continued what they were doing with the lemons as if on autopilot.

"Come on in," Jay said, finally setting the knife aside, scooping up the lemon peels, and dumping them in a container, which he tucked into a small refrigerator under the bar. After wiping his hands on a hand towel, he patted the bar in front of him invitingly. "Park it and introduce me to your friend."

Danny lifted the dog into his arms and carried him to the bar. "Jingles," he said with mock formality. "Meet Jay the Bartender. Jay the Bartender, this is Jingles."

Jay reached out and gave Jingles a chin rub. Jingles gave him a hello lick in return.

With introductions out of the way, Jay leaned forward to study Danny's face. "You've healed," he said quietly, his eyes serious.

Danny nodded, heat rising on the back of his neck, remembering how he must have looked the last time he was here. The things he must have said. How pathetic he must have seemed.

Jay was still tickling Jingles's chin, but his eyes were centered solely on Danny.

"Yeah," Danny said. "I healed. It happens."

"Not too often, I hope. So where's Muhammed Ali?"

"Huh?"

"Your punch-happy boyfriend."

"Oh. He's at work." Danny cleared his throat and looked embarrassed. "So how about a beer? Just for me. Jingles is underage."

Jay laughed as Jingles's tail went into hyperdrive at the mention of his name. Remembering what the kid had ordered the last time he was in, Jay popped open the fridge to grab a chilled glass and filled it at the

Heineken tap. He slid a napkin in front of Danny and set the beer on top of it while Danny laid a stack of one-dollar bills on the bar. Jay plucked a couple of bills out of the pile, rang up the sale, and dropped the money in the till. As Danny took his first sip, Jay studied the dog, now sitting on the stool beside the boy. The dog perched there, looking around like a proper regular who had just dropped in for a pick-me-up after a long day of chasing cats.

"Maybe we've got something for your little friend too," Jay said around a smile. "Can't have him sitting there looking all neglected and forlorn." With that, Jay pulled a bag of doggie treats from a grocery bag he had stashed behind the bar after picking up a few necessities on his way in to work—limes and lemons for the bar, a bunch of celery for Bloody Marys, and a bag of his own dog's favorite Milk-Bones. "Carly won't mind sharing. She's pretty mellow."

Danny peeked around. "Is she here? I'd love to meet her."

"Naw," Jay said. "She's home guarding the cabin."

"So you're a dog owner, then." Danny grinned, settling in, looking more comfortable, sucking some of the foam off the top of his beer. "I knew there was something I liked about you."

Jay flashed a flirty dimple. "Careful now," he said. "I'm susceptible to flattery."

Danny laughed out loud. "Good to know," he said. He peered over the rim of his glass while sipping his draft. "So what breed is Carly?"

Jay leaned on the bar, tucking his elbows on top of a folded towel with every appearance of settling in for a chat. Jingles had chomped up the Milk-Bone like he hadn't eaten in a week and was already looking around hungrily for another, the scoundrel. With a wink at Danny, Jay dipped into the bag and gave him one. "Carly's of the same persuasion as Jingles here. Heinz 57. The closest we can figure is that she hails from a long line of mutts who partake of endless rounds of indiscriminate sex with any other mutt that comes along."

Maybe it was the beer, or maybe it was Jay's easy manner, but whatever it was it made Danny brave enough to flirt a little. "Sort of like me back when I was single."

"Yeah. Me too."

They both laughed. Then Danny appraised Jay for a minute, wondering if he'd spoken the truth, and if he had, what that must have been like. Intriguing, for sure. Definitely intriguing. And if Danny wasn't mistaken, the same speculation was evident in Jay's expression.

Danny pushed away a surge of sexual longing for the man in front of him. Jesus, Joshua would kill him. "Yep," Danny said, forcing himself to push those lusty thoughts aside, although he sure as hell didn't want to. He concentrated on his beer again. Concentrated on the dog. "That's Jingles all over. Heinz 57. He's like the canine equivalent of leftovers night. A little dab of everything in the fridge." After enjoying Jay's smile for a moment, Danny got more serious. "You said we. The closest *we* can figure. Do you have a lover?"

JAY STIFFENED, although he hoped not too obviously. He pushed all thoughts aside of Danny being a slut, which was a damned enticing thought, actually. It took him a few seconds to decide if he wanted to get into the whole Simon story with Danny. It's not like Danny would care, or that he was interested. But the sincere look on Danny's face changed his mind. Maybe he did care. Maybe he really did want to know. And maybe, just maybe, Jay was willing to share a little of his backstory with this young man sitting in front of him.

"The 'we' thing is a force of habit, I guess," Jay said. "I *had* a lover. He's gone now."

"Did you guys split up?"

Jay studied Danny's open, honest face. There was no guile there. He was simply curious.

"He died," Jay said. "Almost a year ago."

"Oh. I'm sorry. I shouldn't have—"

Jay waved off the upcoming apology. "It's okay. Don't worry about it." Still, he thought, a change of topic would be nice. Maybe he wasn't quite as ready to talk about it as he thought. He hated talking about himself anyway. Being a bartender, he was always grateful that few people actually asked him to. They were more centered on their own problems. Most people considered Jay a sounding board, nothing else.

MY DRAGON, MY KNIGHT

It would probably amaze the idiots to learn Jay actually had a life of his own outside the walls of this bar.

A not uncomfortable silence settled over the two while Danny sipped his beer, and Jay studied the boy out of the corner of his eye. Danny had been handsome with a swollen jaw. Uninjured, as he was now, he was a fucking knockout.

"So," Jay said, wondering if he should ask but not really caring if he should or not. "How long have you and Joe Palooka been together?"

Danny blushed. "He's not that bad. We've been together almost a year. The next time we come in together, I'll introduce you."

Jay wasn't too excited by the prospect.

"I mean, if you'd like me to," Danny said, sounding uncertain. Jingles, bored with the conversation and having given up on any more Milk-Bones coming his way, had curled up on the barstool next to Danny and fallen sound asleep.

Jay glanced his way before resetting his eyes on Danny. "I'd like that," he lied. He then surprised himself by doing something he rarely did. "I think I'll join you," he said and turned and grabbed another chilled glass from the fridge. He poured himself a draft like he'd poured Danny. With a smile, Danny lifted his drink, and they clinked glasses. Jay took a long pull, and once again a congenial silence settled over them.

Danny finally broke it. "You said Carly was guarding the cabin. Is that where you live? In a cabin?"

Jay nodded. "Yeah. Just out of town on the side of the San Miguel Mountains. It's just a tiny mountain, so I call it Mount Miguelito. It's about a twenty-minute drive. I like it. Secluded, quiet, no noisy neighbors to bug my ass."

"So it's just you and Carly," Danny said.

"Yep. Just me and Carly. And a couple of cats. And a few chickens out back. And about a gazillion house finches roosting in the rafters who never shut the fuck up."

Danny smiled. "Not that you mind."

Jay returned his smile and nodded. "Not that I mind at all."

Danny's smile widened. "So you're the zookeeper."

"Pretty much."

"Sounds like a great way to live."

"It is."

"You don't get lonely?" Danny asked, then immediately backtracked. "I'm sorry. I shouldn't have asked that."

Jay shrugged. Coming from anyone else he probably *wouldn't* have liked the question. Coming from Danny, he didn't mind, which rather surprised him.

"It's okay," he said. "And no. It doesn't really get lonely. After listening to drunks jabber at me all day, a little peace and quiet is a good thing. I miss my lover, of course, but that's a different battle altogether."

"Is it?" Danny asked, his face somber.

"Is it what?"

"Still a battle. After a year. Do you still miss him that much?"

Jay heaved a long sigh, and while he was heaving it, he stared through the slit between the leather blackout curtain and the jamb of the open doorway that let him peek through to the city street beyond in quiet moments like this one. He never knew what he would see when he peeked through that damn opening. This time he saw a homeless man shuffle by, caught a glimpse of yellow as a cab slid past on the boulevard.

"I'm missing him less and less," Jay said. "It makes me…."

Danny reached over and laid his fingers, cool from the glass, over the back of Jay's hand. "It makes you what?" he asked softly.

Jay turned his eyes to Danny as a tingle shot through him at the touch. "It makes me sad." Jay cleared his throat to strengthen his voice, which had suddenly gotten all wobbly for some reason. "I feel guilty not missing Simon as much as I used to. Sometimes I think I'm beginning to forget him."

Danny's gentle blue eyes speared a path of caring straight into Jay's. His gaze entered Jay like a welcome ray of heat. A warm blessing. He hadn't felt sympathetic eyes fall on him for a long time. It touched him. Touched him deeply.

Danny's next words touched him even more.

"Maybe you aren't missing him less. Maybe you're just reclaiming your own life. Maybe it's been gone long enough. Maybe it's time to resurrect yourself and start all over again."

Jay stared down at his hands. "That's a lot of maybes." He lifted his head and stared at the young man in front of him. Danny had spoken almost the exact same words Jay had been thinking that morning in the graveyard when he took the irises to Simon. His heart squeezed, but not painfully. It was as if Danny's words had formed a gentle fist and gripped him there, trying to prod him back to life.

Before Jay could stop himself, he reached across the bar and laid his hand on Danny's cheek. The cheek that had been swollen the last time they were together. Now it was smooth and lean and warm beneath his fingers. There was the slightest bristle there, as if Danny hadn't shaved that morning—not that it showed. His pale, sparse beard left hardly a shadow on his face.

When Danny leaned into his touch, a lazy smile twisting his lips, Jay smiled back.

"For a kid, you're not so dumb, are you?"

"No, Jay. And I'm not a kid either."

"I know. I'm sorry, Danny." He pulled his hand away, but he didn't want to. He didn't want to *a lot*.

"Maybe I should go," Danny said. He appeared uncomfortable all of a sudden.

Jay wondered if he had gone too far, touching the kid's—*Danny's*—face like he had.

"All right," Jay said. "I guess I'd better get to work too."

"It's not that I want to go," Danny explained, as if he needed to. "It's just that Joshua doesn't like it when I go to bars without him."

"Sure," Jay said. "I understand. We don't want to start a fight."

Danny frowned, rubbing his jaw as if the pain had come sweeping back with the memory. "No, we certainly don't."

Danny gave a reluctant sigh and scooped Jingles into his arms, holding him out for Jay to give the mutt a good-bye pat. He snatched up all the bills still on the bar, leaving two for a tip.

"I guess I'll see you when I see you, Jay."

"I guess you will."

"Thanks for the dog biscuits."

"You bet."

There followed moment of awkwardness, which Jay would spend the rest of the day kicking himself for. He should have tried to lighten it with a joke or a kind word. But he didn't. He merely stood there watching helplessly as Danny set Jingles on the floor, snapped his leash on again, and with a final wave of good-bye, stepped through the curtain and disappeared onto the street.

With a sinking feeling, Jay wondered if he would ever see Danny again.

CHAPTER THREE

JAY'S CABIN wasn't really a cabin. It was an old clapboard house with a wide front porch trimmed at the roofline with spindly, chipped balusters that needed sanding and painting. The same style balusters—only larger and just as in need of sandpaper and paint, as was the rest of the house—also braced the porch railing where Jay would sometimes prop his feet in the morning after dragging up one of the rockers to make himself comfortable. Pulling himself awake in his own sweet time, he would nurse his coffee while contemplating the rocky, secluded landscape stretching down the mountainside before him.

The cabin (for that's what Jay insisted on calling it) had two floors and even a dollop of a third, where a slope-ceilinged garret sat perched atop it all, tucked in among the eaves beside the chimney. The small garret was Jay's favorite room in the house, thanks to an ancient round stained-glass window depicting a dragon and a knight in shining armor that sifted and prismed the light, dressing the walls in splashes of riotous color when the sun hit the window just right.

Jay used the garret as an office. It was there he kept his books, did his taxes, had his computer. The rest of the house was for living. The garret alone was for work. It was hard, but Jay did try to keep the two separate, although now that he was alone, the lines between life and work tended to blur more frequently than they had when Simon was around.

The house also boasted a basement, which Jay steered clear of as much as possible since the day he found a rattlesnake in it. The most disturbing aspect of this story, as Jay always told people, was that after running off to fetch a shovel to kill the snake, he returned to find the damn thing gone. He hadn't seen the snake since and didn't know whether it was still on the premises, but he *did* know he hadn't seen any mice lately. Since snakes *eat* mice, as Jay also told people when relating the story, that was a fairly disturbing development.

Thankfully, aside from the furnace and a few stored odds and ends, there wasn't much reason to go down there anyway. The basement could be accessed from a flight of stairs leading down from the utility room just off the back porch, and also through a sloping trapdoor that stuck out from the rear of the house like an afterthought. The trapdoor wasn't exactly airtight and was probably how the rattlesnake had gained access. Jay kept intending to seal it up a little better, maybe rebuild the door completely since the wood was warped from constant exposure to the elements, but he hadn't gotten around to it yet. If he was totally honest with himself, he probably never would. That particular job simply wasn't very high on his list of priorities. Especially since he didn't know if the snake was still hanging around inside. The last thing he wanted to do was cut off its avenue of escape.

To lessen the creep factor of maybe having a rattlesnake residing in his basement, Jay had named the damn snake George, but as far as the creep factor went, it didn't help much. Jay still avoided the basement every chance he got.

As for the rest of Jay's house, he often thought it looked like it would be more at home sitting on Cape Cod, overlooking a gray, surging sea with screaming gulls wheeling overhead and sand dunes rolling off toward breakers in the distance, rather than perched on a desert mountain (which was really little more than an overblown hill) and drowsing in the Southern California heat, home to rattlesnakes and coyotes and cactus and tumbleweeds.

The cabin sat at the end of a long, winding lane that meandered up the side of the mountain. The lane dodged boulders the size of automobiles and carved its way through the brambles and chaparral, dry as dust in the summer, a muddy mess in the winter when (and if) the rains came.

But Jay loved it. He loved the seclusion the cabin offered. There were no other houses in sight from any window in the place. Jay hadn't lied to Danny when he said he enjoyed a little peace and quiet after listening to people jabber at him all day in the bar. He did indeed enjoy it. But it was lonely too, now that Simon was gone.

That's where the animals came into play.

Carly, the mutt with no discernible heritage except for perhaps a fair dose of German shepherd blood surging through her veins, judging

MY DRAGON, MY KNIGHT

by her looks, was Jay's closest ally. The two cats, Lucy and Desi, both possessing bloodlines just as confusing as the dog's, filled the void when Carly was off chasing rabbits or snoozing in front of the fireplace on winter nights. Even the chickens out back in the wire-enclosed coop (to keep out the prowling foxes and coyotes) were a comfort. And the occasional rare egg they rewarded him with was nice too.

There was no cable TV in the cabin. It was too remote to make cable financially feasible. Instead Jay had an old metal TV antenna poking up the side of the house that gathered all the OTA (over-the-air) broadcasting waves it could snatch out of midair. The TV antenna served Jay's purpose quite handily, since he hardly ever watched TV anyway. He preferred books. Probably because they were silent. Just another way to maintain a little more peace and quiet on the premises after a long noisy day at the bar.

The bar. Perhaps no one was more amazed by the success of The Clubhouse than Jay. He had taken the money he inherited from his parents after their death in a car accident, bought a failing straight cocktail lounge, and turned it around in less than a year to one of the most-frequented gay bars in San Diego. The first couple of years he had worked long hours, making sure his business venture was a success. Now word of mouth and The Clubhouse's reputation did most of the work for him. With financial success came also the opportunity to delegate a lot of the work to a few trusted employees.

Jay learned a long time ago that the best way to maintain his sanity was to take two days off a week from the bar and to almost never work nights. He surrounded himself with reliable people so he could do just that, counting on them to maintain the bar in his absence—accepting deliveries, keeping the place clean, preventing any hanky-panky from going on in the public bathrooms. It was a gay bar, yes, but it wasn't a dive. Jay expected his employees to keep the customers on their best behavior, maintaining a certain amount of decorum in the establishment. No drugs, no toilet-stall blowjobs, no fights. So far they had done his bidding just fine. Things were so well under control that a year or so ago, Jay had begun contemplating taking a third day off every week. Then Simon died and Jay had forgotten about it for a while, thinking perhaps the extra hours would take his mind from his grief. And for a while, perhaps, they had. But now that time had passed, he found the thought of taking an extra day off once again popping into his head now and then. But so far he hadn't taken it any further than the "considering" stage.

He had a feeling that was about to change.

On this Tuesday morning (his days off were Tuesday and Wednesday), Jay stood in front of the bathroom mirror and studied his naked, dripping reflection. He had just climbed out of the old clawfooted bathtub after a long shower. Carly lay in a ball on the bathroom floor drowsily watching him.

Jay stood six two and in his younger years always thought of himself as too thin. Now that he had just squeaked past his thirty-second birthday, he was beginning to see a change in his body. He wasn't fat by any means, just a little… *thicker*. Were those love handles he saw? No, he supposed not. Just a little more meat to pad his aging bones.

His hair was too long at the moment, waving atop his head and dangling a little too far over his eyes for his own comfort. But he didn't care enough to get it cut. He usually let it fly wherever it would, now that Simon wasn't here to nag him about it.

He forced a smile to amuse himself and saw the old dimples pop into view. Simon had always told Jay those dimples were the reason he fell in love with him. The dimples and his dark, brooding eyes.

Jay chuckled inwardly at the thought, squishing his forehead to make his eyes even more brooding than usual. He hunched over like Igor in the old *Frankenstein* movie and glowered at himself a little more. Then he shook his head, wondering if he was nuts.

His chest was fuzzy, his stomach still flat, his long legs hairy and strong from standing at the bar all day and also from his long hikes with Carly up and down the side of his mountain, which he did for enjoyment as much as exercise.

Jay's hips were still narrow, his arms well muscled, his hands strong and capable. His cock, resting now in a nest of sparkling wet pubic hair, was uncircumcised, well fleshed out, and perhaps just beginning to grow tired of the constant lack of attention it had been receiving with Simon no longer around to worship it. Simon. Jay heaved a sigh at that thought. Making love with Simon had always been a gift. A gift he thought they would share forever. There were no taboos in their lovemaking. There was no holding back. Nothing was verboten.

Even thinking of Simon in the throes of passion now made Jay's cock lengthen. He watched in the mirror as it stretched itself out, as the head began peering through the shroud of foreskin where it usually slept. Soon his corona was exposed completely. Bulbous. Fat. Pink and ripe with an infusion of blood as his cock stretched proudly upright.

Jay scraped a thumb across his slit, and at the heavenly sensation, the muscles in his legs tightened. His body rocked with a tiny tremor of desire. His cock stood tall and erect now. He closed his eyes and gently wrapped it in his fist, relishing the rubbery firm girth of it in his hand. He slowly rolled the familiar length and weight of it through his fingertips, his touch lingering, his thumb still caressing the tip with every upward stroke. Already a drop of moisture had seeped through the opening there, causing Jay's thumb to slide over it now more sensually, making his legs buckle slightly, making him reach out with his other hand to grab the sink and maintain his balance.

"Oh, why the hell not," he said in a rumbly voice, and opening his eyes, he watched himself begin stroking his hard cock in earnest. His tongue slid out to moisten his lips as the speed of the strokes increased. His ears went red. His head tilted back.

When his hips began to move with the motion of his hand, he scraped his front teeth over his bottom lip and his eyes acquired that brooding look again. The one Simon used to love so much.

"Come for me," Simon would beg at times like that. And now, standing all alone on his mountaintop with his dog asleep on the floor behind him, Jay rose up on tiptoe and thrust his hips forward.

It was the thought of Simon that did it. His long, lean body. The heat of his groin on Jay's face. The succulent ass, always hungry, always ready.

That thought pushed Jay over the brink.

Jay groaned, and his come shot forth in fat globs, dappling the sink, splattering the mirror. He pumped his cock even faster, and more come dribbled from his slit, with less force now, but just as thickly, soaking his fingers, oozing down over his balls.

Jay released himself then and stood there, still bracing himself with one hand so he wouldn't fall flat on his face, while his heartbeat thundered in his head, and his red cock, slick with his own juices, bobbed in unison with the pounding of his heart. Another string of come dangled from the end, and Jay gathered it on a fingertip before it could fall, shuddering like crazy while he did.

"Holy shit," he gasped as his heart began to quiet and his cock began to wilt.

He swallowed hard and stared at himself in the come-splattered mirror.

"Guess I needed that," he grunted, his voice still weak with release.

Behind Jay, Carly raised her head and stared at him when he spoke. Her tail gave a couple of friendly thumps on the bathroom floor.

Jay gave her a wink. "You didn't see that." He proceeded to wipe himself down with his wet towel.

Later, Carly led him through the mountain brambles on a search for bunnies. At least Jay assumed that's what they were seeking. When they returned home a couple of hours later, Jay dropped into his recliner with a book, his dusty boots still on his feet, and read until his eyes closed in sleep and he softly began to snore.

In front of his chair, Carly snored in her sleep as well. With her eyes squeezed shut and a furrow of worry dimpling her forehead, she lay wondering, perhaps, where the rabbits had gone. They hadn't seen a single one on their walk—not that it was important, really. They had each other, her and Jay. That's all that truly mattered.

Both master and mutt smiled in their sleep while the cats groomed themselves on the mantle over the fireplace, waiting for the evening can of tuna to be dispensed.

That was all the cats really worried about. Tuna. And an occasional butt rub.

"WEAR THE red one," Joshua said, poking his head out of the bathroom.

"I don't like the red one," Danny said. "It hangs funny."

"It's cashmere," Joshua insisted. "It cost me a fortune. Wear the damn thing for once. I insist, babe. Don't piss me off, okay? We're supposed to be happy. We're going to a party."

MY DRAGON, MY KNIGHT

Danny stood naked in the bedroom, studying his glowering expression in the closet door mirror. He was holding his socks in one hand and a pair of underwear in the other.

Some party. Standing around listening to a bunch of CPAs and tax consultants bitch about work when the boss wasn't within earshot, celebrating the anniversary of the opening of the firm, grazing at the catered buffet like a bunch of fat, lazy cows, complaining that the roast beef was tough and the meatballs were cold and grousing about the damned clientele, who always wanted a break on their taxes whether they deserved one or not. Danny had attended last year's anniversary party and had been miserable the whole time. He didn't hold out much hope that this year would be any different.

Joshua leaned around the bathroom doorway again. His chin was coated with shaving cream, and he had a grin on his face. He nodded at the underwear in Danny's right hand.

"And don't wear underwear, Danny. I want to think of you standing beside me naked under your slacks while I'm discussing quarterlies and schmoozing with the clients."

What's that supposed to do for me? But Danny knew it was pointless to argue. He tossed the underwear back in the drawer and perched on the edge of the bed to slip on the socks while Joshua continued to ogle him from the doorway. Joshua was tugging gently at his balls at the same time. He had a heated look in his eye as he stood there staring at Danny still perched on the edge of the bed, naked, legs splayed wide, piddling with his socks.

"I'm going to fuck you silly when this party is over. Just a little heads-up, honey bunny."

Danny tried to smile, but it was a struggle. "I'm not sure I'm up for that, Josh." He tried to copy the lecherous leer he had seen on Joshua's face, but he didn't think he succeeded very well. "I'm kind of sore down there. You got a little rough last night, remember? I know other ways to make you happy, though." He tried to gather up enough enthusiasm to look sexy, but his heart wasn't in it.

Joshua frowned and dropped his balls like they were suddenly radioactive. "Don't be difficult, babe. By the time I'm finished, you'll be as happy getting fucked tonight as you were last night. Trust me. This is a special occasion. I don't want to fight."

No, you just want everything your own way. And you'll get it. You always get it.

Danny stepped into his trousers commando, as Joshua had demanded, and he wiggled his ass around to keep the zipper from snagging his dick. "Fine," he said. "Whatever his highness wants."

Joshua clearly didn't like the tone. "Just for that, maybe I'll fuck you especially hard. Maybe that will cure your attitude."

"Whatever," Danny mumbled and turned to leave the room.

"Jerk," Joshua muttered.

Danny finished dressing in black slacks and the red cashmere sweater in the living room and then sat on the sofa, scowling. Dried off, dressed, and with his hair perfectly arranged, Joshua eventually strode in with his shoes in his hand.

"What's *your* problem?" Joshua asked.

"Nothing," Danny said quietly. He glanced at his watch. "We should probably go, don't you think? You don't want to be late."

Joshua dropped his loafers to the floor and stepped into them. He brushed a dog hair from his trousers and mumbled, "Goddamn mutt."

Danny gazed toward the patio door where Jingles stood on the other side of the glass, staring in. He looked sad, Danny thought. He looked neglected.

Danny tossed him a smile, hoping the dog would understand that was all he could offer at the moment. Then Danny sighed and headed for the front door. "I'll drive," he said. "I've got my keys."

"We'll take my Lexus," Joshua stated flatly. "I can't have the boss see me driving up in your piece-of-crap Toyota."

Danny stopped in the doorway and whirled around. "Hey, it was all I could afford. You know that perfectly well. Why are you being such a cunt?"

Joshua grabbed Danny's arm and pulled him back into the condo, slamming the door shut and sealing them inside away from prying ears. He gripped Danny's shoulders none too gently and pressed him against the wall. "First you don't want to wear the red sweater. Then you don't want to fuck. Now you're bitching because I want to take my car. Someone's being a cunt, I think, but it isn't me."

Danny winced as Joshua's grip tightened.

"I expect you to be congenial tonight, Danny. Not just to me, but to everybody at the party. I expect you to smile and be attentive and make all those screaming queens jealous. Is that so much to ask from a lover?" He inhaled a short, shuddering breath. "Don't mess with me, Danny. Not tonight. You'll regret it if you do."

Danny's eyes teared up, and he hated himself for it. The accusatory words spilled out before he could stop them. "What are you going to do? Hit me again?"

Joshua visibly forced himself to relinquish his grip on Danny's arms. He stepped back, breathing deeply. The anger eased from his face, and he seemed to be calming down, but he never stopped clenching and unclenching his fists.

"I apologized for that," Joshua said. There was no wheedle in his voice. It was simply an icy statement of fact. "If it makes you happy, I guess I can apologize again."

"All right," Danny said quietly.

Joshua's eyes narrowed. The muscles in his jaw bulged. If there was ever love in Joshua's eyes for Danny before, there certainly wasn't any there at this particular moment. In fact, now that Danny thought about it, he wasn't sure there had *ever* been any love for Danny in Joshua's eyes. Lust, yes. Hunger, sure. A pride of ownership, absolutely. Even occasional rage. But never love.

With a trembling hand, as if still trying to control his anger, Joshua chucked Danny gently under the chin. Then his eyes flashed fire, and he leaned in and kissed Danny's lips. Hard.

"Ouch!" Danny said, jerking back when their teeth clattered together. His head hit the wall, and he said, "Ouch!" again.

Still pressing Danny to the wall with his body, Joshua slid his lips from Danny's mouth and pressed them to Danny's ear instead. He breathed his words in a cold whisper. "I don't care how sore you are. Later I'm going to fuck you till you scream. Just so you know."

He stepped back, releasing Danny, and once again yanked open the front door. "Now let's go," he said. "We're going to be late."

Danny bit down on the inside of his cheek as Joshua waved him through the door, trying to ignore Joshua's cold, cold smile when he did.

Danny wasn't looking forward to tonight at all. And not just the party, either, but what might come later. He silenced a sigh as he stepped through the building lobby and into the cool night air.

Joshua took his hand and led him toward the car. His grip was too tight, and Danny was sure Joshua knew it.

"I love you, Danny," Joshua said fiercely, not looking at Danny at all but concentrating on the keys in his hand. "Don't ever forget that."

"I love you too," Danny said back, but he suddenly realized the words meant nothing. Neither Joshua's nor his.

He couldn't help but wonder if Joshua knew it too.

THE PARTY was just as miserable as Danny had expected it would be. He stayed at Joshua's side every minute only because he didn't know what to say to anybody else in attendance.

Danny had to admit Joshua was on his best behavior and at his most charming. He introduced Danny to absolutely everyone, obviously proud to call Danny his lover. Joshua joked with some of his workmates, half of whom were gay, when they threatened to steal Danny out from under his very nose. A large part of the evening was spent with Joshua's hand at the back of Danny's neck, sweetly proprietary, Danny supposed, but annoying just the same, considering the way Joshua had *started* the evening—with threats. When moments of solitude came along every now and then, Joshua whispered words of love in Danny's ear, as if the argument between them earlier had never happened.

For his part, Danny tried to play the role expected of him. He fetched Joshua's drinks, stood with his hand in Joshua's back pocket, displaying ownership just as Joshua was doing to him. He blushed sweetly when the ridiculous comments were made about stealing him away. Usually those comments were made by older guys that Danny wouldn't have looked twice at in any other setting. But here he really had no choice. He had to be congenial. He knew if he wasn't, there would be hell to pay later.

Late in the evening, when an overabundance of cocktails had made the party a bit frenetic and everyone was drunk as a skunk, Danny was horrified when Joshua dragged him into the center of the room and waved his arms around to get everybody's attention.

When he had it, Joshua pulled a tiny box from his pocket and, taking Danny's hand, knelt to one knee in front of him. Blood rushed to Danny's ears as Joshua knelt there on the floor before him. He wanted to run but couldn't. He wanted to disappear but didn't know how.

Oh, sweet Jesus, no.

Pulling one of two simple gold rings from the box and holding it out to him, Joshua gazed up into Danny's eyes with a look of fawning adoration that Danny had never seen in those eyes before. That gaze wasn't meant for Danny, though, but for the audience gathered around them.

On his knees, Joshua spoke softly but loud enough for everyone in the room to hear. "We've lived together for a year," he said, stroking Danny's hand. "It's been the happiest year of my life. We were meant for each other, I think. Please say you'll stay with me forever. Marry me, Danny. Be my husband."

Danny stood speechless, staring down at this stranger on his knees before him. And while there was love in Joshua's eyes, Danny also thought he caught a glimpse of something else in their dark, burning depths. There was a threat there. Danny was sure of it. Joshua was leaving himself wide open here. That was something he rarely did. For the first time since the two of them came together, Danny felt a surge of power go through him. Joshua was at his mercy. In front of his workmates and clients and everyone he'd ever tried to impress, Joshua had left a chink in his armor that Danny could very well exploit.

For a second, Danny considered doing just that. Saying no. He tried to pull his hand away, but Joshua's eyes told him not to do it. Not to even dare. Danny's pulse thudded in his temples. His knees began to shake. Danny knew for a fact there was no love in what was happening. There was no heart in it. Joshua was playing a part and sweeping Danny into his little farce with him. Although he had no doubt Joshua meant every word he had spoken—he did want Danny for his own; he always had—it was not for love that Joshua wanted those things. It was for complete and utter control.

Danny should have seen this coming, he realized. What better way for Joshua to take ownership of Danny outright than by putting a ring on his finger and tying them together legally. Danny couldn't believe he'd let things go this far. He had never been so embarrassed in his life, and he had never been so torn as to what the hell he was supposed to do. Nor had he ever been as afraid to do it, no matter which way he chose to go.

For there was one truth Danny did know. It came to him the moment Joshua dropped to his knees in front of him. It came to him the moment Danny realized what Joshua was about to do.

The truth was this—Danny had lost. If this were a game of chess, Danny had just been checkmated.

Knowing the only way out of this situation—and the only way to survive this horrible moment in time and the night to follow—was to simply acquiesce, Danny twisted his mouth into a smile that felt alien on his face. With a trembling hand, he reached out and touched Joshua's cheek. If Joshua could play a part, so could he.

"Yes," he said, his voice as alien as the smile. He dredged the words up from the soles of his feet. They didn't want to come, but he had to speak them. He had to. "I—I'll marry you."

Once again, Danny saw that cool gleam of triumph flare in Joshua's eyes. He had won and he knew it. He had known he would all along, of course. Joshua knew Danny would never humiliate him in front of all these people by saying no. Danny would never humiliate himself that way either.

Joshua thrust the ring at him more determinedly. "Take it, babe. Please. Read the inscription inside the ring, Danny. Read it for everyone to hear."

Reluctantly, Danny took the ring from Joshua's fingers. He also took that moment to glance at the crowd around them. He saw a lot of conflicting emotions in the sea of faces looking on. He saw an appreciation of romance here and there, he saw simple curiosity, and he saw more than one face wear a smirk of incredulity, as if they too couldn't believe Joshua Stone could be such a twit as to do something like this.

Which was basically Danny's thought on the matter as well.

But instead of admitting it, Danny did as he was asked. He brought the tiny ring up to his eyes and read the inscription inside. He read it to himself, and the words sent a chill through him. He centered his eyes on Joshua's upturned face.

"It's meant to be romantic," Joshua explained.

Danny blinked. "Is it?"

"Yes. Read it out loud," Joshua said again. It wasn't a request, and Danny knew it. It was a command.

Danny swallowed hard and gazed down into Joshua's gloating eyes as he recited the words etched inside the ring for everyone to hear. He didn't have to look at the ring again to say them. The words were already seared into his brain.

"It says, 'Property of Joshua Stone.'"

Danny heard a couple of *aww*s in the crowd, even a murmur of appreciation, but he thought he heard a snicker or two also.

If Joshua heard it, he obviously didn't care. "You're mine now, Danny. And I'm yours. We belong to each other. Come down here and kiss me."

On legs as stiff as firewood, Danny lowered himself to the floor to kneel in front of Joshua. Once there, he let Joshua pull him into his arms. As their lips came together, a roar of drunken hoots and cheers thundered over them.

People moved in then, clapping them on the back while, still in each other's arms, they hauled themselves off the floor. Joshua was all smiles, accepting the praise and good wishes, some of them even sincere, as if he'd won an Oscar or something.

Danny closed his eyes to all the bustle, and the moment he did, some drunken stranger leaned into him and whispered, "You're in for it now, kid."

Danny figured truer words were never spoken.

"PLEASE," DANNY whispered in the darkness, his tears moist on the pillow beneath him. "Not tonight."

"I'll be gentle," Joshua breathed into his ear.

And he was. While Danny was a bit sore from the night before, as he'd said, he was not really in pain. It was simply a ruse to be left alone. One that didn't pan out, of course. Still, Joshua didn't know it was a ruse, thank God. He assumed Danny truly was tender down there, so when he entered him, his cock swollen and hungry but at least encased in a condom this time, Danny relaxed beneath him to make the entrance as easy as possible.

"Tell me again how much you love me," Joshua gasped as his cock forged a path through Danny's ass and began to move, to slide deeper, even as his cock swelled ever harder, ever fatter.

Hating himself for it, Danny closed his eyes and let Joshua take him completely. He even began to enjoy the piercing. As he always did. As Joshua *knew* he always did.

When Joshua came, his rocking motions became frantic. He lost all sense of rhythm as he cried out in Danny's ear. At the same moment, raising his ass in the air, meeting Joshua's uncontrollable thrusts and stroking his cock beneath him, Danny cried out at his own release as well.

Later, Joshua lovingly cleaned him up with a warm washcloth, cooing gentle words as he did.

But still, beneath the softness, beneath the caring, tender actions, Danny felt a stirring of dread building deep inside him. Deeper even than Joshua's cock had gone.

He slept that night in the arms of the man he was beginning to hate. And for the life of him, he didn't know what the hell he was supposed to do about it.

One thing he knew for a fact was that Joshua would kill him if he tried to leave. Danny didn't doubt that for a minute.

The other thing Danny knew for a fact was that he didn't want to marry this man. Being lovers should be enough. Hell, sometimes it was *more* than enough.

But marrying Joshua, actually signing the papers and making it legal, would be the stupidest thing Danny could ever do. And he damn well knew it.

HAVING FORGOTTEN during the course of the day, Jay strolled the half mile down his lane in the dark to check his mailbox, which stood where the lane met the county road that meandered up the side of the mountain. Jay wasn't expecting anything important in the mail. He was simply bored and thought he needed a little fresh air. He carried a flashlight with him because the rattlers had been known to curl up and sleep on the still-warm dirt of the trail after the sun went down. Stepping on one of them would be enough to ruin *anybody's* evening.

While Carly ranged noisily far and wide in the surrounding chaparral, barking and acting like a twit, Desi, one of the cats, followed regally along at Jay's heels, purring softly, looking neither left nor right.

The moon above Jay's head was fat and full and cast bluish shadows over the desert mountainside. The heavy reek of sagebrush lay on the air around him. Simon used to hate the scent of sage on the mountain air, but Jay had always loved it. It smelled of the wild to him. It smelled of freedom.

He could almost imagine himself centuries earlier, living on the edge of an as-yet-unexplored wilderness. A mountain man, maybe, decked out in rawhide with moccasins on his feet. Trapping and hunting for his livelihood. Surviving off the land.

It was a pleasant phantasy that Jay milked for all it was worth until it was shredded by the sight of a satellite streaking across the heavens. So much for the Old West.

With a roar of triumph, Carly flushed a rabbit out of the bushes. The rabbit tore a path straight for Jay, and when the startled creature burst onto the trail at his feet, Jay let out a whoop and jumped straight up in the air. Then he jumped again when Carly rushed past in front of him, hot on the trail of the rabbit. Mountain man indeed. If he jumped when a rabbit crossed his path, what the hell would he do if a bear came after him?

Jay laughed at himself, then scooped Desi off the trail and perched him on his shoulder. "Best get you up out of the way before you get run over," he said. "The wildlife seems to be stampeding all over the place tonight." The cat said thanks by nuzzling Jay's ear with his cold nose, purring up a storm and settling in for the ride.

With Desi happily anchored to his shoulder, Jay checked the mailbox, gathered up the couple of letters and the sheaf of worthless fliers he found inside, and headed back to the house. Halfway there, Carly joined them, coated with brambles, still panting, her tongue happily flopping around.

Jay figured he would have to brush her down before he let her inside the cabin.

Not that he much minded. It was worth it to see her look so proud of herself.

He gazed up at the sky. What he did mind was not having someone to share that fat, beautiful moon with.

Someone like… Danny.

The moment that thought crossed his mind, a stab of guilt struck him right between the eyes. He stopped and gave his head a sad little shake.

"I'm sorry, Simon," he whispered into the sagebrush-scented air before slowly walking on.

CHAPTER FOUR

JINGLES WASN'T stupid. He knew exactly where they were headed. His tail whapped back and forth, and he bounced around on the end of his leash like a kite in a hurricane. While Danny laughed at his antics, he also took a moment as he walked down Broadway to gaze into a passing store window or two, straightening his shirt and running fingers through his hair to make himself more presentable. Since it was kind of a windy day, he didn't want to look like he'd just fallen out of an airplane.

Danny had some serious problems to consider, but at the moment he refused to think about them. What he did now, he did for himself.

These noontime visits to the bar had become a habit Danny enjoyed. Jingles obviously enjoyed them too, not least because there was always a Milk-Bone or two waiting for him. Danny enjoyed the visits for reasons other than the doggy treats. Which is not to say they were reasons he was actually willing to admit to himself. Not yet anyway.

But he did admit to having found a friend in Jay Holtsclaw. At the present time in Danny's life, with all the restrictions Joshua put on his time and now with the fucking proposal to worry about, it was nice to have found someone he could talk to. The fact that Jay was handsome and sweet and caring did not escape Danny's notice either. It was also nice that Jingles could be himself for once, gratefully accepting his two Milk-Bones, then hopping down and exploring the bar while Jay and Danny chatted over a beer. At home, Jingles's movements were so limited by Joshua's threatening presence, he barely left the balcony at all anymore, which broke Danny's heart a little bit. So perhaps Danny wasn't the only one who'd found a friend in Jay. Maybe Jingles had too.

Since he hated both his job and night school, dropping in at The Clubhouse for an occasional beer and chat had become the high point of Danny's existence. He tried not to go overboard, limiting his visits to two or three times a week, but on the days he didn't go, he always felt something was missing from his life.

Today was no different. Danny's pulse quickened as he stepped through the blackout curtain hanging in the doorway. At the first sight of Jay standing behind the bar serving Bloody Marys to a trio of older gay men, Danny felt a stab of disappointment, knowing on this day he would have to share Jay's time with his customers. Danny liked it better when it was just the two of them—or three, counting Jingles.

Still, it was nice to see Jay light up when Danny stepped through the door. That welcoming smile made Danny's pulse quicken. He couldn't deny it. And when Jay pointed to the far end of the bar where the two of them could have a little privacy, Danny smiled wide and accepted the invitation eagerly.

By the time he got there, his beer was waiting for him, and alongside the beer sat two dog biscuits on a napkin. Jay had poured himself a beer too, Danny noticed, which was nice. It meant he wouldn't be drinking alone.

It was a funny thing about these noontime trysts, if that's what they were. Jay's and Danny's conversations sometimes picked up at the exact place they had left off the time before, as if no time had passed at all. Today was one of those days, or Jay tried to make it so. Unfortunately, his plans didn't exactly pan out.

After waving away Danny's offer of money, Jay leaned his elbows on the bar and rested his chin in his hands, bringing his face even with Danny's. That way they could talk more quietly.

"You were telling me about night school," Jay said, and Danny's mood darkened at the mention. Jay must have recognized the shift because he quickly corrected himself. "Or fuck school. Maybe we were talking about something else. So how have you and the mutt been? How's Rocky Balboa? Oops. I mean the boyfriend." Danny was relieved for a second at the change of direction, but then the mention of Joshua disturbed him all over again.

Looking like he wanted to pull his tongue out with a pair of tongs from the garnish tray and slice it off with his fruit knife, Jay reached out and touched Danny's hand. "I'm saying all the wrong things today. How's about *you* take the helm and steer the conversation where *you* want it to go."

Jay delivered the lines like lighthearted banter, but the humor was lost on Danny. He stared down at Jay's cool fingers resting on his arm and then covered them with his own. He'd had no intention of talking about Joshua with Jay today. But now that he was here, he realized he had to. He had to talk to *somebody*.

"He asked me to marry him," Danny said.

A THUD of unease jolted Jay. There was no celebration in Danny's voice. His lips were thin, and he gazed up into Jay's face as if he had just admitted to some horrible wrongdoing. The poor kid looked like a deer stunned by a pair of headlights. A thrill had jolted through Jay when Danny touched his hand, but hearing about a marriage proposal from that jerk Danny was with was the last thing Jay wanted. The look of fear, the look of being *trapped* that crossed Danny's face when he said it, made the announcement even worse.

Because he felt he should, Jay made a concerted effort to keep his voice neutral. He was ranting and raving inside. On the outside, he was calm. Or at least he hoped he was. "So what did you tell him, Danny?"

Danny tore his gaze from Jay and made a quick reconnaissance of the bar, either to see where Jingles had gone or to avoid looking Jay in the eye. Jingles had curled up under his barstool and was softly snoring. Jay couldn't see him, but he could certainly hear him. Eventually, Danny turned back to Jay.

"I told him yes."

Now it was Jay's turn to avoid Danny's eye. He stared down at his fingers resting atop Danny's arm. As if he had no control over his own appendages whatsoever, he watched like a bystander as his fingertips slipped down Danny's arm over the bony ridge of his wrist and scooped Danny's fingers into his grasp.

Jay clutched Danny's hand gently as he said, "So you really do love him, then."

Danny's thumb stroked the back of Jay's hand. "I told him yes because I didn't have a choice. He picked the worst time ever to propose, in front of everybody he works with. He made a bigass production out of it. I'm surprised he didn't post it on YouTube. I kept expecting a line of chorus boys to come dancing out of the wings. I—I didn't know what else to do, Jay. Josh would have killed me if I had humiliated him by saying no in front of his friends."

"Maybe that's why he asked you when he did," Jay said quietly.

Danny nodded. "Yeah, I think it is."

Jay had an almost uncontrollable urge to bring Danny's hand up to his lips, but he didn't quite dare. Danny had enough crap to worry about without being hit on by the one person that maybe he felt he could trust.

"He even bought the rings," Danny said, looking down at his bare finger.

"You aren't wearing it," Jay responded.

"I didn't want to." Danny looked so sad it nearly broke Jay's heart. "I'll have to put it on again before he comes home from work."

Danny continued staring at their two hands lying there clasped together. Wishing for eye contact, Jay gave Danny's hand a little squeeze to get his attention. When Danny's eyes rose to his, he asked, "So what are you going to do?"

"I don't know."

"Do you want to marry him?" Jay's heart gave a lurch the moment those words were out of his mouth. Jesus, did he really want to know the answer to that question?

Jay almost smiled when Danny said, without a moment of hesitation, "No." Danny didn't give him a chance to respond, though God knows what Jay would have said. Anger flared in Danny's eyes. He sat up straighter on the barstool. His grasp on Jay's hand grew tighter.

"He doesn't love me, Jay. He just wants to own me, I think. If I marry him, I'll really be trapped. I can love Josh sometimes. I can. There are moments when he's good. He can even be fun. But there are other times...."

"There are other times when you're afraid of him," Jay said, and this time he threw all caution to the wind and did raise Danny's hand to his lips. He kissed the pad of Danny's thumb and gazed in amazement at the beauty of Danny licking his lips, staring at him wide-eyed, stunned, perhaps, by what Jay had done. But he didn't pull away. That was all Jay knew.

Danny didn't pull away.

"There's something else," Danny said, his voice barely audible over the laughter of the three customers yakking at the other end of the bar.

Jay was alarmed to see a tear slide down Danny's cheek.

"What, Danny? What is it?"

Danny's fingers tightened around Jay's, and Jay held on in return just as tightly.

Danny's words came out on a shudder of breath. Just a whisper of sound, like the distant stirring of leaves on a tree. "I'm afraid to leave him, Jay. I'm afraid of what he'll do."

A silence fell over the two.

"Then that's reason enough to leave right there," Jay finally said, his lips still on Danny's hand.

Danny simply stared back while another tear slid down his cheek.

"Where have you been?"

"I went out for a beer."

"There's beer in the fridge, Danny. You could have stayed home and had a beer."

"Jingles needed a walk. I killed two birds with one stone."

"Where'd you go? The Clubhouse?"

"Yeah."

"You've been going there a lot."

"No. Just once in a while. And only for a few minutes. It's in walking distance. Would you rather I drive somewhere and get picked up for drunk driving on the way home?"

"What I'd rather is for you to stay home altogether."

"Christ, Josh, I'm an adult. I should be able to have a beer when I want. Besides, Jingles needs to be taken out."

"They let you take that stupid dog into the bar?"

"They don't mind."

"I'm pretty sure that's against a health law or two. Maybe I should report the bar for endangering public welfare."

"Jesus, Josh, why would you want to do that? That's just mean and spiteful."

"You think I'm mean and spiteful?"

Silence.

"I asked you a question, Danny. Do you think I'm mean and spiteful?"

"No."
"Where's your ring?"
"What?"
"Where's the ring I gave you?"
"I—I took it off earlier to wash my hands."
"So you know where it is, then?"
"Yeah. It's by the sink in the kitchen."
"No, it isn't. I was just in there."
"But I—"
"It's only been a week and you've already lost the ring."
"It's in the kitchen, I tell you."
"Go look if you don't believe me."
"If it isn't there, then you've got it."
"Maybe you're not so dumb after all. Yes. It's right here. Do you want it back?"
"Well, sure."
"I'd like to know why you feel you have to take my ring off when you go to the bar."
"What?"
"You heard me."
"It wasn't like that. I took the ring off to wash my hands. Later I went to the bar. The two actions were not connected."
"If you don't like the ring, I can take it back. I can take a lot of things back, Danny. Is that what you want?"
"N-no."
"Don't start that sniffling shit. Why are you crying?"
"You're scaring me."
"Good. You need to be scared once in a while. And don't go to the bar again."
"I don't see why I can't—"
"Danny!"
"All right. If that's what you—"
"Never take this ring off again either. Promise me."
"I—I promise."
"Tell me you love me."
"Y-you know I do."

"You disappoint me, Danny. Come here and take this ring before I come over there and cram it up your ass."

"Josh, please—"

"I said come here. Closer. Come closer."

"I'm practically on top of you now."

"If I ever thought you were cheating on me, you know what I'd do, right?"

"I'm not cheating on you."

"I asked you a question, Danny. Do you know what I'd do if I thought you were cheating on me?"

"You—you'd hurt me."

"Bingo."

And the fist came out of nowhere.

ON A Thursday when the California sky had opened up and the city was deluged with an early rain, Jay stood at the bar staring at the curtain separating him from the world outside.

Last week Danny had stopped by three times for a noontime beer.

This week Danny hadn't shown up at all, and Jay was worried out of his mind.

He had begun to enjoy the visits from his young friend—begun to enjoy them a little too much, maybe. But still, what the hell did that have to do with anything? The simple fact was he still missed Danny every single morning he didn't show up at the bar.

The unwanted proposal of marriage Danny had told Jay about was bad enough, but a whole weeks' worth of missed visits was really starting to frighten Jay.

He had visions of Danny lying in a hospital bed somewhere, beaten to a pulp, one or two limbs encased in plaster, his appendages strung up on some godawful hospital trapeze contraption while he healed from his fucking injuries—injuries inflicted by his asshole lover, Joshua.

Oh yeah, Jay knew the guy's name now. He and Danny knew a lot about each other after all the talks they'd shared over the occasional beer, while Jingles, more times than not, sat on the barstool listening in.

Jay still cringed remembering the first time he and Danny had spoken. That was the day Danny came in with his jaw puffed out like a cantaloupe. Jay still saw red every time he thought of it.

Danny had never brought Joshua to the bar to meet Jay, because if he had, Jay knew, it would be tantamount to admitting that Jay and Danny got together now and then to talk about the jerk. And they *had* talked about him. They had talked about Joshua enough for Jay to know that Danny was afraid of him. While Jay made a promise to himself he wouldn't try to interfere with their relationship, it was a promise he was having a hard time keeping.

There was nothing Jay hated worse than a cheater. Someone who either cheated on his lover, or someone who wormed his way into a position to make somebody *else's* lover cheat. Jay didn't want to be that other guy. While he thought it would be the best thing to ever happen to Danny if he tore himself free from Joshua altogether, Jay still didn't want to be the one who created the breach.

It had taken Jay a long time to admit it to himself, but what he wanted—what he *really wanted*—was for Danny to make the decision on his own. *And then come to me of his own free will.*

So yes, Jay had finally admitted to himself he had feelings for the boy. Sorry. Feelings for the *man*. There was nothing Jay wanted more than to wrap Danny safely in his arms and protect him from the world. And from Joshua.

But it had to be Danny's decision. Not his.

Standing behind the bar, Jay turned his attention to the street door for the twentieth time that day.

It was funny how quickly the temperature had dropped. It seemed like yesterday that San Diego broiled under summer skies. Now it was autumn. Jay stood listening to the rain, feeling the cold damp air blowing through the open door, whistling underneath the leather blackout curtain, stirring the napkins on the bar. He sighed a heavy sigh. When the cold air made him shiver, he didn't even mind. His thoughts had exploded into a thousand fragments, and unfortunately there were no customers in the place to distract him from those thoughts. Yep. Jay figured a distraction about now would definitely be a good thing.

He eased around from behind the bar, crossed in front of the pool table, and began pulling the front door closed to block out the wind. It was cheaper than turning on the furnace. Before he blocked the day out completely, he stood in the doorway and stared out at the city, the crisp familiar lines of the downtown high-rises blurred by the downpour. The ever-present crowds of passersby on the sidewalks were quickly dispersing, hustling themselves in out of the rain. Passing cars threw great sheets of water from beneath their wheels, making the pedestrians run even faster.

Not for the first time, Jay wished he had Danny's phone number. But he had never asked for it for fear a moment like this would come along and he would use it.

Then another thought entered Jay's head. A clever thought. A *sneaky* thought.

He knew for a fact that Danny still worked at Macy's. Danny's shift started later in the day. Maybe Jay could simply happen to be strolling through the men's department of said establishment, and maybe he would accidentally run into Danny when he did. It's not like he'd be asking for trouble. Hell, a lot of people shop at Macy's. And Jay needed a new coat since winter was coming up. No shit. He really did.

He glanced at his watch. Tommy would relieve him in a few hours. Danny would still be on duty in the shopping center then. On duty in the Macy's store where he worked. At the shopping center. Only a few blocks away.

Yep. I definitely need a new coat.

Whistling, Jay set to work prepping the fruit for the night ahead. While he worked, he still kept an eye on the front door. But once again, Danny never showed up.

Cutting limes, Jay gnawed his lip and worried. Then he worried even more because of what he was about to do. And what he was about to do was cross that line he had always held sacred. Don't get involved with anyone already in a relationship. And don't tempt anyone else to get involved.

On the other hand, maybe involvement had nothing to do with it. Maybe he was simply worried about a friend. Or better yet, maybe the only thing he was about to do was simply buy a fucking coat.

He chuckled in the darkness. Jeez, even *he* wasn't stupid enough to believe that one.

Jay's knife slashed through the limes while the rain pounded down outside. His heart felt lighter just knowing he would see Danny later.

That lightness of heart probably wasn't a good sign. And yeah, Jay could admit it to himself now—he had a crush on the kid. But that didn't mean he still couldn't be just a friend. It didn't mean he was anything more than concerned for Danny. It's not like he was about to make any grand announcements. He wasn't going to declare his undying love or anything. He just wanted to make sure Danny was safe. That's all. Really. That's all he wanted to do.

Plus buy a coat.

While he worked, he remembered Danny's smile. How sweet it was. How open and honest and handsome. Jay cast a silent prayer skyward that when he finally found Danny, that smile would still be intact.

Hell, who knows. Maybe it would even be aimed at him. A guy could hope.

He coughed up another wry chuckle. That hope probably wasn't a good sign either.

IT WAS midafternoon. Jay rushed out of the bar two minutes after Tommy relieved him. Rather than drive his Jeep the few blocks to Macy's and fight the traffic, Jay sloshed through the downpour with his collar turned up and a baseball cap pulled low over his forehead. His mind was so filled with worrying about Danny by this time, Jay hardly noticed the rain at all.

Foot traffic in the mall was sparse. After shaking himself off, Jay strolled through Macy's Men's Department between racks of shirts and slacks, trying to ignore the godawful Muzak, peeking around displays, hoping he looked inconspicuous and not like a shoplifter, all the while searching for a blond-headed clerk. Finally, in the distance, he saw one standing at a cash register, ringing up a sale. The clerk's back was to Jay, but it was Danny. Jay knew it by the pale hair and the way the guy was standing. Something about the posture. Something about the line of the shoulders. The slim build.

Jay took a moment just to stare at him. My God, even from behind Danny was beautiful.

Jay lingered at a shoe display, studying a pair of tennis shoes he didn't give a shit about, waiting for Danny to finish with the transaction. As soon as the customer gathered up her bags and Danny bent to drop a bunch of hangers into a box by the counter, Jay stepped in front of him with a broad smile on his face, fighting the urge to say "Tada!" like a magician pulling a rabbit out of his hat. Then he got a good look at Danny's face and almost laughed.

"What's with the sunglasses?"

Danny gave a start. "Jay! What are you doing here?"

Jay spread his arms wide and twirled around in a circle like some sillyass ballerina, trying to be funny. Trying to be charming. "Shopping. What else?"

Danny stood watching him. His smile appeared forced, Jay thought. Maybe this hadn't been such a good idea after all. Then he noticed Danny's ears getting red. He looked uncomfortable.

Jay stepped closer and rested his hands on the counter, hating the fact that the big fucking chunk of plywood and plastic was preventing him from getting any closer.

"Danny?" he said quietly. "I haven't seen you at the bar. I was worried. So I thought I'd come and see if you were okay."

Danny almost smiled at that. "I thought you said you were shopping."

"Yeah, well, that too," Jay said. "I need a coat. At least I think I do." He leaned in closer and studied Danny's face. "You didn't answer my question. It's raining cats and dogs outside. Why in the world are you wearing sunglasses?"

Danny bit down on his lip before answering. "You don't want to know."

The smile fell from Jay's face. He tightened his lips into a tense line. "I think I do."

Danny stiffened. "Don't get mad. Everybody's always mad at me these days."

Jay blinked. "I'm not mad at you, Danny. I might be afraid for you, but I'm not mad." A silence settled over the two. The silence went on just long enough to become uncomfortable. "Danny. Take off the glasses. Please."

"Jay—"

"Please."

With a trembling hand, Danny slipped the sunglasses off his nose. His right eye was almost swollen shut. The flesh around it was green and purple, and beneath it hung a sack of blood, as black as chocolate pudding.

Jay bit down on his own fist. Before he could stop it, his anger spewed out. "I'm gonna kill that fucker!"

Danny reached out to Jay's other hand, covering it with his own. "Jay, please. It was my fault. I started it. I shouldn't have been going to the bar so much. It's only natural he got jealous."

Jay stood staring, incredulous. "Please don't tell me he did this because of me!"

"No, he—"

"And don't make excuses for him! How long have you looked like this?"

Danny hesitated.

"How long?"

"Almost a week. But it's getting better."

"This is *better*?"

"Jay, please. Did—did you really want a coat? What kind were you thinking about get—"

And again, before Jay could stop himself, he broke every vow he'd made to himself about not interfering. "Danny, you have to leave him. You can't go on like this. One of these days he's going to go too far, and you're going to end up seriously hurt."

Danny dredged up a Joan Rivers impersonation while pointing at his injured eye with a trembling finger. "What? This isn't serious enough?"

"Don't joke, Danny. I mean it."

Danny heaved a sigh and slid the sunglasses back in place. "I think you'd better go, Jay. I don't want to get fired. I need this job."

"I know, but—"

Danny's hand still covered Jay's on the countertop. "Please, Jay. We can't talk about this here. My boss is already a little unhappy that I have to wear sunglasses to work."

"I think this is more important than your job, Danny. This is your life we're talking about."

Danny leaned in close and hissed in an angry whisper. "I know it's my fucking life! And I know I have to leave him! But I can't do it without setting aside enough money to get an apartment of my own."

"I'll loan you the money."

"I don't want you to loan me the money, Jay. I'm tired of owing people. I owe Josh, and look where it's got me."

"What do you owe Josh?"

Danny sighed again, casting his gaze around the store as if making sure the boss wasn't watching. When he turned back to Jay, he was vibrating with anger.

"I owe Josh because he took me in and gave me a nice place to live."

"Where he constantly abuses you," Jay argued.

Danny ignored him. "He convinced me to start night school so I could one day find a good job."

"In a field you care nothing about."

"I'm trying to make something of myself, dammit."

Again Jay objected. "The only thing you're making of yourself is a victim. He's going to kill you one of these days, Danny. Can't you see that?"

Danny stood mute. Furious now. It was the first time Jay had ever seen him angry. He wasn't convinced that was a bad thing at all. Danny *needed* to be angry.

Jay clutched Danny's hand, trapping it in his own. "Goddammit, Danny. Listen to me. You have to get away from this guy. He's nuts. He's crazy."

There were still a couple of empty hangers resting on the counter. Danny used his free hand to scrape them into the box on the floor with all the others, where they landed with a clatter. He whirled on Jay, his voice a seething hiss of desperation. "Do you think I don't know that? Look, I'm doing the best I can! These things take time. I can't just leave today. What about Jingles? What about all my stuff?"

"I told you. I'll help you."

"No!"

"Why not?"

Danny was clearly trying to calm down. He was so mad he was shaking. So was Jay.

"I just can't leave him right now," Danny said, his voice weak, resigned. He looked like he was collapsing in upon himself, like a man who was simply worn the fuck out.

Jay wasn't worn out at all. Jay was bristling with energy.

"Why not, Danny? Tell me why the hell not? Why can't you leave him today! Why can't you leave him this very goddamn *minute*?"

When Danny spoke, his words were drenched in weary emotion. The hand in Jay's fist was cold and small. Shaking.

Danny leaned close, whispering fiercely, tears brimming in his eyes. "Because he'll kill me if I do."

CHAPTER FIVE

JAY STOOD on his front porch watching the sun slide down the western slope of his tiny mountain. The rain had stopped, but not before it turned his winding lane into a muddy mess. Thank God his Jeep had four-wheel drive or he never would have made it home.

The one good thing about the rain was that it produced a most spectacular sunset. Jay looked out on a sky ablaze with streaks of tangerine and red, slashed through with arrows of razor-sharp golden flame. The remaining dark splotches of storm clouds skimming away in the distance were limned with the fiery light of the setting sun.

If only Jay hadn't been too upset to appreciate the beauty in front of him.

The scene at Macy's with Jay trying to convince Danny to get the hell away from his lover while he was still able to had infuriated Jay. It was a frustrating, confusing fury too, for Jay wasn't exactly sure who he was maddest at: Danny himself, or the brutal man Danny had let himself get involved with. Joshua.

While the anger still burned inside him, there were other forces at play too. There were truths buried within him he couldn't quite sort out. Truths about the way Jay was beginning to think about Danny. Truths about the hunger Jay was starting to feel when he thought of Danny, about the clenching sensation he felt inside his chest every time Danny was near. Truths about the *real* reason Jay wanted Danny to flee the relationship he was in.

Selfish truths.

Jay bent and twiddled Carly's ear. Carly repaid his tenderness by pressing her snout into his hand and licking his palm. Jay smiled down at her.

"He's too young for me," Jay said.

Carly's ears stood up, as if she were considering the statement.

"And he's way too cute for someone like me."

Carly tilted her head so far to one side that one long ear fell over her face and dangled there atop the other. She didn't look convinced.

"He's vulnerable right now. The last thing I should do is try to push myself on him."

Carly's tail thumped on the wooden porch floor.

Jay's lips tightened as he stood there staring down at the dog. A furrow formed between his eyes. Carly whimpered, watching him. Her eyes grew worried too.

"He's in a dangerous situation, Carly. And he's frightened. I could protect him, I think, if he'd let me. But he won't. He's too afraid of that bastard he's living with. Hell, maybe by now he's too afraid to trust *anybody*." Man and dog stared at each other. "To make matters worse, Carly, it's entirely possible that anything I try to do to help him might put him in even more danger than he's already in."

Aside from perking up a little at the sound of her name, Carly finally appeared to grow bored with the one-sided conversation. She dropped to her belly again, laid her chin across her paws, and closed her eyes.

Jay smiled sadly down at her before staring back at the sunset, no wiser than he had been before. Still unsure as to what he should do. Or if he should do anything at all.

He shivered as the cool evening breeze brushed his face. It would be downright cold tonight at this higher elevation. He didn't need a weatherman to tell him that. Maybe he'd build a fire in the fireplace. Fires are great for toasting your toes while sitting in front of the flames, sucking on a beer and pondering life's mysteries. Plus, Jay felt lonely and, strangely, heartsore. A fire would keep him company, keep him distracted.

He set off to gather an armload of firewood from the stack at the back of the house. As he traipsed across the muddy yard, Carly at his heels as always, one word kept time with Jay's footsteps. One name kept tapping its rhythm through the darkness inside his head, incorporating itself into his thoughts. Flowing in tempo with every breath he took. That name was almost a part of him now. It continually thudded through him like a heartbeat.

Danny—Danny—Danny—

DANNY STOOD at the dining room table, staring at the gaily wrapped package. The rain outside the condo windows had lessened. It was coming on to dusk, and Danny thought he saw a glimmer of clear sky on the horizon. Maybe the rain wouldn't last much longer. He was still upset by the confrontation with Jay at the store earlier, but he was trying not to think about it. Danny tore his eyes from the horizon and stared back at the package in front of him, at Joshua standing there offering it to him.

"What's this?" Danny asked for the second time.

Joshua smiled a handsome smile. "Take it, baby. It's for you. It'll help you with school."

Danny didn't want the package. He didn't care what was in it; he didn't want it. "You didn't have to do that."

Joshua reached out and removed the sunglasses from Danny's face. He leaned in closer to examine the damaged eye. "It's looking better."

"I know."

"Does it still hurt?"

"A little."

"I'm sorry I did that, Danny. I'm sorry I hurt you. If you hadn't moved when you did, the smack I gave you wouldn't have caused so much damage."

Danny almost laughed. Now it was Danny's fault for moving wrong while Josh was throwing a sucker punch.

"I'm sure that's what happened," Danny said. "I moved wrong."

Obviously Joshua didn't detect the note of sarcasm in Danny's words or Danny would no longer be standing. While still holding the gift out like an offering, all Joshua said was, "Anyway, I'm sorry. Maybe this present will help make up for it."

You mean until next time? Danny wanted to ask. But of course he didn't. He wasn't that stupid.

Since he couldn't do anything else, he took the package. It was only a few inches thick, but heavy. Maybe a foot and a half across.

"Open it," Joshua said around a smile. He was handsome, standing there all excited about giving Danny a gift. He really was. Danny had to admit it. But Danny had seen too many glimpses into the reality of what lay *beneath* all that handsomeness to be taken in by it anymore.

Danny set the package on the dining room table and began pulling at the gift paper, trying to ignore the gleams of light bouncing off the ring shining on his finger. The ring Josh had given him. The same as the ring

Josh also wore on his finger. Danny hated that ring now. Still, he never removed it. He didn't dare.

Danny already hated whatever was inside the package too, but he didn't dare show that either. He carefully set the lengths of ribbon aside like his aunt May used to do, not that Danny wanted to save the ribbon. No. What he was actually doing was simply stalling for time because he just didn't *care* what was inside the fucking box.

"I'm sorry I hit you, Danny. It won't happen again. I promise."

Danny stopped what he was doing and stared at Josh. He had heard that promise before. In fact, Danny heard that promise every time Joshua whacked him. The promise had lost a little of its fizz by now. If it was veracity Danny was looking for, he knew better than to try to find it in one of Josh's insincere apologies. It was all he could do to even *pretend* to believe what Josh was saying.

But Danny could be a liar too. He proved it by saying the same thing he always said at times like this. "I know you're sorry. It was my fault too. I shouldn't have done what I did."

Although for the life of me, I don't know what the fuck it was.

Danny didn't expect to hear any argument, and sure enough he didn't. It was fairly obvious that Joshua believed their little altercation had been all Danny's fault.

Through the jumble of torn gift paper, Danny spotted the Apple logo on a gray slab of cardboard. He tore the rest of the paper away and stood there staring down at what Joshua had given him.

"It's a MacBook Air," Danny said.

Joshua beamed. "I told you it would help you with your schooling."

Danny nodded, trying to dredge up a little enthusiasm but not being very successful about it. His eye was aching, and just having Josh standing this close to him was starting to piss him off. Still, Danny knew he was in dangerous territory here. If he said the wrong thing, he might very well be sporting *two* black eyes for the next month.

He walked into Josh's arms and pressed his face to Josh's chest, just so he wouldn't have to look at him. "Thank you," he mumbled.

Josh's arms slid around him. "I love you, Danny."

Danny nodded. "I love you too," he lied.

And for the first time, Danny truly admitted to himself it *was* a lie. A cold, bald-faced lie.

Afraid the nearness would spur Josh into wanting sex, which was the last thing Danny desired, he splashed some phony glee onto his face like aftershave and stepped back, rubbing his hands together. "Let me see if I'm smart enough to get this thing up and running. I've really needed a laptop. Thanks again, Josh. This is great."

It worked. Josh watched, pleased, while Danny began excitedly uncrating the MacBook Air. Josh would have been surprised to read Danny's real thoughts at that moment. He probably wouldn't have been too thrilled to know that what Danny truly wanted to do was heave the fucking laptop off the balcony and watch it explode into a million chips of plastic on the street below.

Then he would have liked for Jingles to take a dump on Josh's fucking foot. At that thought, Danny did smile. Luckily, Josh never knew what brought the smile to life.

If Danny had known what would happen before the week was over, he wouldn't have brought Jingles into the equation at all.

ON SUNDAY, Jay went to The Clubhouse early. He stripped the back of the bar of all liquor bottles, rows and rows of them. Then he removed the cocktail glasses and stemware and various other tools of the trade, setting it all atop the bar out of the way. When the shelves were empty, he went to work scrubbing them down. When that job was completed to his satisfaction, he began cleaning the mirrors that covered the walls behind the shelves. With the mirrors clean, he wiped down all the bottles that were on the bar. He worked as if his life depended on it. The bar wasn't really that dirty, of course. Even Jay knew what he was really doing was working off his frustrations. Of which he had many.

While he worked, he made sure the front door of the joint was open in case anyone needed an early-morning libation. He was in attendance, after all. He might as well be open for business while he cleaned.

Besides, you never knew *who* might drop in.

It had been days since Jay confronted Danny at Macy's, and Danny still hadn't set foot in the bar again. Jay missed seeing him. He missed their short talks, even when those talks sometimes touched on unhappy matters—such as Danny's stormy relationship with Joshua. Stormy relationship. There was an understatement if Jay ever heard one. Still, Danny must know Jay was worried about him. Was this Danny's way of letting Jay know he didn't appreciate being confronted on his own turf and told how to live his life? Or was Danny *afraid* to visit the bar because of what Joshua might do if he found out?

Jay was glad he didn't have Danny's phone number. If he had, he was pretty sure he would have made a fool of himself by now by calling every five minutes and quite possibly endangering Danny even more than he was endangered already.

Jay worked for hours. A couple of customers dropped in, taking their drinks at one of the tables in the back since the bar was buried in liquor bottles. Jay played the jukebox while he worked, another unsuccessful attempt to take his mind off Danny.

By two o'clock, when one of his bartenders relieved him, Jay had the place put back together.

Still no Danny.

With a sad heart, Jay gathered his crap, waved good-bye to everybody, and headed home.

He walked Carly down the mountainside that evening, still dodging puddles from the rainstorm earlier in the week. With winter coming on, Jay wore his heavy coat with a bright red woolen scarf that used to belong to Simon wound around his neck.

Even in the cool of approaching winter, the wildflowers were blooming. They showed up as splashes of yellow trailing down the mountain among the boulders and the crusty chaparral that no amount of rain ever seemed to make supple and green. It was those familiar smears of sweetly scented yellow blossoms along his mountainside that always heralded winter for Jay. That's how he knew cold weather was really about to set in. Not down in the city, perhaps, or along the coast. But up here on Mount Miguelito, which Jay called home, the winters could be pretty chilly for Southern California. The cabin even got an occasional dusting of snow in the colder years.

As night began to settle in, Jay and Carly wended their way back up the mountainside, heading for home. Jay hummed softly to himself as he walked, and Carly shot off in one direction or another, chasing down whatever took her fancy at that particular moment.

Back at the cabin, Jay prepared a simple dinner for himself. Sandwiches, a beer. He fed Carly and the cats and scattered some bran out back for the chickens. If he'd had a rat in his possession he'd have tossed it down the basement steps for the fucking rattlesnake. Or maybe not. Later, he enjoyed the fire for a while, letting it burn down to embers so he wouldn't have to worry about burning the cabin to the ground while he slept. Finally he headed off to bed.

Turning off the lamp beside the bed in his second-story bedroom, he listened to the animals stirring around here and there in the cabin, settling in for the night themselves. Lucy came and joined him, taking up residence at the foot of the bed, adding her gentle purr to the symphony of house finches singing their good-night song in the rafters above the garret.

The moment the cabin settled down for the night and darkness truly closed him in, a face appeared in Jay's imagination. It was a beautiful young face with blue eyes—not just blue, but blue upon blue—with blond lashes and more blond hair hanging over a smooth, golden-skinned forehead. It was Danny, of course. It was Danny's face. And it was undamaged.

In his imagination, Jay reached out and trailed a finger along Danny's smooth cheek. He smiled lying in his bed as in his vision he saw Danny turn his head into Jay's touch. Danny's warm lips brushed the skin of his finger in gentle acceptance.

At that moment, Jay sat straight up in bed, startling Lucy, who took off running.

Simon! Jay had forgotten Simon. Today was Sunday, and for the first time since he'd died, Jay had forgotten to put flowers on Simon's grave.

As if that wasn't bad enough, he came to another unnerving realization. Jay threw back the blankets and slung his bare legs over the side of the bed, ignoring the goose bumps that rose on his skin because the room was so cold.

"I have to tell him," Jay said, speaking into the darkness, into the shadows. His words were aimed at no one. At nothing. Or more appropriately, aimed backward at himself. And at Simon as well.

"I don't care what happens, Simon. I don't. It has to be done. I'll go crazy if I don't."

Sitting there in the darkness, he didn't have to explain himself to anyone. Jay knew exactly who and what he was talking about.

Danny, he thought around a dawning smile. *I have to tell Danny how I feel.*

JINGLES WAS bored. Perhaps that was enough to explain what happened. Or maybe Fate simply decided to ratchet up the drama, as if Danny didn't have enough drama in his life already. Whatever the reason, Danny woke up at first light knowing—*just knowing*—something was wrong.

He eased out from underneath Joshua's arm. Joshua's soft snore stopped for a moment, then resumed. Danny heaved a sigh of relief and wormed his way out from under the covers, trying to jar the mattress as little as possible.

He snatched up the pajama bottoms that lay in a muddle on the floor beside the bed, then dragged the pajama shirt from the top of the dresser where Josh had tossed it the night before. As he pulled the pajamas on, Danny realized his ass ached a little. Josh hadn't been particularly gentle in his lovemaking again last night, which Danny hated to admit he rather enjoyed. If Josh would stop being a jerk and limit their interaction to sex with no sucker punches, Danny might not hate the guy so much.

And make no mistake about it, I really am starting to hate you. Love is hard to maintain in an atmosphere of fear. Danny knew that above all other truths. How could he not? Gingerly, he touched his still-swollen eye. *I have the scars to prove it.*

He stepped through the bedroom door as quietly as he could, then carefully latched the door behind him. Looking up, he spotted Jingles sitting at the end of the hall, watching him. The moment Danny saw the shame on Jingles's face, his heart sank. Jingles had that hangdog look that told Danny he knew he had done something wrong.

Danny's whisper was a desperate hiss. "Oh God, baby, what did you do?"

Jingles's tail didn't move. He just sat there, head down, eyes forlorn.

Trying to keep his footfalls as silent as possible, Danny rushed down the hall and stepped through the doorway leading into the living room. He gazed around. Everything seemed to be just the way it always was. Jingles hadn't chewed a hole through the carpet. He hadn't gnawed a leg off the dining room table. The drapes were still hanging.

Danny almost wept with relief.

Then he spotted a crumpled sheet of paper peeking out from behind Josh's leather sofa. He took one step closer to peer around the end of the sofa and saw another piece of paper, this one shredded to oblivion.

Danny recognized it as a page from a ledger. Josh's ledger. From work.

"Oh no."

Jingles whimpered as if he knew exactly what Danny was thinking.

Already certain World War III would commence the minute Josh crawled out of bed and saw what Jingles had done, Danny braced himself and peered around the sofa to see the full extent of the damage.

"Oh, shit, fuck, damn, fuck, shit, balls, fuck."

Not only was Josh's ledger shredded into a million pieces, the satchel he carried to work every day was thoroughly chewed up, the strap gnawed in two. What was left of Joshua's top-of-the-line Samsonite soft-sided leather attaché was peppered with teeth marks and glistening with dog spit.

Danny closed his eyes, already starting to tremble at what he knew was about to happen.

Josh had been itching for a reason to get rid of Jingles. There was nothing Danny could do to stop that from happening now. Nothing.

Danny took a moment to bend down and stroke some of the fear from Jingles's face. Jingles responded by whimpering again. The poor little guy was shaking like a leaf.

"Don't worry," Danny whispered. "I'm going to get you out of here. We'll find you someplace safe, I promise. At least until this all blows over." *If it ever does.*

Danny jumped at the sound of footsteps in the bedroom. Joshua was up. Danny heard the bathroom door close. He didn't have much time.

He rushed into the bedroom, threw on a shirt and jeans, and pulled tennis shoes over his bare feet. Panic beginning to build, he raced around trying to find his car keys, finally discovering them tucked in among a pile of crap on Josh's desk in the spare bedroom. After dropping his keys in his pocket, along with his wallet and cell phone, Danny latched a leash to Jingles's collar and headed for the door.

Before he could reach it, Josh stepped naked from the hallway, rubbing sleep from his eyes.

"I woke up and my baby was gone," Josh said. He blinked back a yawn and studied Danny a little more closely. "Where are you going? What's wrong? You look like you've seen a ghost." He trailed his gaze from Danny to Jingles, who was cowering on the end of his leash at Danny's feet. "And what's wrong with the mutt? He looks like he's seen a ghost too."

"Nothing's wrong," Danny said hastily. "He just needs to be taken out. I'll be back before you know it."

Joshua stiffened. "No. Something's wrong." He eyed Jingles again. "Why is he looking so frightened? What the hell did he do?"

Danny dropped the leash and raced forward, pulling Josh's body, naked and sleep-warm, into his arms, pressing his face to Josh's chest.

"Please, baby, don't be mad. He didn't do it on purpose."

Joshua stiffened in Danny's arms. He gripped Danny's shoulders and pushed him to arm's length, his voice already seething. "What did he do?"

Danny couldn't prevent his eyes from sliding for the briefest of seconds toward the sofa and what lay behind it. When he saw Joshua follow his glance, the fear inside Danny blossomed into pure terror. Terror for Jingles. Terror for what Joshua would do to him.

Without thinking, Danny dropped to his knees at Josh's feet, trapping Josh's bare legs in his arms, pressing his face to Josh's soft cock, inhaling his scent, trying to find a remnant there of the man, of the body, he once loved.

"Please don't hurt him," Danny pleaded, his lips on Josh's stomach now, his eyes peering up the long length of Josh's naked torso. The torso that once thrilled him so. The torso he once worshiped. "Please don't make me get rid of him, Josh. I'll do anything you want. Just please don't take it out on Jingles."

"Move," Joshua growled. Coldly pushing Danny aside, he stepped around the side of the sofa to see what the hell had happened.

Danny cowered on the floor, watching him. Josh's spine stiffened. Danny reached out, pleading, "No!" when Josh's hate-filled face turned to stare at Jingles, still trembling among the loops of his leash by the front door.

"You little fucker!" Joshua bellowed, and before Danny could move, before he could do *anything*, Josh stomped across the room and kicked Jingles so hard in the ribs the dog crashed against the door, rattling its hinges.

Jingles's cry of pain tore through the condo, and Danny was on his feet before he knew what he was doing. When Joshua raised his foot to give Jingles another kick, even while Jingles was still whimpering in pain and scrambling around trying to stand, Danny panicked and grabbed the first thing he could get his hands on.

He snatched up the brass table lamp from the end table and, ripping the cord from the wall, swung the heavy lamp like a baseball bat and smashed it into the back of Josh's head with a horrible hollow bonking sound, driving Joshua to his knees.

"You fucking bully," Danny screamed. "You fucking asshole. Leave my goddamn dog alone."

It was Joshua's turn to cower on the floor as he brought himself up to his hands and knees and tried to shake the cobwebs out of his head from where Danny had whacked him with the lamp.

"I'll kill you for this," Joshua gasped, still shaking his head to clear away the pain. "I'll kill you both."

Danny leaned over and screamed in Joshua's ear. "You'll have to catch us first!" He brought the heavy brass lamp up again and threw it with all his force into Josh's back, driving him back to the floor. "And consider the marriage *canceled*!"

Josh furiously pushed the lamp away, spitting curses. He tangled his hand inside the shade and ripped it to shreds, then hurled the lamp halfway across the room. Before he could get to his feet, Danny grabbed up Jingles from the floor, eliciting another whimper of pain, raced through the front door, and slammed it shut behind him.

As Danny ran toward the elevator, he heard Joshua bellow from the condo.

"I'll kill you both for this! I'll kill you fucking *both*."

Too mad to cry, Danny stood in the elevator with Jingles cradled in his arms while the doors slowly closed in front of them.

"Get some new material," Danny whispered to himself on a shaky breath.

As if agreeing with him wholeheartedly, Jingles licked Danny on the chin.

After what seemed an eternity, the elevator began to move.

CHAPTER SIX

LOCKED SAFELY inside his car, Danny sat there like a statue for about two minutes, gripping the steering wheel and trying to get a handle on his emotions.

Finally calm enough to start thinking rationally, he turned to Jingles sitting in the passenger seat beside him.

"Are you hurt, boy? Did he hurt you?"

Danny ran his fingers gently over Jingles's ribs. When Jingles didn't wince, Danny figured his injuries weren't too bad. Thank God Joshua had been barefoot when he kicked him, not wearing shoes. Otherwise the damage might have been considerably worse.

As he stroked Jingles, Danny noticed for the first time that he hadn't escaped the fracas without an injury of his own. His finger was cut. Probably from grabbing the brass lamp the way he had and swinging it like a club. The cut didn't look deep, but already there was a smear of blood across the steering wheel and his finger was beginning to smart.

Danny wrapped his finger in a tissue he found in the console to absorb the blood, trying to clean himself up. When he thought the bleeding had stopped, Danny cupped Jingles's face in his hands and rested his forehead on Jingles's snout.

"He'll never hurt us again, baby. I promise," Danny whispered.

But as soon as the words were out of his mouth, he wondered how he was going to manage it. Danny had no friends he could stay with, no one who could even take the dog. In fact, Danny hardly had any friends at all. Joshua had seen to that, running all Danny's old friends off the minute the two of them got together.

And I let him do it, Danny thought, sitting there in his crappy Toyota in the condo's underground parking garage, shaking his head, not quite believing he could have been so damn stupid as to let Joshua take control of his life the way he had. And he was *still* in control! Even now!

But Danny had to get past all that. He had to at least figure out what to do with Jingles until Danny could tear himself away from Joshua and find a place of his own. But how the hell was he going to do that? He didn't have enough money to rent an apartment. Hell, he barely had enough money to check into a hotel for a couple of days, and most hotels probably wouldn't take a dog anyway.

No, what he had to do was find a place where Jingles could stay until Danny could make arrangements for himself. Until he could save up some money. Until he could find a place. Rent some hole-in-the-wall apartment. He didn't care how crummy it was; he had to try to get his life back together. On his own. Danny needed to be *on his own*.

With a sinking heart, Danny realized the only way he could do that was to go back to Joshua. At least for a while. Beg to be forgiven. Without Jingles, Danny was pretty sure Josh would accept him back. In fact, with or without Jingles, Danny was pretty sure Josh wouldn't let him go at all. Ever.

Of course that didn't rule out the possibility he would pound Danny senseless first for decking him with a lamp.

Danny dropped his head on the steering wheel, remembering the lamp smashing into the back of Joshua's skull. Much to his own amazement, Danny smiled a wicked smile.

Jeez, that felt good. I mean from my end. Probably not so much from Josh's.

On the other hand, after Danny almost killed him with that fucking lamp, maybe Josh wouldn't take him back at all, no matter what sort of arrangements Danny made for the dog.

Danny blinked himself back to an awareness of his surroundings. Good Lord, he was still sitting in his parking space in the condo's underground parking. In the slot next to his, not two feet away, sat Joshua's Lexus.

That was pretty stupid. He had to get out of here.

Danny cranked up the engine, pulled out of his space, and headed for the exit. He still didn't know where he was going, but he knew he couldn't figure it out sitting where he was.

As he drove, mindlessly turning down this street and that, he tried to think things through. With one hand nestled in Jingles's soft coat, comforting himself as much as the dog, Danny tried to make a plan. There had to be *someone* who would take Jingles for a while.

All the time Danny was thinking these thoughts, he knew, he already *knew*, who he would be turning to for help.

He checked his watch. It was still too early. Maybe he would head to Balboa Park. Walk Jingles. Grab himself a bite to eat in one of the park kiosks that sold coffee and pastry. Kill some time.

He wished he had a toothbrush. His mouth tasted like fear and last night's dinner. As he thought of Joshua's cock piercing him roughly the night before while Danny lay beneath him begging for more, hating it, loving it, he felt a shame he had never felt before.

How could he let a man he'd grown apart from, a man he'd grown to *despise*, use him like that? And how could he enjoy it when he did? *Christ, am I that much of a slut?*

He remembered the early days, back when Joshua and Danny were just beginning their relationship. Josh had been kinder then. Kinder and sexy as hell. The sexy part was still there, Danny supposed, but somehow in the passing of time the kindness had morphed into cruelty. Mutual respect had become a one-sided battle for control. And Danny was on the losing end of the battle. Sometime during the past year, their relationship had become a matter of ownership, not love. Somehow Danny went from being an object of affection to a possession. Danny wasn't sure how or when it happened. It just did.

Danny drove, his cheeks once again damp with tears. He missed those early days. He missed the gentleness of them. Soft promises in the dark. Lazy caresses. Mind-boggling passion. And sex, always sex. Sex with the person he loved. What an addiction it was. And oh, how Danny had craved it back then.

But like any addiction, after a while the old highs are unobtainable and there's nothing left but that horrible clamoring need. But need isn't love. It's not even close.

Danny checked his watch again as he crossed the Laurel Street Bridge into Balboa Park. It was still early in the morning. The park was almost deserted. A few joggers clomped past. A couple of homeless people shuffled along, their worldly possessions slung over their shoulders in garbage bags, their eyes empty, their bodies slumped, an aura of hopelessness surrounding them like fog.

That could be me.

Pulling his mind away from that horror, Danny found an out-of-the-way place to park in a secluded lot beneath the low-hanging branches of a pepper tree. He snapped the leash to Jingles's collar and they exited the car, heading deeper into the park on foot, past the organ pavilion, past the natural history museum, the carousel.

Among a riot of dew-soaked roses on a winding cobbled path inside the rose garden, Danny stopped, an unbidden sob rising up inside him. He closed his eyes, fighting against the tears while Jingles waited patiently at his feet.

He had only one hope for Jingles, and if that hope failed him, what then? The pound? He couldn't do that. He *wouldn't*. He'd die before he sent Jingles to that awful place.

When Danny opened his eyes, the threat of tears had passed. For a while, at least. His mind was filled with the image of himself sitting on a barstool. The bartender in front of him was pressing his lips to Danny's hand, speaking comforting words and offering kindness where kindness had been most sorely lacking. Offering Danny what he couldn't get from his lover.

Remembering that day, Danny's frown dissolved, and he almost smiled for the first time that morning.

"Come on, boy," he said quietly, tugging gently on the leash. Jingles yipped happily, also for the first time that morning, and followed Danny through the roses as the dew began to burn away beneath the rising sun.

At the same time, Danny's fear began to burn away too. He began to rediscover the joy of friendship. He rediscovered the appreciation of it too. It was the friendship offered by a man who had no ulterior motives other than Danny's safety. His welfare. He had offered advice as well at the store that day. Advice Danny knew now he should have listened to but had been too fucking stubborn—or frightened—to take.

Jay. Jay was the friend who had offered those things to Danny. Jay would help him. Danny didn't doubt it for a minute, even though he blushed now, remembering how he had spoken to Jay in the store when he came to offer advice. Advice Danny had ignored. He felt a rush of shame knowing he had purposely not gone to see Jay at the bar since.

What a dick I am.

Still, he had to wait. Jay hadn't started work yet, and since Danny didn't have his phone number, or even know his last name, he had no way to contact Jay other than through the bar. Danny couldn't hang around outside The Clubhouse waiting for Jay to open up. Jay's bar was only four blocks from the condo. The odds were too great Joshua might see him there.

So, afraid to go home and afraid to hang around on the street, Danny spent the morning walking. And thinking. He traversed trails through Balboa Park that he didn't know existed until he stumbled on them that day.

When his legs began to ache and his stomach started yowling for sustenance, he parked himself under a metal umbrella at a snack bar not far from the entrance to the zoo and scarfed up a couple of hot coffees and three donuts (two for him and one for Jingles). After contentedly licking the glaze from his fingers and watching a bunch of schoolkids parade past, caterpillared hand in hand on their way to a field trip at the zoo, Danny checked his watch one last time and headed back to the car.

JAY HAD just dropped his bags behind the bar and flipped on the lights when Danny walked in the door behind him. At one glance, Jay knew something bad had happened.

"Christ, you're bleeding!"

Danny froze. "Wh-what?"

"There's blood on your face."

Danny looked down at his hands. "Oh. I cut my finger. I must have—"

But Danny couldn't seem to finish what he was trying to say. The words stuck in his throat as he stood there in the doorway. He began to shake.

Jay rushed across the bar and pulled the street door closed. Only when he had latched it so no one could enter did he pull Danny into his arms and hold him tight, making shushing noises in Danny's ear. In no time at all, Danny's tears had soaked the front of Jay's shirt. Danny's arms came up and held on to Jay even more tightly than Jay was holding on to him.

The top of Danny's head was a perfect height to tuck under Jay's chin, so Jay pressed his lips to Danny's blond locks, cooing gentle words. "It'll be all right, Danny. Don't worry. Stop crying now. It'll be all right."

"He hurt Jingles," Danny sputtered.

"What?"

"Joshua kicked Jingles, so I hit him in the head with a table lamp."

Jay gently eased Danny to arm's length so he could look into his face. "No shit?"

Danny nodded, tears streaming. "Yeah. Twice."

Jay couldn't help it. He felt a grin coming on. When Danny saw it, he grinned too. Even in the midst of crying his heart out.

Still grinning, Jay said, "Well, good. It's about time he got a taste of his own medicine. Say. You didn't kill him, did you?"

"No. He was on the floor cussing when I left."

"I'll bet he was," Jay said, reaching up and ruffling Danny's hair, which was looking a little wild this morning. After what he'd been through, Jay supposed he couldn't fault Danny for that.

Danny sniffed, sucked in a long wobbly breath, and tried to blink away his tears.

Jay turned his attention to Danny's hand. "Let me see your cut."

Danny held his injured finger out like a little kid who'd just fallen off his bike and gone to his mother for sympathy. The movement was so sweetly innocent, Jay's grin spread, all sympathetic around the edges. He carefully took Danny's hand in his and kissed the bloody finger. Then he gazed into Danny's eyes.

"There," he said. "Feel better?"

Danny nodded, mute, staring up at Jay with eyes as big as Ping Pong balls. Even the puffy black one was wide open.

"Come on," Jay said. "Let's wash the dried blood off your face and get this finger cleaned up. I've got some Band-Aids behind the bar."

But Danny didn't move. "I don't know what I'm going to do, Jay."

Jay tutted when Danny's tears began to leak out again. He reached up and squeegeed them from the boy's cheeks, using his thumbs like windshield wipers. "We'll figure it out, kid. Come on, now. Let's get you patched up."

"I'm not a k-kid."

Jay cupped Danny's face in his hands, leaned in to press a kiss to Danny's forehead, then pulled back to study those tear-filled eyes. "I know you're not a kid," he said. "Sorry. But come over to the bar. Let me clean you up, and we'll decide what to do together. Okay? I won't let anything happen to you or Jingles. I promise. We'll get this sorted out."

Danny leaned forward and dropped his forehead to Jay's chest. "I knew you would help me," he said softly on a staggered breath. "I knew you'd be a friend."

Jay laid his hand to the back of Danny's head, pulling him close, rocking him, patting Danny's back. Making shushing noises again. Trying to comfort. Trying to calm. "I'm glad you knew it, Danny. I'm glad you came to me."

Danny looked up. "Really?"

"Really. But if you die of lockjaw because you didn't let me clean your mangled finger, I'll never forgive myself."

Danny almost smiled. "We can't have that."

"No, we can't. Come on."

Jay took Danny's hand and led him to the bar. Danny obediently followed along, and Jingles followed *him*. Jay parked Danny on a barstool, then picked up Jingles and placed him on the barstool next to Danny.

"I don't have any dog biscuits," Jay said to Jingles, as if he were a customer, not a terrier. "How about a jerky stick instead?" Jay reached into a big jar behind the bar, pulled out a long stick of beef jerky, unwrapped it, tore it into manageable lengths, and set it on the bar in front of Jingles, who went to town on it right away. Then Jay turned his attention to Danny.

He soaked a clean cloth under running water in the sink beneath the bar and gently swabbed the smear of dried blood from Danny's cheek, wiping away a few new tears in the process. He even patted Danny's hair into place, since it was still sticking up all over.

"You look like you just crawled out of bed," Jay said.

"Actually, I wasn't up more than thirty seconds when the fight started. Stopping to style my hair before I ran out the door would have been suicidal."

Jay chuckled. "I suppose it would've."

Turning his attention to Danny's cut finger, he carefully dabbed it clean, speaking softly as he did. While he worked, he ignored the pounding of his hopeful heart. "What do you need me to do for you, Danny? How can I help?"

Danny reached out with his free hand and brushed through the hair on Jay's forearm with his fingertips almost idly, as if the touch of Jay's skin helped him think. He left his hand there. "You're so gentle," he said.

Jay grunted, embarrassed but pleased. "Thanks. Tell me what I can do."

"I need you to take Jingles for a while. Just until I can save up enough money to get my own apartment."

Jay stopped what he was doing and gazed into Danny's face with an expression of disbelief. "Don't tell me you're going back to him!"

"I have to. I can't live on the street. My stuff is still there. I don't even have a pair of socks with me."

"I'll loan you some socks."

"Don't be stupid. All my clothes are there. The only shirt and pants I have with me are the ones I'm wearing. Even living on the street I'd need a change of pants now and then."

"I'll loan you pants."

Danny clucked at that. "You're eight feet tall. I'd walk right out of your pants."

Now there was an intriguing idea, Jay thought. "That's something I'd like to see," he said, making Danny blush.

Biting back a smile, Danny said, "I was being serious."

Jay wasn't smiling at all. "So was I."

At that, Danny stiffened. "Look. This is a piss-poor time to flirt. I have to go back to him and set things right. I have to act like I want to make up with him so I can stay with him at least long enough to get my life in order. And I need you to watch Jingles while I do that. I won't take him to the pound, Jay. That's not an option. And I won't bring him within kicking distance of Josh again either. If you won't help me, I don't know what I'll do."

"Don't worry, Danny. I'll be more than happy to take Jingles home with me. On one condition."

Danny was torn between emitting a sigh of relief and trying not to look suspicious. "What condition is that?"

"You have to come with him."

MY DRAGON, MY KNIGHT

A furrow formed in Danny's forehead. "What do you mean?"

Danny's finger was clean and dry. The cut didn't look too bad, Jay thought, so he carefully spread a Band-Aid over it, wrapping the sticky ends all the way around the finger so it would lock on to itself and stay in place. Only then did he raise his eyes and gaze at Danny's face.

"I mean you can't go back to him, Danny. God knows what he'll do to you if you do. You can stay with me until you save enough money to get your own place. I have an extra bedroom at the cabin. And I'll be good. I promise. No unwanted advances or anything. I just want to help. I just want you to be safe."

"I'm not sure the advances would be unwanted," Danny said softly.

They stared at each other for a minute. The only sound in the bar was of Jingles still licking his chops after devouring the jerky.

"Good to know," Jay answered just as softly.

They studied each other in the silence until Danny finally tore his gaze away and stared down at the Band-Aid on his finger.

"But I can't do it," he said. "I have to go back. All my stuff is there. My books for school. My clothes. *Everything.* Don't make this any more difficult for me than it already is, Jay. Please. Just watch Jingles for me until I get my life sorted out. It won't be more than a few months. That's all I ask."

"No."

Danny blinked. His chin trembled. "No? But my stuff, Jay. Everything I own, which I admit isn't much, is all back there in Josh's condo. I can't afford to buy all-new clothes. I can't afford to—"

"I'll go with you to get your stuff."

"You'll what?"

"I'll go with you, Danny. Maybe I'll even take my bouncer along with us, just for a little extra security."

At long last a smile twisted Danny's mouth. "Your bouncer? You mean the gorilla who cards people at your door every night?"

Jay smiled right back. "That's the one. His name is Ernie. And while we're there, you and me and Ernie, you can return something that belongs to him."

"Him who? You mean Joshua?"

"Yes."

Danny looked confused. "What do I need to return to Joshua?"

"This," Jay said, lifting Danny's hand. It was the hand with the ring on the finger. The ring that matched the one on Josh's hand.

Danny stared down at it. "My God. In all the excitement I forgot it was still there." He wrenched the ring from his finger and dropped it on the bar, where it spun, catching the light, until Jay snatched it up and slipped it in his pocket.

"I'll give it back to him myself," Jay said, a wicked glint in his eye. When Danny looked dubious, Jay relented and said, "Or we'll let the gorilla give it back. At high velocity. Wrapped in a fist."

Danny finally threw his head back and laughed. Jay laughed with him while Jingles whapped his tail on the back of the barstool and looked hopefully across the bar at the bigass jar of jerky sticks still sitting there like the Holy Grail.

Jay took the hint and gave him another stick before turning his attention back to Danny, his eyes warm, his face somber. He took Danny's hand in his, and with the tip of his finger, he rubbed the place where Danny had just removed Josh's ring.

"I'm not going to let you go back to him, Danny. This isn't about me wanting to get you in my clutches or anything. This is only about keeping you safe. I don't trust him. After you nailed him with a lamp—*twice*—do you really think he's going to just forgive you and act like nothing happened? He might really hurt you this time, Danny. Hell, he's probably so mad he might even kill you. I mean *really* kill you."

Danny's eyes were misting up again. Jay wasn't sure if that was a good thing or a bad.

"I can't just move in with you, Jay. I—I mean, I have some pride left. I've got nothing. A few bucks in the bank. I didn't come here for charity. I came here for Jingles, not for me."

"I'm sorry, Danny. I won't help one without helping the other. I'm not asking you to sleep with me at the cabin. I'm not asking you for sexual favors. I'm asking you to occupy my spare room while you get yourself straightened out. Rent-free. You can come and go as you please. Do whatever you want. Have people over, I don't care. All I'm asking is that you live in a place where Joshua won't know where you are and where you won't have to be afraid every time you turn around. A place where you and Jingles will both be safe from Joshua's fists."

"Safe," Danny said on a sigh. "It's been a long time since I felt safe."

Once again, as he had so many weeks ago, Jay lifted Danny's hand from the bar and touched his lips to the heel of Danny's thumb.

"I know it has," Jay said, his lips brushing Danny's skin as he spoke. "Let me do this for you, Danny. Please don't go back to him. I'm too afraid for you to let that happen. He'll never forgive you for what you did. You know he won't. Come with me where you'll be safe. Please."

Jay clutched Danny's hand, his lips still on it, his warm breath flowing over Danny's wrist.

"Please, Danny. You'll be safe on my mountain. He'll never find you. I'm offering you a place to heal where you won't be bothered by that bullying fuck until, like you said, you can take control of your life again." Jay reached up and gently brushed his fingertips over Danny's black eye. "I won't let him do this to you again. I don't think I could stand it, Danny, if he did. I—I like you. I don't want to see you hurt anymore."

"You're my friend," Danny whispered. "Aren't you?"

"Yes, Danny. I'm your friend."

Danny dropped his head to rest it atop their two clasped hands. "I knew you were. Ever since that first day we talked."

"Yes, Danny. Ever since the very first day I talked to you right here in the bar. You had a swollen jaw then. Remember? Today you've got a black eye and a torn finger and a bruised dog. Between those four injuries, you've had a host of others at the hands of a man who says he loves you, but who would never have done those things if he really did. He'll kill you if you go back. You know it as well as I do. Maybe not today and maybe not tomorrow, but sooner or later, he'll kill you."

"Maybe."

"It's not a maybe, Danny. It's a reality, and you know it."

"I never wanted to be a pest like this, Jay."

"You're not a pest. You said it yourself. You're a friend. Friends help each other. This isn't a new concept, kid. Friends have been doing it since the beginning of time. You know that, right?"

Danny lifted his head and nodded, silent.

"So that's a yes?" Jay asked, his heart suddenly flooded with more hope than he could ever remember feeling since Simon died. "You'll come? You'll come and live with me?"

Danny's words barely stirred the air. "Yes, Jay. I'll come. But I have one condition of my own."

"Oh yeah? What's that?"

Danny offered a fake snarl. "Stop calling me kid."

Jay crossed his heart like a good Boy Scout. "I promise."

They stared at each other for a couple of heartbeats, but even with the best of intentions, Danny couldn't keep his emotions from taking over.

"Oh shit," Danny said as tears began to flow again. "I'm going to start crying again. I'm really not a wuss, you know. I've cried more in the past three months than I've cried in my whole life. I swear." He angrily sniffed. "I'm sorry."

"Don't be," Jay crooned, reaching across the bar to wipe Danny's tears away with a napkin. "And wusses don't beat the crap out of abusive lovers with lighting fixtures. Only butch people do that. Anyway, you go ahead and cry. You cry, I'll wipe." He grinned. "It's called division of labor."

Danny hiccupped. "I guess getting wiped dry is better than getting punched senseless."

Jay offered up a sardonic smile. "Or nailed in the head with a lamp. Twice."

They sat in silence for a couple of minutes, Jay thrilled that he'd gotten his way while Danny looked stunned by Jay's generosity.

"I don't know how to thank you," Danny finally said. "I—I really don't."

Jay gave his head a tiny shake. "You already thanked me by saying yes. Let's just leave it at that."

"I can't just leave it at that," Danny said. And standing on the rungs of his barstool, he leaned over the bar and pulled Jay close in a hug, planting a kiss on his cheek in the process. "Until you're better paid," he said.

Jay's ears burned. "That's all the pay I need. Best paycheck ever, in fact."

Danny laughed at that. "Oh, please."

Jay stepped away from the bar, still embarrassed. "Well, then. Maybe I'd better call up Ernie the Gorilla and see if he has time to flash his muscles around for an hour or so while we collect your stuff."

"Josh will shit," Danny said. He wasn't smiling when he said it.

"That's the idea," Jay answered. He smiled wide enough for both of them.

Danny looked suddenly uncomfortable all over again. Jay laughed when Danny pointed behind the bar and asked, "Can I have a jerky stick too? I didn't get much breakfast."

Still laughing, Jay gave him two.

ERNIE THE Gorilla was as dumb as a post, as sweet as pie, and as broad and tall as a garbage truck. When Joshua opened his door to find Ernie on his doorstep, he looked him up and down like a tourist staring for the first time at a giant sequoia.

"What the hell do you want?"

Ernie's brow furrowed. "That's not a nice way to greet somebody," he said, and reaching in, he lifted Joshua by the armpits and set him to the side so Jay and Danny could enter.

Jay caught the smirk Danny tried to hide at the shocked look on Josh's face and the cold compress he was holding to the back of his neck where Danny had nailed him with the lamp. A lamp missing a shade, Jay noticed, had been placed on an end table. Its shade was lying in a mangled heap by the wall. On the coffee table lay the chewed-up leather attaché case and all the shredded ledger sheets Danny had told Jay about. It looked like Josh had been trying to salvage what he could, which wasn't much.

"I'm calling the cops," Josh said.

"Danny lives here," Jay said, speaking calmly, figuring that would be the best way to piss Joshua off even more than he already was. Jay didn't like Joshua. Pissing him off seemed like a really good idea. "Or at least Danny *did* live here. He's come to collect his stuff since he's decided to move out. You'd be wise not to try to stop him, or the cops might be just as interested in Danny's black eye and the litany of other injuries you've inflicted on him in the past year. Just let Danny gather up his belongings, and we'll be off."

Joshua's eyes narrowed to mean little slits. Part of the effect was lost to the fact that he was still holding the compress to the back of his neck like an old lady with a headache. "I know you. You're the guy who owns the queer bar down the street."

Ernie loomed over Josh like a thundercloud. "Don't get mean," he said, his voice pleasant but his posture deadly. "You can't fix yourself by breaking someone else."

Josh stared at Ernie with his mouth hanging open like he'd suddenly noticed the guy had two heads. "What kind of New Age claptrap is that? Are you for real?"

Ernie flapped a warning finger in his face. "Hush, now, or I'll pick you up by your feet and hang you upside down until you pass out."

Joshua tried to push him away, but it was like pushing a wall. "Don't threaten me, you fat moron." He aimed a hateful glare at Jay, but the way he kept watching Ernie from the corner of one eye made it clear Ernie was really starting to make him nervous. "So you're the reason Danny kept going to the bar. I knew he was cheating behind my back."

"I never cheated on you," Danny said quietly before turning on his heels and heading for the bedroom. "I should have, but I didn't. And be nice. You used to know how to do that."

"Fuck you, Danny. You're pretty brave when you've got your goons with you. You hurt me when you hit me, Danny. You hurt me bad."

"No more than you've hurt him," Jay interrupted. And to Danny, he added, "Go collect your stuff."

Ernie tapped Josh on the shoulder. The expression on his big round face made it clear he was wounded to the core. "I'm not fat. I'm big-boned."

Josh ignored him, still yelling after Danny. "Where do you think you're going to live? You don't have any money!"

Danny looked uncomfortable, shaking his head as he walked away. But his posture was straight. He didn't slump. He was obviously determined to finish what he came here to do and try to salvage as much pride as he could while he did it. "I don't need money," Danny said over his shoulder. "I have friends. You might try getting some sometime. They really come in handy."

"Touché," Jay mumbled under his breath.

"Very sagacious," said Ernie, nodding his head up and down like Gandhi. He turned to Jay. "That word was in the *New Word for Today* calendar you gave me at Christmas, boss. It comes in handy all the time. I use it almost as much as the book you gave me for my birthday, *Proverbs to Live By*."

Jay laughed, heading off to follow Danny. "I'm glad you liked them both."

"When eating fruit, remember the one who planted the tree," Ernie yelled after him. "That's a proverb! See how they fit into any situation?"

Jay choked back a laugh. "Jesus, Ernie, shut the hell up."

Joshua stared from one to the other like he'd just landed on the moon and these were the first two aliens he'd bumped into.

Danny was in the bedroom by this time. He'd started removing his clothes from the closet. Still on their hangers, Danny laid them in Jay's outstretched arms. When Jay's arms were full, he draped a few things over Jay's broad shoulders.

"You're handy," Danny said, trying to joke his way through the terror he must have felt being so near to Josh. "Like a big walking coatrack."

Jay grinned. "Thanks." Since his hands were full, Jay aimed his chin at a table by the window. "Is that your laptop?"

"Yes," Danny said. "It was a gift. But I don't want it."

They both heard Joshua sputter curses in the other room. He must have overheard.

When Jay was in possession of all of Danny's clothes, Danny headed for the kitchen, where he grabbed a garbage bag from beneath the sink. With the garbage bag in hand, and ignoring Josh as if he didn't exist at all, Danny hurried into the spare bedroom where he collected all his stuff from the desk—ATM card, assorted paperwork, checkbook, his favorite paperbacks, the two schoolbooks, various other odds and ends. After that, he scooped up everything that belonged to him from the bathroom drawers and the medicine cabinet. He even brushed his teeth while he was in there, causing Jay to jokingly comment, "Look at me, Danny. I'm still a coatrack. You want to hurry it up?"

All the time Danny was doing what he had to do, Ernie stood in front of Joshua like the Berlin Wall, arms crossed, as if nothing would make him happier than for Josh to start some shit.

Joshua called out over Ernie's shoulder. "You don't have to leave, Danny. We can work this out. I forgive you for this morning."

"No, we can't!" Danny shot back. "And I don't forgive you. You kicked my dog! Only an asshole would kick a little dog."

This was evidently too much for Joshua. "He ate my fucking briefcase! He destroyed important paperwork!"

Danny leaned his head around the doorjamb and screamed right back. "He was bored because you never let him come inside."

"Obviously for good reason."

Ernie loomed over Joshua like a disappointed thundercloud. "You're getting mean again." With that, he raised a huge fist, held it up in front of Joshua's face, and when Josh least expected it, Ernie flipped Josh on the nose with his index finger.

"Ow!" Josh yelled, backing away.

Ernie snickered. "I love doing that."

Jay followed Danny back into the living room, Danny weighted down with the garbage bag filled with his belongings, and Jay still balancing all of Danny's clothes on his outstretched arms. By carefully tilting his cargo, Jay was able to reach into his trouser pocket. Ernie stepped aside as Jay stood directly in front of Joshua, holding out the ring Danny had taken from his finger.

"This is yours, I believe," Jay said.

Joshua gaped at the ring in Jay's hand. When he brought his eyes up to stare at Danny across the room, there was such fury in them, Danny took a step backward.

"You were supposed to marry me," Joshua fumed. Fists clenched, he stormed toward Danny, but he only took about two steps before Ernie grabbed him by the collar and dragged him to a halt.

Jay stepped in front of Josh and thrust his face forward until the two men were nose to nose. He was even madder than Joshua.

"If I ever hear of you coming after him, or trying to hurt him, or trying to exact any sort of revenge against Danny for leaving you, I swear to God I'll beat you to within an inch of your life. I don't like people like you, Mr. Stone. You give gay people a bad name. Hell, you give *humanity* a bad name. So leave Danny alone. Just let him go. He doesn't want to be with you anymore."

Joshua glared back with hatred in his eyes. His tongue came out and licked his thin lips. His eyes darted from Jay to Ernie to Danny. And finally back to Jay.

"You'll pay for this!" he seethed. "I'll make you *all* pay for this!"

Ernie tsked, an unhappy schoolmarm. "Wrong answer," he said. And catching Joshua by surprise, he executed another finger flip, this time on the ear, making Joshua jump and howl in pain.

Jay was too mad to laugh at the startled look on Joshua's face. He leaned in one final time. "Don't forget what I said. Leave Danny alone. Do we understand each other?"

"Just get out," Joshua hissed. "All of you, get the fuck out of my house!" He turned spiteful eyes to Danny. "You too, whore. Get the fuck out!"

Danny hurried through the front door, hugging his belongings to his chest, head down, never looking back. Jay and Ernie followed right behind. Since Ernie was last, he pulled the door closed behind them, but not before giving Joshua a friendly finger-waggle of good-bye.

"Kindness is a gift," Ernie said in his best professorial manner. "You should give it once in a while."

"Get the fuck out of here!"

"Here's another one," Ernie said. "Those who light up the lives of others always have light inside themselves."

"Leave!"

Ernie was not to be deterred. He seemed to be having more fun tormenting Joshua than he had had in a long time. "I guess you're a lost cause on that one," he said, "so how about this? A closed mouth gathers no feet. Or you can't stop a pig from wallowing in the mud. Or you can't make a silk purse out of a—"

Joshua kicked the door shut in Ernie's face. Chuckling, Ernie galumphed down the hall, striding happily toward Danny and Jay, who were waiting by the elevator.

BACK IN the condo, shaking in anger, Joshua glared down at the ring in his hand. With a scream of rage, he flung back his arm and threw the ring as hard as he could. Danny's ring sailed through the open patio door and disappeared over the balcony railing, arching down toward the city street below, catching the light for one brief moment like a tiny meteor hurtling from the sky. Glaring down at his own hand, Joshua pulled off the matching ring and flung it after the other.

Trembling with fury, he stared through the patio door as the mocking silence of an empty condo settled in around him.

CHAPTER SEVEN

DANNY, JAY, and Ernie stood outside the bar. Jay had just contacted one of his bartenders and asked that he come in early so Jay could have the day off.

"I still don't know how to thank you for everything," Danny said, gazing up at Jay. He turned and gazed even farther up at Ernie. The guy really was a tree. A big wide tree. "You too, Ernie. The finger flips were particularly enjoyable."

To Danny's surprise, Ernie blushed. Still blushing, Ernie scooped Danny into his arms like a rag doll, flung him around like a kid playing airplane with a toddler, and crushed him in a bear hug that squeezed all the air from Danny's lungs. By the time Ernie set him down, Danny's clothes were askew, one shoe was off, and they were both giggling like idiots.

Ernie molded his face into one of intense deliberation. "You're well shed of that Joshua guy, Danny. He's not a nice person. Evil is as evil does."

More proverbs? Really?

Danny chewed on a grin. "The deceitful have no friends," he offered.

Ernie's face lit up. "It takes two to tangle."

"Dickheads are assholes."

Ernie gazed off at the horizon and scratched his head. "That one's not in my book."

Jay looked on like a proud father, mumbling skyward, "My two best boys, mangling proverbs."

Sniffing back a happy string of snot, Danny retrieved his shoe from the gutter. Ernie bent to pet Jingles, then waved good-bye and trundled off down the street, shoulders hunched, hands in pockets.

"I think that man has a crush on you," Danny said, watching him go.

Jay gazed in surprise at Ernie disappearing down the street. He smiled at the way people stepped out of Ernie's way as if a dump truck was coming at them. "Don't be silly," he said. "I'm not even sure Ernie's gay."

"And here I thought you were smart," Danny said, eyeing him sideways.

But Jay didn't respond. "Follow me?" he asked instead, clearly anxious to get on the road.

Danny nodded. "Just don't drive too fast. My Ferrari's in the shop, and the Toyota's sort of on its last legs. Or wheels, as the case may be."

"Gotcha," Jay said with a snort. "Twenty miles an hour it is."

"Well, you might hit thirty if it's downhill."

They took Danny's car to where Jay had parked on the street a few blocks over. Once there, Jay climbed into his Jeep Sahara and took off toward his mountain with Danny hot on his bumper.

Danny's first glimpse of Jay's house on Mount Miguelito, and the seclusion it promised him, brought Danny to tears for the very last time that day. Before they bumped to a stop, one car behind the other, Danny wiped away all evidence of his emotions. Jay had seen him cry enough. Hell, Danny had seen *himself* cry enough. It was time to get his life in order. Time to move on. And thanks to Jay, he had a place to retreat to while he did it.

He climbed from the car just as Jay hopped out of the Jeep on his long legs, his dark hair flying.

"That's quite a lane," Danny said, tearing his eyes from Jay long enough to check under his Toyota to make sure the engine hadn't tumbled out, jarred loose by one of the potholes.

"You may not be able to drive up here in your car at all when the winter rains really start. But we'll cross that bridge when we come to it." He slipped an arm over Danny's shoulder and turned to face the cabin. "So what do you think?"

Danny stared up at the old house, taking in the second-floor windows and the third-floor garret with the lovely round stained-glass window depicting a dragon and the knight attempting to slay it. Lastly, Danny studied the broad front porch with its mismatched chairs and a coffee cup still sitting on the railing where Jay had presumably left it. "It's great. And wow! It's really big." He saw three fuzzy faces staring out from a front window. "Those must be your kids," he said, pointing.

Jay beamed proudly. "That's them. And the clucking sound you hear is coming from the chickens out back. Before we haul your stuff inside, maybe we'd better introduce the critters to Jingles."

Jingles was still locked inside the car, staring through the windshield and trembling with excitement. Danny kept him there while Jay unlocked the front door and Carly came barreling out, tongue flopping, tail wagging, toenails tapping excitedly as she flew across the wooden porch and down the steps. The cats were a little more reserved, but they did brush themselves against Jay's pant legs to say hello while Carly hopped around like a fool, as dogs usually do.

All three animals froze when Danny opened the car door and Jingles came flying out. Jingles whimpered a leery greeting to the mob of creatures staring at him. Carly barked back an enthusiastic hello. Lucy and Desi apparently decided formal introductions could come later, so they took off running back into the house. Jingles strained to follow, but the leash in Danny's hand held him back.

"You might as well let him go," Jay said to Danny. "Let them get to know each other on their own terms."

Danny did as Jay suggested, and the next thing he knew the two dogs were fast friends, chasing each other around the house. When they heard a pandemonium of clucking and squawking and flapping wings, Danny knew Jingles had been introduced to the chickens. With the first rush of friendship accomplished, Carly and Jingles tore through the front door to finish their tour of the premises. The cats, being the reticent creatures they were and having a modicum of common sense, simply hid under the couch and growled.

With the animals off doing their own thing, Jay turned to Danny, who was still standing by his car door. Danny was suddenly shy. Shy and hesitant about what to say, what to do. But Jay reassured him with a smile and said, "Let's get your stuff inside and get you settled. Then I'll fix us something to eat. I know you're hungry."

Danny nodded, and before Jay could do anything else, Danny stepped forward and walked into his arms to hug him fiercely. He laid his head against Jay's chest. "I'll never be able to thank you for this. I think maybe you just saved my life."

Jay rested his fingertips at the back of Danny's neck. "I can't think of a life I'd rather save. Now that I've met your boyfriend, I gotta tell you, Danny, I think your mangled proverb was right on point. That asshole really is a dickhead."

"He's not my boyfriend anymore," Danny said quietly, his cheek still pressed to Jay's broad, welcoming chest.

"No," Jay said. "No, I guess he isn't."

The hug lasted another minute while Danny stood breathing in the scent of the man holding him, and the scent of Jay's mountain as well. After a lifetime in the city, the air seemed alive with new smells. Alive and clean and full of promise. Not the least of these was the heady aroma of Jay himself and the luscious feel of his strong, gentle arms surrounding Danny.

"Your mountain is beautiful," Danny said.

Jay smiled. "The house is big. The mountain's bigger. Just remember, this is your home now, Danny. As long as you're under my roof, I want you to feel safe. But I want you to be happy too. You'll have plenty of room to spread out and do your thing without us bumping heads every five minutes."

"I don't mind bumping heads," Danny said softly. Then he bit his lip, wondering if maybe he had said too much.

Jay pressed his lips to Danny's hair. "Neither do I," he whispered. Jay eased himself out of Danny's arms. "Let's get you unpacked, and after we eat, I'll take you and Jingles on a tour. How would that be?"

"That would be great," Danny said, his hands still on Jay's chest, reluctant to let him go, thrilled to sense the reluctance in Jay as well. Still, he gave himself a mental shake and pulled away. He was two minutes out of his relationship with Josh. This was no time to go diving headlong into another. Besides, Jay was his friend. That was good enough for Danny at the moment.

It should also be good enough that he believed himself safe for the first time in months. He had so much to thank Jay for. Not the least of which was that here, on this secluded mountain, Josh would have no way of finding him. None at all. For that alone, Danny felt blessed.

Still, Danny was plagued by thoughts that strove to push aside all the good things that were happening and leave him feeling lost and miserable all over again. As he and Jay began unloading the car, Danny tried to push them away, but they kept stabbing their way back inside his head to threaten him with fears that should no longer be an issue.

Thoughts of Josh. Disturbing ones. Thoughts that made Danny ache inside. The exploding pain of Josh's fists. The cruel words. The way he fucked Danny as if he wanted to make it hurt—and too often succeeded. The way his voice turned cold when Danny displeased him in any way. The look of fury that sometimes burned in Josh's brown eyes. Eyes that at times showed kindness but could turn to rage in a heartbeat. The loss of contentment when the fear of those hateful eyes came thundering in. The loss of love. The helplessness.

And the final words Joshua had spoken—*screamed*—at Danny as they left the condo earlier with all of Danny's belongings.

"You'll pay for this!" Josh had yelled. *"I'll make you* all *pay for this!"*

God help them, Danny had a horrible feeling that, given the chance, Josh would do exactly that.

"I HAVE class in a couple of hours at City College," Danny said.

The words were the first Danny had spoken for several minutes, and Jay had remained silent as well, respecting Danny's mood. They were sitting on the porch, plates in their laps, sodas on the floor beside their chairs. The hamburgers were eaten, the butter-soaked baked potatoes gobbled up. Carly and Jingles lay snoozing in the yard side by side. Lucy and Desi were purring and grooming each other on the steps, regally ignoring the dogs.

Jay gazed over at Danny while wiping a glob of catsup from his lip. "How many nights a week do you go?"

"Two."

"Do you like it?"

Danny sighed. "I hate it. But Josh insisted I study bookkeeping. Wanted me to be like him, I guess. Wanted me to get around to earning a decent wage. I suppose I shouldn't fault the guy for that."

Jay considered for all of thirty seconds whether he should butt in or not. Actually it was more like twenty seconds. Maybe fifteen. "Danny, Joshua isn't running your life anymore. Earning a decent wage is a noble goal, but not if you earn it doing something you hate. You're too young to be settling for that. If you don't like the class, drop it. Pick something else to study if you want. It isn't all about him anymore. It's about you. It's about what makes you happy. You deserve a little happiness, I think, after all you've gone through."

Danny studied Jay sitting there beside him, slouched comfortably in his chair, his legs propped up on the banister. He didn't speak; he merely stared until Jay had to fight the urge to twitch under Danny's scrutiny. Finally Danny tore his gaze away and looked down the mountainside, where a fluff of clouds scudded low across the horizon.

Quietly, he said, "Josh was good to me in the beginning, you know. He wasn't always—violent."

"Danny, if you're going to start blaming yourself for how your relationship with Joshua turned out, I'm going to go finish my dinner on the roof. I've never understood why victims tend to blame themselves. It doesn't make any sense to me at all."

Danny tucked his chin into his collar. His face grew contemplative. "I'm not blaming myself. Well, not for all of it. But I do think it's my fault for letting it go on so long. I should have left him the first time he hit me. But I couldn't. I—"

"You what?"

"I still loved him." Danny avoided Jay's eyes.

"Do you love him now?" Jay asked.

Danny stared down at his hands. "No. I think the love died a long time ago." He twisted his mouth in a wry smile. "Probably about the same time I sported my third or fourth black eye."

"And don't forget, you've *still* got one," Jay said. "You're *still* wearing the marks he gave you."

Danny touched his black eye as if he had almost forgotten it was there. "I—I know. But this one's the last." He said the words as if he meant them. "I'll never let anybody hit me again."

"Good," Jay mumbled. He reached out and patted Danny's arm. "And as for school? Really. If you hate the class, don't go. Shoot them an e-mail and tell them you're dropping out."

"I don't have a computer. I always used Josh's."

"I have one, Danny. And you're welcome to use it anytime you want. Use it for schoolwork, even, just as soon as you decide what courses you want to take. Preferably ones you might actually enjoy."

Danny pushed his strawberry-blond hair back off his forehead where the wind had tossed it. He held the hair back from his eyes while he stared at Jay's face. "I've never known anyone as fiercely kind as you."

Jay's ears went hot. "I'm just trying to be a friend."

Danny smiled. "I know." Again, he looked away, staring down at his hands. "I hope I can be as good a friend to you."

Jay squinted with humor. "You ate my cooking. That makes you a friend right there. Not a very bright one, maybe, but a friend."

Danny laughed. But in the midst of his laugh, his face grew somber. "I want to talk business."

Jay blinked himself serious. But only mockingly so. "Oh, crap. This can't be good."

"I don't want to live here rent-free, Jay. I want to pay you something."

"Danny, I thought we came to an agreement on that. My spare room is sitting there whether you're sleeping in it or not. I'm not out anything by having you here. Why should you pay me?"

"What about food?"

Jay set his plate on the floor beside him, and while his long legs were still propped on the porch railing, he toed off his shoes. They fell over the rail and landed in the yard, startling the cats, who went to investigate.

"Fine," Jay said. "If you feel you absolutely have to buy groceries once in a while, be my guest. But don't spend much, and don't make it a habit. You're here to save up for a new life, remember?"

"Jay?"

Something about the tone of Danny's voice made Jay stop scratching his ankle and turn to him. "What?"

Danny twisted in his chair, facing Jay more squarely. His eyes were sad. Or were they fearful? Jay couldn't be sure.

Either way, he didn't like it. "What's wrong, Danny? What are you thinking?"

Danny's words came out in a rush. "When I start my new life, will you continue to be a part of it? Can we stay friends? I mean, if you want to. Can we keep seeing each other even when I'm not living here anymore? As friends, I mean?"

Jay wasn't entirely sure, but he suspected his heart had just done a somersault inside his chest. He reached out again, this time taking Danny's hand. "Danny, I'd like it if we were friends from this day forth till the day we keel over dead from old age. And if you're still living in my spare bedroom then, that's okay too."

Danny's face grew sad. "I wasn't joking."

Jay stared at him. "Neither was I."

Danny took a shuddery breath, echoed by Jay's own. "So we're really friends, then? You're not just doing all this out of—you know—pity."

Jay dropped his stockinged feet to the floor and stood up. He plucked Danny's plate from his lap and set it aside on the floor beside his own. When that was out of the way, Jay pulled Danny out of his chair and wrapped him in his arms. Speaking softly, he whispered in Danny's ear.

"I've liked you since the first time we talked that day in the bar. I wanted to be your friend even then. It makes me happy to be doing what I'm doing, having you here and all, keeping you safe. I've never known anyone who deserved a little compassion, a little *safety*, more than you do. Please, if you're my friend too, don't ever question me again about whether I honestly like you or not. Okay? Let me just enjoy having you here, Danny. Let me just watch you blossom into the happy guy you were meant to be. The happy guy you *can* be now that you're not being used as a punching bag anymore. Now, say it out loud so I'll know it soaked in. Danny and Jay are friends."

Danny leaned back from Jay's embrace just far enough to gaze up into his face. He was smiling when he did. They both were.

"Danny and Jay are friends," he said, standing up straight, a ninth grader reciting Milton. "How's that?"

Jay shook his head, feigning a lack of conviction. "I didn't hear much enthusiasm. Maybe you should try again."

Danny dug a finger into Jay's ribs, making him jump. Jay barked out a laugh, and Danny tried again, his blue eyes shining brightly. "Jay, the big hunky owner of The Clubhouse, is my friend. He's not just my friend. He's my *best* friend. We're even roommates. We live in a big old house on top of a beautiful little mountain with a shitload of pets running all over the place, and he makes me hamburgers. *Friends.*" He tilted his head and eyeballed Jay like a real wiseass. Only cuter. "Was that better?"

Jay hadn't even been listening. He was lost in contemplation of Danny's beauty. Danny's sweetness. He shook himself back to the present and tried to catch up to the fact that it was his turn to speak.

"Uh, yes! Absolutely. Friends. Roommates. Hamburgers. Was there anything else?"

Danny giggled. "Jeez, try to keep up."

"So you're not going to school tonight?" Jay asked. He gave Danny a quizzical look, as if he'd been waiting all this time for an answer.

"Uh, no, Jay. I don't believe I am. I never wanted to be a bookkeeper anyway."

"Goody," Jay said. "I'll make popcorn later, and we'll build a fire and get to know each other better."

"Getting to know each other better sounds like the best idea ever."

And that was the end of bookkeeping class.

THE DAY had been one Danny would never forget. Exhausting. Exhilarating. Empowering. Frightening.

He had spent the afternoon packing his few belongings away, trying to make Jay's spare bedroom feel like home. Jay had told him to spread out, think of the entire house as his, but Danny couldn't do that. Not yet anyway. He felt out of place. He felt like a nuisance. Jay's kindness was still almost more than Danny could accept without tearing up and making a sobbing fool of himself all over again.

As the hours of their first day together drew to a close, Danny grew quieter and quieter. Jay had some raw hamburger and buns left, so he whipped up a pot of sloppy joes, added a bigass bag of Ruffles, and they had dinner, once again on the porch.

"Hope you're not into health food," Jay joked.

"This isn't health food?" Danny joked right back, but as soon as the words were out of his mouth, he grew serious again, melancholy about everything that had happened. After dinner, Jay asked Danny to walk with him. As dusk began to darken the mountaintop, he sought out Danny's hand while they strolled along a game trail.

Appreciating the gesture, Danny twined his fingers through Jay's as they walked. Carly and Jingles were off in the brambles somewhere chasing rabbits. Every few minutes, their excited yelps let Danny know they were still close, still safe.

"I hope you don't mind me holding your hand. This path can be tricky if you don't know it. I don't want you to fall," Jay said.

"I don't mind at all," Danny said. "I like holding your hand."

Jay opened his mouth as if to respond but quickly closed it and said nothing. Danny wondered what Jay had meant to say but didn't ask. He had further words of his own he wanted to speak, but they were hard to get out. Jay wasn't looking at him, which should have made it easier, but before Danny could try again, he stumbled on a stone. Jay's broad hand anchored him and kept him from falling. The anchor metaphor wasn't lost on Danny.

"You've kept me steady all day, Jay. I never could have done what I did today without your help."

Jay grunted. "Friends," he said, as if that was enough to explain his actions.

Danny fought the urge to drop his head to Jay's shoulder as they walked. He was so drawn to the man. Everything about Jay excited Danny. But that wasn't why he was here. He was here to get his life back on track. He was here to escape a relationship that was, frankly, killing him. Jay had been right about that. One day, Joshua really would've gone too far, and whether by accident or design, Danny would have paid the ultimate price. He didn't doubt it for a minute. Joshua would have killed him.

It was Jay's touch that gave Danny the courage to say what he had to say. Jay's touch and Jay's gentleness. It was all a brand-new experience for Danny. With Josh he had been forced to weigh every word he spoke. With Jay those scales were tossed aside.

The freedom was almost mind-boggling.

"Jingles has been with me since high school, you know. I could never have let him go."

Jay ran a thumb across Danny's fingernail and smiled gently. "Of course not. How we feel about our pets is a complicated thing. Losing them is like losing family."

"I don't have to go to school, Jay. I can work two jobs instead."

At that, Jay did stop. And being an anchor, he dragged Danny to a stop with him. "No. You need to go to school. You need to learn a trade. Believe me, one day you'll regret it if you don't."

Danny chewed his lip, thinking. "I suppose."

Jay smiled. "Sometimes I forget how young you really are. Nothing much scares you at twenty-one, does it?"

Danny sobered. "Joshua scared me."

"Josh would have scared anybody, Danny. Ernie was right. You are well shed of him. I hope you realize that."

"I do, but—"

With a gentle tug of Danny's hand, Jay began leading them farther down the path. "But what, Danny? What's bothering you?"

Danny eased closer and drew comfort from the feel of Jay's muscled arm brushing against his as they walked. "I don't think he's just going to let me go." The dogs were off in the distance, sniffing around a clump of chaparral, and Danny kept his eyes fixed on them to avoid looking at Jay. Nonetheless, he sensed that Jay was studying him.

"You've already left him, Danny," Jay said at last. "There's nothing he can do. This isn't a feudal state. You weren't indentured to him as a sex slave. He didn't buy you on the block. You were his lover. Or should have been. He relinquished the right to receive love from you in return by treating you the way he did. Don't ever regret leaving him, Danny. And don't ever think it isn't over. It *is* over. You escaped. You're safe. He doesn't know where you are. He can't hurt you anymore."

"He knows where I work."

"He won't start anything at the store, Danny. What would be the point? He must know by now he's lost you. Hell, he's probably already out there cruising the bars looking for a new punching bag."

Danny eased even closer, finally giving up the battle and resting his head on Jay's shoulder as they walked. "You don't know him. He's… ruthless."

Jay shook his head. "I didn't see much ruthlessness today. You may have noticed he let you go without a fight."

"There wasn't much he could do with Ernie there."

They reached the spot where Jay had apparently been leading them. A shed-sized sandstone boulder perched precariously at the edge of a steep drop-off. He released Danny's hand and clambered up onto the boulder, then reached down and offered a hand up to Danny. Patting the rock beside him, he invited Danny to sit. Danny was surprised how comfortable a resting place the boulder made. He sat beside Jay, and the two of them swung their legs over the precipice. The evening breeze chilled Danny's heated face after the strenuous hike up the mountain. Before them, the whole world lay spread out at their feet as the setting sun burned red on the horizon. "I guess you don't know about Ernie," Jay said.

Danny tucked his hands between his legs, thinking he might have overstayed his welcome in the hand-holding department. "What about Ernie?"

Jay laughed. "He's a wienie. He wouldn't hurt a fly. He's never been in a fight in his life. Don't get me wrong, he's not a coward. It's just he doesn't know how to fight. Or have the will to do it."

"But he's your bouncer."

Like teeny tiny sinkholes, Jay's dimples popped into place. Danny caught a glimpse of white teeth inside a gentle laugh.

"As a bouncer, all he has to do is stand there like a rogue elephant and look threatening. Nobody in their right mind is going to pick a fight with the guy or disobey him. He's a bulldozer. Or at least he gives that impression. In reality he's a hippie's Volkswagen camper with daisies painted on the side and a big peace sign spray-painted across the back."

"Josh was afraid of him."

Jay swung his feet like a nine-year-old. "Who wouldn't be?"

"I hope you're right about Josh letting me go, Jay. I really am."

"He has no choice. You've left him, Danny. He got what he deserved."

The mountain silence settled around them. A pair of catbirds, fat and brown with orange pantaloons, played atop a tall cactus. Courting maybe. Singing their trilling song. Danny smiled, watching them. Jay once again sought out Danny's hand and cupped it in his gentle grip. Danny stared at their two hands while another minute of mountain silence swallowed them whole. The catbirds had moved on, so it really was silence this time. Then somewhere behind them, Carly barked, and immediately afterward, Jingles let out the same crisp yip.

Danny apparently wasn't the only one with something on his chest. Jay's voice broke the silence. "There's something I want you to know."

Danny scooted a little closer until their legs touched. Jay pulled Danny's hand onto his thigh and rested it there, giving Danny a sudden tremor of hunger at the solid heat of Jay's leg, the muscled strength. He didn't speak, he merely waited. Jay coughed, clearing his throat. "I want you to know I'm glad you're here. It's been—oh, man, I can't believe I'm saying this—it's been lonely up here on this fucking mountain since Simon died. I've missed having a face to look at. I've missed having someone to share my meals, to pass the time, to maybe listen to me bitch about stuff." He snorted. "Forget that last one."

Danny grinned. "Forgotten."

Jay turned and gazed into Danny's eyes. "I've missed having a friend too, Danny. Just like you have, I think. If I overstep my bounds, tell me. If I do something you don't like, don't keep it to yourself. Let me know. And honestly, Danny, don't worry about rent or anything for a while. Save your money. Get yourself back on solid footing. Like I told you earlier, without you in it, that room would be sitting there empty. Just like the house. Empty except for one old lonely bartender rattling around the place wishing he wasn't alone."

"You're not old."

"I am compared to you." Jay's eyes slid to the horizon, then back to Danny. "I just want you to know I like you, and I want you to be happy here. And—and I want to be your friend."

"Oh shit," Danny said.

Jay frowned. "What? What's wrong?"

"Nothing. It's just that my eyes are watering up again. After all the crying I've done today, I'll probably die of dehydration."

"Well, we can't have that. If you'd like, we can go back to the house and have a beer or ten. Liquids, man. Liquids. They're key to good hydration. I'm a bartender. I oughta know."

Danny ignored the invitation. He even ignored the joke. With eyes misting over, he continued to stare at Jay's face. "I've never known anyone like you."

Jay frowned again. "Uh-oh."

And Danny smiled. "No. That's a good thing."

"Oh. *Phew.*"

"I'll try to be a good friend too, Jay. I swear I will."

Jay stroked the back of Danny's hand. "I know you will. I've never doubted it for a minute."

"But please…." Danny furrowed his brow and clung tighter to Jay's hand.

"What?" Jay asked, his eyes wary but avid. "Please what?"

Danny stared again at the sliver of red sun still trembling at the edge of the earth. The shimmering sunset was like the last flicker of a candle's flame, he thought, just before it went out. He impatiently brushed away a tear that trembled, just like the sun, just like that imaginary candle, on the edge of his eyelash, about to fall, about to slide off into oblivion.

"Please don't underestimate Joshua," Danny said. "Please don't talk yourself into thinking it's all over. I don't trust him. I don't want you to get hurt."

Jay squeezed Danny's hand and, with his other hand, hooked a finger under Danny's chin, dragging Danny's face toward him. "Ernie's the wimp, Danny. Not me. In a fight, I think I can take your nasty ex-lover. I don't care how much he honed his boxing skills on your poor unsuspecting head. But trust me, Josh won't come after either one of us. It's over for him. He's lost you forever. I'm sure he knows that. I'm sure he's accepted it."

Danny nodded but didn't speak. Fighting the urge to bury his face in Jay's chest, he wrenched his head around to catch the very last ray of sunshine as it glimmered on the horizon. When that tiny flame of light flickered out and night truly began to settle over the mountain, Jay got up and pulled Danny to his feet, and the two of them walked silently home over the darkening trail while the dogs scampered around their legs.

Danny held Jay's hand along the way, feeling guilty for it but still not letting go.

CHAPTER EIGHT

DAYS PASSED. Days turned into weeks. On the surface, life became simple. At Jay's urging, Danny looked into other night classes, but new courses wouldn't begin until the next semester, which was two months away, and Danny still didn't know what career he wanted to work his way toward, so he made do by extending his hours at Macy's. Jay was pleased that when Danny needed advice, he relied on Jay to give it to him, and he almost always heeded Jay's suggestions.

Jay's simple life went back to normal as well. On the surface. He enjoyed Danny's company at the house, and they quickly became close. Since they both worked days, they inevitably spent their evenings together. Playing with the animals. Sharing dinner. Hiking the mountain afterward. Talking. Always talking.

The habit of holding hands with Danny on their strolls up and down the mountainside became one of the things Jay most looked forward to. Danny laughed more now too. That was something else Jay looked forward to. Even *remembering* the sound of Danny's laughter made Jay smile. To actually hear it next to him, as they explored the mountain together, made Jay as happy as he could ever remember being. Not since Simon passed away had Jay found such peace in his life.

And it was all because of Danny.

The one thing Jay did not share with Danny, though, was his longings. His secrets concerning Danny. Not until an evening in October, when Jay and Danny once again rambled down the mountainside, following the game trail again, squinting against a light drizzle that came out of nowhere and caught them without hats. Danny didn't seem to mind the rain. Jay barely noticed it at all. He had other things on his mind. They had been on his mind all day. No. They had been on his mind for *weeks*.

Today was the day Jay decided to share those thoughts with the young man beside him. Come hell or high water, he couldn't live with them buried inside himself for another minute. He had to let them out. He had told himself to tell Danny how he felt weeks earlier, even before Danny moved in. But life interceded. The right moment never came. Well, now the right moment was here.

As always, Danny's hand nestled snugly in Jay's as they rounded a bend in the game trail. Squinting against the cold sprinkling mist, they hiked to one of Danny's favorite places on the mountain. It was on the eastern slope, out of sight of the cabin, where ancient tectonic upheavals had pushed a scattering of sandstone boulders to the surface. Huge boulders. Boulders as big as automobiles. The game trail meandered here and there among the great stones. It was the same place Danny once hid behind a rock taller than his head and jumped out to scare the crap out of Jay when Jay didn't know he was there.

Among the boulders, where an overhang shielded them from the cold rain that was beginning to grow a little stronger, Danny pulled Jay to a stop. They stood there, shaking the droplets from their hair, while Jay wondered how to best say what he was determined to say.

"Let's wait here a few minutes. Maybe the rain'll let up," Danny said.

As if agreeing wholeheartedly, Carly and Jingles, the best of buddies now, joined them under the overhang, shaking themselves dry just as the humans had, then settling in to lick their muddy paws and maybe catch a few z's while the humans did whatever the hell it was humans did.

Jay smiled down at them, then back at Danny. There was a waist-high stone placed conveniently beneath the overhanging rock. Jay motioned toward it, and Danny joined him. When they had hopped on and wiggled their asses around until they were comfortable, Jay again laid his hand over Danny's.

"You're cold," he said.

"No," Danny answered. "I'm not cold."

Aside from the lazy patter of rain on the outcrop of stone above their heads and the clattering chatter of the droplets smacking the bushes a few feet away, silence moved gently in, but only for a moment. Danny spoke before Jay could gather his nerve to begin.

"Tell me about Simon," he said, his voice soft. "What was he like?"

Jay stared into Danny's azure eyes, then looked away. He could get lost too easily in those eyes. If Danny really wanted to talk, Jay wouldn't be able to put two sentences together if he had to stare into Danny's eyes. He gazed out into the gray haze instead, watching a bank of silver fog rolling through the scattered boulders toward them, and let his thoughts go back to the man he once loved. Now it was almost routine that a smile lit his face when he did. Before, when the pain of losing Simon was still fresh, those memories brought only misery. *Thank God for time. It's like Neosporin for the soul.*

Jay closed his eyes as he spoke, as he remembered back. The better to feel the cleansing breeze on his face. The better to block out all distractions, not least of all the man sitting beside him holding his hand.

On a sigh, Jay began his tale. "Simon was beautiful. He was quiet, but when he wanted to be funny, he was hilarious. Nobody could tell a joke like him. Nobody could make me feel as important as he could." He paused, still purposely not opening his eyes to see Danny watching him, then went quietly on. "Our walks remind me of him. He sometimes held my hand too as we strolled the mountain. You're the first person I've shared these paths with since he left. The first person I ever *wanted* to share them with."

Danny didn't speak, and Jay glanced at him, wondering what Danny was thinking. He was staring at Jay so intently it was almost disconcerting, so Jay looked away again and let his memories flow. "Simon was a terrible driver," Jay said, smiling at less painful truths. "I once saw him hit two parking meters in one day. A bunch of coins fell out of the second one when he hit it, and laughing our fool heads off, we jumped out of the car and gathered them up, stuffing them in our pockets."

Danny laughed.

"He cooked for me every day because he got off work before I did. Back then I worked later at the bar, but he was a physical therapist, so he worked normal hours. It was Simon who adopted the cats because he thought Carly was lonely when the two of us were at work. It was Simon who bought the chickens too, because he thought fresh eggs would be nice." Jay chuckled. "I think we saw four fresh eggs in two years."

"You miss him," Danny said. It wasn't a question.

Jay shrugged, swallowing an old familiar pain, and swallowing other words, too, that he couldn't yet bring himself to say. Words about the young man beside him. "I miss Simon less than I used to. I guess that's a good thing." He didn't even sound convinced to himself.

Danny's fingers tightened around his. "Jay."

"Hmm?"

"Do you—do you think you'll ever be ready to love again, now that Simon's gone? I mean, do you think you'll ever be able to move on to someone else?"

At that, Jay opened his eyes and centered his gaze on Danny's face. "Yes," he said softly, without hesitation. "I think maybe I'm finally ready."

"Do you think…?"

"What, Danny? What do you want to know?"

But Danny shook his head and looked away. He changed the subject instead. Or seemed to. "Do you remember the first time we really talked at the bar? The day the old guy was cruising me and you came and parked yourself in front of me to get me out of the line of fire?"

Jay nodded. "I remember. Your cheek was swollen from one of Joshua's punches. I made you an ice pack, hoping we'd get the swelling down."

"Do you remember what I called you that day?"

"Yes, Danny, I remember."

"Say it," Danny said, obviously startled by the answer. "Tell me what it was."

Jay blushed. "You called me your hero."

IN A heartbeat of time, Danny lost all fear of the words he wanted to speak. He had sat quietly, listening to Jay talk about Simon so sweetly. Thrilled to be sharing the moment and never more so than when Jay admitted he might be ready to move on. Danny had been waiting for the proper opening into which he could slip his own words. His own revelations. For they were coming, had been coming for a while now. Danny could sense them wanting to burst forth, like a thoroughbred at the starting gate, aching to run free.

He twisted around, facing Jay on the stone beside him. The hand he held, Jay's hand, he clasped with both his own now. He snuggled closer, letting Jay's heat warm him.

"You *are* my hero," Danny whispered, locking his eyes on Jay's, leaning in and pressing a kiss to Jay's cheek. A sigh escaped Jay's lips. Jay's warm, sweet breath, exhaled in a shudder. It flowed across Danny's face, sending a shiver down Danny's spine as he studied Jay's face, his clean profile, the dark lashes over his brown eyes. He admired the too-long hair, wet with mist, falling over the smooth forehead, pushed aside occasionally by one of Jay's broad, strong hands. He eyed the five o'clock shadow on Jay's angular jaw and longed to feel the coarseness of the stubble on his fingertips, longed to reach out and stroke it.

Danny released Jay's hand and reached up to push the damp hair out of Jay's eyes. His fingers lingered there in the dark locks while Jay closed his eyes and laid his mouth over the tender skin of Danny's wrist.

Chills shot through Danny, and he struggled to find his voice. "A hero isn't all you are to me, Jay. Surely you know that by now."

As if he had lived only to hear the words, Jay spoke in a voice that trembled like the clump of chaparral stirring in the rain-soaked breeze beside them. "I hoped. But I didn't want to hurry things."

"We're not hurrying."

"I didn't want to catch you on the rebound."

"I'm not on the rebound."

Jay cupped his hand to the side of Danny's cheek, their faces inches apart. "Then tell me. Tell me what else I am to you, Danny. Please. I want to hear you say it."

"You're—you're the man I want to be with."

"Is that all I am?" Jay offered him a sad little pout, as if trying to be funny.

"No," Danny said, his eyes focused solely on Jay's mouth, because he couldn't bear staring into Jay's eyes another second. Not yet anyway. Not now. "Please don't joke."

"I'm sorry. I didn't mean—"

Determination hardened Danny's expression. "Fuck it," he said, dragging his eyes to Jay's after all. "I don't care what happens. I have to get the words out. I can't live with it trapped inside me anymore."

Jay stroked Danny's temple with his thumb while his fingertips caressed Danny's ear, which was chilled by the wintry drizzle. "What words, Danny? Tell me."

Danny's pulse quickened, but he remained mute. His courage had abandoned him.

Jay leaned in and laid a chaste kiss to the tip of Danny's nose. "Tell me. Don't be afraid."

Danny couldn't do it with Jay's eyes on him. He just couldn't. Once again, he looked away and pressed his face to Jay's chest. He breathed in Jay's scent, Jay's heat, and the moment he did, he found the courage he needed. The words spilled out, surprising even him.

"I—I can't spend another night listening to you stir around in the other bedroom where I can't get at you. You snore, you know. It's cute. But it's annoying. I want to be there beside you in your big four-poster bed, all sleep-warm and toasty. Then when you snore, I can kick you in the leg and make you shut up. I want to be able to reach out anytime I want and feel you sleeping there beside me. I want your breath on me when *I* sleep. I want you to want me the same way I want you. I want you to lay claim to me as if I belonged to you, Jay, and I want you to know damn well you can do anything you want with me, because whatever the hell it is, you can pretty well figure that's exactly what I want as much as you do!" He clapped his mouth shut like a car trunk, then sputtered, "Holy shit! Where did all that come from?"

Danny swallowed hard, almost collapsing in upon himself, winding down, stuttering to silence. The words had been like an ejaculation. One of those really great ones. Tearing out of his body, leaving him exhausted, drained. Empty.

He pushed his face harder into Jay's chest, and when he did, Jay wrapped his arms around him, pulling him closer, giving him a warm place to huddle away from the cold air. A safe harbor.

Danny realized he wasn't completely empty after all. He still had a few words to go. These words were the most important. These words were the ones he had agonized over the longest. As he spoke them, his lips brushed Jay's shirtfront, and behind the shirt, behind the warm flannel, he heard the pumping of Jay's heart. It was that sound that gave Danny the courage to speak those final words.

"I'm in love with you, Jay. I want to be your lover. I'm not sure, but I think maybe you love me too. At least I hope you do, otherwise I'm making a really big ass of myself right now. Tell me I'm not. Tell me I'm not being stupid. Tell me your heart is pounding in my face like a turbine engine for a reason and you're not just having a heart attack or something."

At that, Jay barked out a laugh. He squeezed Danny so tightly in his arms, Danny heard something pop, but whatever it was it caused no pain so Danny ignored it. Jay pushed him to arm's length and beamed down at him, his face alight with happiness. His eyes misted over all of a sudden.

"Don't cry," Danny said. "That's my job."

"Shut up."

Danny blinked. "Okay. But you still haven't answered my question. Getting a little anxious here. I'm hanging in the breeze like a windsock. Do you think maybe you might like me back? At least a little bit?"

"What do you think?" Jay asked softly, and a split second later he covered Danny's mouth with his.

The taste of Jay's lips on his was something Danny knew he would never forget. Ever. It wasn't just your run-of-the-mill kiss either. It was a *terrific* kiss. It was a *spectacular* kiss. And the darn thing went on and on until finally Danny pounded on Jay's broad chest and broke the kiss himself.

"Well?" Danny asked, caught between sex-driven heat and pure fucking anger. "Tell me, dammit! Give me an answer!"

Jay's grin looked amazingly like one of Carly's goofyass smiles.

"Yes, Danny," he said, his eyes burning bright, his cheeks red from either the cold air or the kiss, which Danny could still taste. "I loved you even before you moved in. I've wanted to tell you for weeks."

"So why didn't you?"

"Chicken, I guess. Afraid you'd say no."

"Promise me you won't be afraid of me saying no again. About anything. Except maybe your lasagna. That really sucks."

"Thanks. There was another reason I didn't tell you, Danny."

"What was it?"

Jay stumbled around for the words. "Well, I have this thing about not cheating, see. I mean, well, I don't cheat. Ever. On my lover, if I have one, or anybody else's."

Danny frowned, confused. "That's a noble attitude for sure, but what does it have to do with me? I'm single now."

"Yeah, but when you first came here, you were *barely* single. I had to make sure you had really left Josh. That you had no intention of going back."

Danny gave an exasperated grunt. "You didn't know that already?"

Jay's ears got as red as his cheeks. "I wasn't sure."

"My God, you're dumb."

Jay snorted. "Thanks again."

Danny grew serious. He tore his eyes from Jay's face long enough to gaze down the rain-soaked mountainside. "It's not letting up," he said. "The rain, I mean."

"No, it's not," Jay agreed, poking his hand out from under the overhang and letting the icy raindrops sprinkle his palm. "If anything it's raining harder. But do we care?"

Danny blinked when a distant streak of lightning strobed across the mountainside. "Not much," he said, just before the thunder grumbled over their heads, tumbling away into the distance.

Danny turned from the sky and snuggled into the alternate universe he liked better. The universe inside Jay's arms. With Jay's heartbeat against his face, and with his nose pressed into the delicious aroma of Jay's warm shirt, he said, "Let's go home."

"But not as just roommates," Jay said, all attempts at joking aside. He had never sounded more serious. "Not this time. Please."

"No," Danny said. "Not as just roommates. Never again as just roommates. I mean, if you really want me."

Jay laid his lips to the crook of Danny's neck and sucked lightly at Danny's skin. Danny relished the sensation, relished the soft brush of Jay's bristle against his cheek.

"Trust me, Danny. I really want you. I want you more than anything. I always have." Their mouths came together one more time before Jay pulled gently away. "Thank you," he said, as his fingers splayed over the Danny's cheeks and their gazes joined. Jay's lips were still moist, swollen from Danny's kiss. "I'll never hurt you, Danny. I want you to know that."

Danny dropped his forehead to Jay's chin, smiling to himself. "I knew that before I knew anything else," he said. "There's something gentle about you, Jay. Gentle and honest and kind. I knew it the first time I saw you."

Jay closed his eyes. "Good." Danny found Jay's warm mouth again and kissed him until the rain and the cold and all his worries disappeared.

JAY LED Danny up the narrow staircase leading to the second floor. He shrugged out of his coat and kicked off his shoes as he went, and Danny followed. Behind them, the last flickers of fire in the fireplace showed the four animals, both cats and both dogs, sprawled out on a rag rug in front of the dying flames. Their heads all pointed in the same direction, directly at the fire, as if absorbing all the heat they could before it went out for the night.

At the top of the stairs, Jay turned and whisked an already trembling Danny into his arms. Danny stood on tiptoe to claim a kiss. When their lips met, his hands slid under the tail of Jay's shirt and stroked the soft skin of his back. His fingertips brushed a fluff of hair at the base of Jay's spine, and he smiled against Jay's lips. With his other hand, Danny began unbuttoning Jay's shirt.

"I've wanted this for so long," Danny muttered.

While Danny worked at the shirt, Jay led Danny through the bedroom door and quietly closed it behind them. By then, the last button had been undone, and Danny pushed the shirt off Jay's broad shoulders, exposing his chest completely.

While the shirt slid down Jay's back and puddled at his feet, Danny muttered, "Oh, man," and laid his mouth to the heated skin of Jay's chest. Danny's lips brushing against the scattering of hair on Jay's chest made Jay shiver with need.

"Oh, man," Danny muttered again.

Jay couldn't seem to talk. His voice box was on vacation or something. He simply nodded, and surprising even himself, he reached down to undo Danny's belt buckle. With a yank, he slid it out of the loops and tossed it aside. Next he popped the button at the top of Danny's jeans, plucked out the shirt tucked there, and pulled it over Danny's head.

"Ouch," Danny giggled. "My nose."

Jay's arms were already around Danny's torso, their bare chests meeting in a heated embrace. Jay had never felt anything as incredible in his life. He lifted Danny off the floor and held him tight, burying his face in Danny's throat, loving Danny's fingers tugging at his hair, trying to draw him even closer.

"Fuck your nose," Jay said around a sigh.

"If you want," Danny gasped, and before either of them could laugh, their mouths met in another kiss.

Still cradling Danny in his arms as if he weighed nothing at all, Jay pulled back and twisted his face into a deliberately sexy grin that definitely got a reaction.

"It's been a month since you moved in," Jay said. "It's taken me all that time to get you into my bed."

"Slowass," Danny said, wrapping his legs around Jay's waist, a hungry gleam in his eye, his fingers buried in Jay's hair.

As Jay's mouth found Danny's yet again, he carried Danny across the room and lowered him carefully onto the bed, breaking their kiss at the last moment.

"Don't go," Danny pleaded as Jay stepped back to look down at him sprawled across the bed.

But Jay only smiled, and bending down, he grabbed the cuffs of Danny's jeans and stripped them away in one swift tug and slung them across the room. Danny lay before him naked, now, but for the white socks on his feet.

Staring down at him, Jay froze, passion heating his flesh and widening his eyes. Danny was beautiful. His legs were coated with fair hair, his stomach smooth, unblemished, and pale. His cock was perfect, erect and strong, rising up from a bush of strawberry-blond pubic hair.

When Danny reached down to grasp his own cock, Jay gently bent forward to ease Danny's hand away. "No, please," he said. "Let me." Danny's gulp echoed Jay's, almost comically, as Jay stood upright again and slid his trousers down over his hips and legs, peeling the boxer shorts away at the same time. His cock sprang free, as hard as it had ever been. As he stood there before Danny in nothing but socks and a blush, Danny sat up on the bed and slipped his cool fingers around Jay's erection, almost reverently, gently easing the foreskin back.

"You're not circumcised," he whispered, and a second later he pulled Jay down onto the bed beside him.

They came together in their first complete embrace, cocks grinding against each other, their bare legs entwined. Before Jay could make a move toward Danny's cock, Danny took the initiative. He pushed Jay back on the bed and straddled his waist to hover over him. After resting his hands on Jay's chest and staring down at him for a moment, Danny lowered his face to Jay's mouth. While Jay massaged Danny's thighs, Danny slid his mouth away from the kiss and dragged his lips down over Jay's chin and across his unshaved Adam's apple.

Never stopping but grazing downward, Danny's mouth brushed Jay's chest, taking side trips to each nipple as he went. From there, heading ever south, Danny pushed his face into the warmth of Jay's stomach and inhaled deeply. Then he slid his tongue through the trail of dark hair that blossomed at Jay's belly button and continued downward, until his chin bumped Jay's cock.

Only then did Danny raise up and stare into Jay's eyes while Jay lay there, riveted by everything Danny was doing. Danny smiled, his eyes still locked with Jay's, and tilted Jay's hard cock toward him. Taking his sweet time about it, he slid his tongue around the corona, dipped it under the foreskin and over the sensitive shaft beneath. Danny slid Jay's foreskin back and laid his mouth to the tip to kiss away a drop of liquid shimmering there. Jay bucked beneath him, overwhelmed with sensation.

Jay dragged himself to a sitting position and lifted Danny's face to his. He kissed Danny hungrily, but a kiss was not what he really wanted.

"Turn around, Danny. Face the other way. Lay with me that way. Please."

Danny did as he was asked. Without releasing Jay's cock from his gentle grip, he jackknifed himself on the bed until his cock was in Jay's face, right where Jay wanted it, and Jay's own cock was in Danny's.

Jay breathed a sigh and wrapped his arms around Danny's waist. He pulled Danny close and tucked that golden cock into his mouth, drawing a shuddering gasp from both of them. Danny began to tremble when Jay's mouth engulfed him. In return, Danny slipped his fist around Jay's cock and took it deep into his mouth. His hands caressed Jay's ass, and Jay did the same to him. Jay touched a fingertip to Danny's opening, just the gentlest of touches, and Danny cried out in either laughter or agony, Jay couldn't be quite sure which.

"It's been a long time," Danny muttered, barely audible. He bucked and writhed beneath the attentions of Jay's mouth. "Jay, stop!"

"No," Jay said around him, smiling a mischievous smile to himself before taking Danny's cock all the way in and manipulating the corona with his tongue, sliding it deliciously over the seeping slit, loving the taste of the juices he found there. Wanting more. Wanting more *now*.

Danny arched his back, and Jay's cock slipped back into his mouth. If his plan was to take his mind off what Jay was doing and prolong the blowjob, it didn't work. Certainly not for Jay.

"Oh God, Danny, I'm going to come."

"Me too."

"That was quick."

"No shit."

Again Jay smiled around Danny's cock, and when the beautiful young body beside him arched again and Danny tore at Jay's hair with his one free hand, Jay arched right back.

"Yes," Danny breathed, and a moment later, they both came. Jay filled Danny's mouth at the very same moment that Danny's cock slipped free and spilled come across Jay's face.

Jay reclaimed Danny's shooting cock and clung on tight, accepting everything Danny offered as he spilled his own seed into Danny. Even when the fury of their eruptions began to subside, their mouths continued to draw sweet juices from each other. Jay's cock softened as Danny continued worshiping it. Danny, too, softened in the moist heat of Jay's mouth while Jay clutched him tightly in his arms, his fingertip still on Danny's tender opening, his nose buried now in the soft pillow of Danny's pubic hair. Danny's come lay hot on the skin of his face until he wiped it free with his fingertip and pushed it into his mouth, where he swallowed it with all the rest.

Slowly, they relaxed. Their muscles unwound.

Jay's cock slid free from Danny's mouth and lay against Danny's lips, still leaking, while Danny rested his heated face against Jay's stomach. Danny's heart thudded in unison with Jay's, echoing through the pulse in Danny's groin as they continued to hold on to each other as if afraid to let go. Danny stroked Jay's legs, his palms grazing the hair softly. As the rush of that first hunger abated, Jay found the beauty of Danny's thigh and, pressing his mouth to it, tasted it on his tongue, relishing the heat and softness of Danny's skin, the gentle tickle of Danny's leg hair on his nose.

"Thank you," Jay whispered. The words barely reached his own ears. It was as if Jay's strength had been spent. All of it. It was all he could do to even utter a word. A sound.

Danny made a move as if to spin back around on the bed, but Jay held him in place where he lay. "Please, Danny, no. Stay just like this for a while. I love the feel of your leg against my mouth. Jesus, you taste great."

Danny relaxed, once again resting his cheek on Jay's stomach. He slipped his hand around Jay's flaccid cock and snuggled it against his cheek.

"You're beautiful," Danny said. "Your cock is beautiful. So soft and gentle now, when it was so hard and heavy before." Smiling, Jay pulled him close, sliding up on the bed just far enough to bury his face in Danny's stomach, just as Danny was doing to him.

"It's you that's beautiful, Danny. You're even more beautiful than I thought you'd be."

Danny didn't answer. They let the silence of the night settle over them. Slowly, as they lay cuddling, Jay began to move his hands again. Not in an impatient way. Not driven. But idly. Almost casually. As if he were calmly and happily exploring Danny's secrets. Danny responded in kind.

Finally Jay asked the question he'd wanted to ask since the two of them stood in the rain at the side of the mountain. Only minutes ago, it seemed, but a lifetime ago too. Back in a time when secrets had yet to be shed.

"Danny?"

Danny seemed too content to speak, enjoying the moment too much to go to all the trouble of forming words. "Hmm?"

Jay pressed his lips to Danny's belly. He found courage there.

"Danny, do you really love me?"

At that, Danny lifted his head and gazed at him. Their eyes met. Danny brushed his fingertips over Jay's mouth, as if remembering the happiness those lips had given him just moments before.

"Yes," he said simply. "I want to be your lover. Please let me do that."

Jay nodded, unable to speak. He pulled Danny in tighter and closed his eyes, losing himself in the feel of the man beside him.

Finally two words escaped Jay's lips. "My lover," he murmured. And those were the last words he spoke or heard before the darkness of sleep settled over him.

AS THE first faint hint of dawn stole through the window, Danny opened his eyes. Sometime in the night, he and Jay had squirmed around into a proper sleeping position and were now cuddled together under the blankets, wrapped in each other's embrace.

Jay's arm lay across Danny's chest. Danny had slipped down into the warmth of it with his face tucked into Jay's armpit. He decided immediately it was his new most favorite place to be. He thought it pretty cool that he loved this position so much he could even find it in his sleep.

Jay's body was sleep-warm and heavenly against his own. His armpit hair lay fuzzy and cleanly fragrant against Danny's nose. Danny woke with an erection. No surprise there. The surprise was how great it felt finding his dick snugged up against Jay's thigh with Jay's leg hair scraping the tender underside of his swollen corona. Danny pressed the gentlest of kisses to Jay's rib cage, then carefully slid out from under the arm that pinned him lovingly to the bed.

As quietly as he could, Danny padded barefoot across the cold bedroom floor to the bathroom. There he relieved himself, did a little cleaning up afterward, and gargled with mouthwash while staring at his groggy reflection in the bathroom mirror. That done, he padded down the hall to his own room, snatched a condom from his nightstand in what seemed the first time in forever, then slathered some lubricant over his hole. Planning ahead never hurts, right? Afterward he navigated the dark hallway back to Jay's bedroom, slipped back into bed, and resumed his old position. Jay grunted in his sleep, and his warm arm once again pulled Danny close against him before he settled back into slumber.

The slumber didn't last long.

With Jay's long naked body lying against his, Danny's erection returned with a vengeance. Keeping the covers over them both to block out the cold morning air, Danny slowly slid deeper into the bed, dragging kisses down Jay's rib cage as he went. By the time his mouth was grazing Jay's hip bone, he noticed a definite tenting of the covers up ahead.

Smiling, Danny cupped Jay's balls gently in his hands and oozed across the bed to where he could press a kiss to the tip of Jay's cock, which bounced in response. Danny took that as a good sign.

A hand came down and massaged the back of Danny's neck as he took Jay's cock into his mouth, tasting it, giving it just a moment's attention. Jay's legs opened wider, and Danny crawled over one of them to position himself between the two on elbows and knees. There, he slid his mouth from Jay's cock and tasted his way down the shaft until Jay's balls were right where he wanted them. Slathering them with kisses and scooping one into his mouth, or trying to, he was rewarded with Jay's fingers tightening in his hair and a heavenly groan erupting from Jay's throat.

While he continued to worship Jay's balls with his mouth and Jay continued to groan and thrash around, Danny quietly extracted the condom from the wrapper and, after positioning it carefully over the head of Jay's cock, began expertly rolling it down the shaft.

Jay's voice was a passion-rattled baritone. Deep and sexy. "What's my baby doing, I wonder?"

"You'll see," Danny murmured.

With everything ready to go, Danny straddled Jay's legs and squirmed his way toward the head of the bed until his thighs were clamped around Jay's hips and his mouth had found Jay's in the darkness.

They kissed as Jay's hands came up to stroke Danny's smooth back. Reaching farther, Jay cupped the globes of Danny's ass and pulled him up a little more.

"You're not so dumb," Danny whispered into the kiss, and reaching down, he guided the head of Jay's latex-covered cock to his premoistened hole.

Obviously noticing the lubricant, Jay mumbled, "Somebody planned ahead."

Danny broke the kiss and said with a grin, "Shut up."

Still hovering over Jay, he planted his hands on Jay's chest for support and forced himself to relax. Slowly, Danny gave in to Jay's gentle prodding to be let in, and once his anal ring accepted the inevitable—happily, it must be said—Danny lowered himself onto Jay's straining cock. Gasping for air at about the halfway point because Jay was so much bigger than Josh, Danny bit back a cry of ecstasy as he carefully forced himself to envelop the shaft completely. As he hunkered there, pierced to his very heart, it seemed, Jay's pubic hair scraping his tender opening, Danny's entire body gave a great shudder.

Jay held Danny in place, considerately allowing Danny to adjust in his own time. But his voice was ragged with lust. "Am I hurting you?"

Danny gave a staggered laugh. "God, no."

Jay smiled. Then his smile vanished as he struggled visibly to restrain his blood-infused cock. Still trying not to hurt him, no matter what Danny said.

Danny continued to hover over Jay on hands and knees, impaled, unmoving. Adjusting to Jay's girth. Bending down in the darkness under the covers, he sought Jay's mouth with his own. Finding it, he melted against Jay's welcoming lips. Jay smiled into the kiss as his hands caressed Danny's ass. He gently eased Danny's cheeks wider, helping Danny adjust. His breath came in shattered puffs, and a cutoff gasp escaped when Danny's tongue found his.

Oh, so slowly, Danny raised his hips, dragging his tender channel over Jay's cock. Pulling away. At the point where Jay could almost slip free, Danny lowered himself onto Jay's erection once again. Forcing that heavenly cock into himself as far as it would go.

Danny's movements began to quicken. Jay's hands clutched tighter. Their tongues moved more frantically inside the kiss for a moment. Then Jay raised his knees from the bed, bending his legs to better position himself and jarring Danny loose from the kiss. But once situated, once Danny was cradled comfortably over Jay's moving cock, Danny accepted it as part of himself.

"Now," Danny whispered, once again finding Jay's mouth in a kiss. He relinquished control to Jay, giving himself to the man completely in that moment to do with him as he pleased.

Jay accepted the reins as eagerly as Danny offered them, but still his movements were gentle. His lunges controlled. Regardless of his own enjoyment, he strove to please Danny with every stroke, every push. When Danny gasped in delight as Jay's cockhead reached the proper depth to stimulate Danny's prostate, Jay concentrated all his efforts on that spot until Danny could no longer be restrained by a kiss. He flung himself up on his knees, arching his spine over Jay—his head flung back, the tendons in his neck quivering—and cried out every time Jay's bulging corona scraped the magic spot. Jay's expression was blissful as his cock tunneled deep, burying, retreating, burying itself again.

While Jay fucked, Danny stroked himself, sometimes stopping long enough to cup his own balls while his stiff dick stood upright, bobbing in tandem with his thundering heart. At those times, Danny closed his eyes and threw his head back, his mouth slack in blind sensation. Jay released one hand from Danny's ass and circled Danny's standing cock. When Danny clamped his knees tighter around Jay's chest, Jay began to stroke Danny's shaft with a look of pure hunger on his face. On every upward stroke, Jay slid his thumb across Danny's weeping slit, at times releasing him long enough to carry the silver drops to his mouth and lay them on his tongue.

Suddenly, Danny lurched uncontrollably. His back arched, thrusting his torso forward. He took his hands from Jay's chest, dug his fingers into Jay's tousled hair, and held on like a rider hanging on to a bucking horse's mane for dear life. Jay wrapped his fingers around Danny's pulsing cock, and the moment he did, a geyser of come shot from Danny and splattered Jay's chest, his chin, his lips. Jay immediately licked away Danny's come, and Danny shuddered.

A moment later, Jay convulsed, and wrapping his arms around Danny in a bear hug, he drove his cock deep and began spilling his seed inside the condom with a cry of joy that startled Danny with its ferocity.

While Jay convulsed below, Danny shuddered above, riding Jay with a smile on his face, groaning happily when Jay cried out beneath him. Finally, as Jay's lunges slowed, Danny collapsed over him, wrapped Jay's head in his arms, and cradled him, cooing soothing sounds into Jay's ear. While Jay's iron cock continued to stab through him, less insistently now, almost lazily, like a gentle sword piercing a willing heart, Danny comforted Jay to the end of his explosive climax. And only when Jay's lunges and cries subsided completely did Danny ease his grip, softening his embrace, cooing muted words, crooning gentler sounds.

When Jay stilled, only then did Danny relax over him. *This is how it should be. This is how it should always be.*

Jay's warm lips, still fragrant with Danny's come, brushed lightly over Danny's ear. His bristly jaw scraped Danny's smooth cheeks. He whispered words, grumbly and sweet, that brought a contented smile to Danny's face. "I know what my baby likes now."

Danny couldn't stop himself. He had to speak the words. He had to. "You were so gentle," he sighed. He tilted his head enough to bury his face in Jay's mop of hair, closing his eyes as the softness of it covered his nose, brushed his tender mouth. Jay's cock still rested deep inside him, dwindling now but remaining a presence. A wonder. Jay's long, powerful body lay beneath him, as thrilling to the touch as it had been the first time Danny had explored it the night before.

Jay's arms tightened around him. "Why wouldn't I be gentle? I love you."

"Still…."

Jay pulled Danny closer, wrapping him more securely in his arms as if postponing the inevitable detachment for one more moment, one more second. "Did Josh cause you pain, Danny? I mean, you know, when you fucked? Did he try to hurt you?"

Danny struggled to answer, but the best he could manage was a mere wisp of sound. "Sometimes."

"Maybe he didn't mean to," Jay consoled. "Maybe he didn't know."

"He knew."

With his own cold words still ringing through his head, Danny closed his eyes and buried his face in the heated crook of Jay's neck, letting the man's goodness seep into him. At last feeling safe. At last feeling loved.

As if fully aware of what Danny was thinking, what Danny was feeling, Jay held him in his arms until the sun peered through the bedroom window to stir them into a brand-new day.

CHAPTER NINE

GRADUALLY, AS time passed, Jay learned how sweet and kind Danny truly was, how committed a lover he could be. Danny learned the same from him. Their trust in each other grew quickly. Apart from Danny, Jay felt unfinished. When they came together, it was like two pieces of a jigsaw puzzle clicking into place. They became complete. A single perfect unit.

Their days were spent at their respective jobs, where Jay counted the hours until he could rush home again and they could be together. Danny glowed with a happiness he swore he had never known. Jay had known it with one other, yet even those halcyon years he had spent with Simon had not brought him the sheer joy he felt knowing Danny loved him. And Jay did know it, for Danny proved it to him every day.

In return, Jay strove to prove to Danny that love could be a gentle thing. It did not have to come with heartache and pain and black eyes and angry fists and screaming, hurtful words. Love could lie dormant and calm, always there waiting until the simplest touch or the most innocent of kisses stirred it to life. Yet even when the passion rose and the hunger came rushing in, gentleness could still be a part of it. And Danny never seemed less than astonished by that fact.

Jay began whistling to himself at work. A smile rarely left his face. His clientele at the bar and the other bartenders kidded him about it. Ernie, most of all, seemed content to see Jay's sudden happiness after the many months of sadness following Simon's death.

"Danny's good for you," Ernie whispered in Jay's ear one day at the bar as he leaned over the waiter's station to steal a handful of maraschino cherries.

"Those cherries are coming out of your paycheck," Jay kidded.

Ernie kidded back. "Danny's *still* good for you. Even if you are a cheapskate. I'm glad you guys are happy together."

Jay remembered what Danny once told him about Ernie having a crush on the boss. He supposed it was possible but still gave it little thought. All matters of love were centered on Danny these days. Jay had neither the need for, nor any interest in, any other. Still it was nice having the big guy's blessing, the big guy's friendship.

"Thanks, Ernie."

To Jay's surprise, Ernie popped a cherry in his mouth and leaned in even closer. "He came in last night."

Jay looked up. "*Who* came in?"

"The guy Danny was with. Joshua."

Jay considered that. "Did he cause any trouble? Did he say anything to you?"

"No. Since he's obviously old enough to drink, I didn't card him. He just glided past me like I wasn't there, and I let him go. He had one drink, chatted with the bartender a little, and left."

"And that was it?"

"That was it."

Ernie had such a worried expression on his great heavy face that Jay reached over and patted his cheek like he might a child. "Well, don't worry about it. The guy's gay, we're a gay bar, and he only lives four blocks away. He's bound to come in once in a while. Unless he starts something, just let him be."

Ernie didn't look convinced, but he tipped Jay a salute anyway. "Will do," he said. "Just thought you oughta know."

Jay nodded, watched Ernie walk away, and promptly forgot about it when the four guys playing pool in the corner shouted out an order for a round of drinks.

IT LOOKED like it was going to be a cold, wet California winter on top of Jay and Danny's mountain. Not that a little bad weather could wipe the happiness from Danny's heart or chill his ever-present hunger for Jay. Danny accepted the weather the same way Jay did, the way they accepted everything else—bravely together, on a communal front. In each other's arms, in each other's hearts. Whatever happened outside their little bubble of love never quite reached them. They had found their safe harbors. The world outside could blow and storm all it wanted. With Jay's strong hands at Danny's back and Danny's head on Jay's chest, Danny feared nothing. His contentment was impenetrable.

Now it was Jay who left work first, so it was Jay who cooked dinner every day. He would have it ready, some simple dish or other, when Danny walked through the door, shed his coat and scarf while calling out for Jay, then kicked his shoes off and stomped through the house in his stockinged feet until he located him. After which he'd throw himself into Jay's arms as if they'd been apart for weeks.

After dinner they would hike their mountain and speak softly, in the sage-scented air, of inconsequential things. Always holding hands, never more than a whisper's distance apart. They would hurry home to make love and speak quietly there in the upstairs bedroom, bound together in each other's arms until sleep claimed them or their lazy hunger for each other brought them together for a second round of sex. Or a third.

As contented as he had ever been in his life, Danny became an extension of Jay, and Jay, Danny felt sure, of him. They kept no secrets, hid no longings, except for one.

It was a week before Thanksgiving, after they had been together as lovers for almost a month, when Danny aired his one secret longing.

They were sitting downstairs in front of the fire. Jay was sipping a beer, juggling two cats in his lap, and reading a book. Danny was simply staring into the flames, his toes digging through Jingles's coat as he lay by the fire at his feet. Carly was upstairs running around, the staccato clatter of her toenails tapping through the house like the echo of distant gunfire. God knew what she was doing.

"I've been thinking about Simon," Danny said.

Closing his book, Jay gazed over at him in surprise. "Why?" he asked.

"I want to meet him. I mean, I want to go with you to the graveyard and see his grave. You still take flowers there sometimes. I know you do. The next time you go, I want you to take me with you."

Jay's face softened. "All right. We're off work tomorrow. We can go then if you want."

"Thank you," Danny said. He turned to face the fire again but kept a corner of an eye on Jay.

Jay stared at Danny's profile for a moment, then reopened his book. After a minute or two, though, he set the book aside and reached between their two chairs to grasp Danny's hand.

Danny smiled, and as always when he did, Jay smiled too.

Later, when their joined hands didn't seem to be enough anymore, Danny eagerly followed Jay up the stairs to their bed.

IT HAD only been a few days since Jay had brought flowers to the grave. Since a week hadn't yet passed, the old flowers were still there. Already dying, they drooped sadly in the cup by the flat, cold stone with Simon's name carved into it. Before Jay could make a move to remove the flowers and make room for the spray of fresh red and white carnations he held in his hand, Danny reached down and plucked the dead blossoms out and carted them off to the trash can placed a few graves over near where Jay had parked the Jeep.

By the time Danny returned, Jay had positioned the new flowers and brushed the gravestone free of debris. Danny took his arm, and together they stood at the foot of Simon's grave, staring down.

"It's so sad," Danny said, his voice hushed by the surroundings, by the solemn gravestones standing like sentinels on the hillside around them. Hushed too by the sound of taps being played somewhere over the hill, where a funeral was taking place on this cold November morning and strangers mourned another soul—a friend or family member, maybe—lost forever, relegated to silent memory. "Simon was younger than you when he died."

"I know."

"Do you still miss him, Jay? Do you think about him a lot?"

Jay paused as if to consider the question for a moment before turning to stare into Danny's eyes. "Sometimes you remind me of him."

"I do?"

"Yeah. Simon could be annoying too," Jay teased.

Danny laughed. Slowly, his laugh faded and he stared back at the stone, at the flowers so pretty beside it. But they too had been torn from life, Danny realized. Doomed to wither now, their stems snipped, their roots gone, no longer connected to the earth that bore them.

Danny clung to Jay's hand as they stood side by side at the foot of the grave. The air was filled with the sweet smell of the honeysuckle that climbed along a wrought-iron fence only a few feet away. Ravens wheeled overhead, crying out their joy for life while the graveyard lay silent as death beneath them. A perfect dichotomy. "I'm sorry you lost him, Jay. I'm sorry you were hurt like that."

"It's part of life, Danny. We all lose people. We all get hurt sometimes."

"I don't know what I'd do if I lost you."

Jay's grip tightened on Danny's hand. "You'd survive. We always do. Then you'd find somebody else."

"Like I found you?"

Jay nodded. "Like we found each other."

Danny bent to straighten a blossom that had slipped from the other carnations. It was one of the red ones. As red as blood. He gently coaxed it back into place, and while on his knees in the grass, he ran his fingers over the cold stone, over the sharp letters of Simon's name gouged into the marble. "I hope you know I'm taking care of him for you," Danny softly said, his fingers still buried among the carnations. "I'll love him as much as you did, Simon. I promise. I'll do everything I can to make him happy."

Jay lowered himself to his knees beside Danny and slipped an arm around his waist. They stared down at the stone together.

"Thank you," Jay whispered.

Danny nodded, dropping his head to Jay's shoulder.

THEY HAD a lunch of prawns and clam chowder in a seafood restaurant at the edge of the bay. By the time they finished eating, their melancholy moods had been shed, and they were laughing like loons at the antics of a seagull that was bound and determined to steal Danny's napkin.

Leaving the mainland behind, they stared out over the ships on the bay as they traversed the long sloping bridge that connected the coastline to Coronado Island. With hordes of tourists in town for the Thanksgiving holiday, it took Jay a while to find a place to park, but once he did, they strolled the quaint streets of Coronado until they reached a smooth expanse of white beach in front of the Coronado Hotel.

The air sweeping in off the ocean was icy, but they merely wrapped their coats more tightly around themselves and strolled the sands hand in hand.

Danny longed to remove his shoes and dig his toes through the sand as he walked, but it was too cold. He did find a gray stone, rubbed smooth and round by countless eons of surf and sand. He slipped it into his pocket to remember the day, flushing a little when Jay smiled at him.

"You're a romantic," Jay said.

Danny shrugged. "I'm just happy." He stopped and pulled Jay into his arms. There was no one else on the beach, no one else to see, not that Danny would've cared anyway, and he was sure Jay wouldn't have either. Homophobia barely existed in San Diego. Not inside their little bubble of existence anyway. For that Danny was truly grateful.

Wrapped in each other's arms, Danny's head on Jay's chest, they stared out at the foamy breakers sweeping in from the sea. The wind tossed their hair and reddened their cheeks with cold.

"I'm happy too, Danny. Every day is like a new adventure for me, being with you. I still can't believe you love me. I still don't know what I ever did to deserve you."

Danny snuggled closer. Jay made a great wind blocker. Danny tucked his nose under Jay's scarf for a little extra warmth. "You were right, you know."

"About what, baby?"

"About Josh. He let me go. Like you said he would. He didn't come after us. He didn't try to hurt me. I haven't seen him once."

"He hasn't tried to call you?" Jay asked.

"He did at first. But not anymore. I guess he gave up when I wouldn't answer. Thank God."

Jay gave him a look Danny couldn't interpret but then shook his head. "I'm sure Josh has his own life to live, Danny. He's an asshole, but even assholes have to punch the clock, live from day to day, worry about work, try to find a little happiness, try not to get arrested for beating the piss out of ex-lovers. I don't suppose he knows we're together, but he does know you want nothing more to do with him. He's accepted it and moved on. Just let him go and try not to think about it. I told you once, and I'll tell you again. He can't hurt you anymore. You're with me now, Danny, and I'll never let any harm come to you."

Danny closed his eyes and tucked his hands under the tail of Jay's coat. "I love you so much," he whispered.

Jay kissed his hair. "I love you back."

"Should we go home? The kids'll be anxious."

Jay laughed and dipped his head to kiss Danny's forehead. "I suppose we'd better. Jingles and Carly might be plotting to kill the cats by now."

Danny grinned. "My money's on the cats."

Jay slapped Danny's ass. "Come on. Let's go. I'm freezing. This is San Diego. Why is it so damned cold?"

"Coldest November on record."

"In that case I'm glad I'm not sleeping alone anymore."

Danny's eyes burned suddenly hot. He slid a finger along Jay's jawline. "Ooh. Me too."

They crossed the beach, following their own sandy footsteps back to where they started. Passing the hotel, they headed for where they'd parked the Jeep. "I think I know how I might warm us both up," Danny teased as they strolled through an open-air cafe, still holding hands, not caring what anybody thought.

No one even glanced their way.

"I'm intrigued. Now what could you possibly do to warm me up?" Jay answered, a mischievous fire erupting in his warm brown eyes.

"And don't I love it when you're intrigued," Danny giggled, tugging him down the street at a faster clip.

JAY KNEW something was wrong the moment he opened the front door.

The house was cold, as if a window had been left open. He stood in the doorway, wondering why no animals came rushing out to greet them. Danny stood at his back, peering over Jay's shoulder.

"Where is everybody?" Danny asked.

Jay shook his head. "I don't know." He called for the dogs. "Carly! Jingles!"

No answer.

Danny raced across the living room, headed for the kitchen and the utility room behind it. "We left the door open!" he cried, and Jay hurried to join him.

Jay stared at the door, then at Danny. "Maybe it blew open," Jay said. "Sometimes it doesn't latch properly. Still, I thought I locked it before we left." Jay gazed around. "Wait."

He eased Danny aside and stepped toward the door leading down the stairs into the basement. The door stood ajar. The simple hook and eye with which Jay kept it locked lay on the floor at his feet, along with a few splinters of wood and a muddy footprint.

"Somebody broke in," Jay said. He couldn't believe it. "Someone's been in the house."

Jay spun around and tore from room to room, checking the TV sets, clomping up the stairs to make sure the computer was still in the garret, rummaging through the drawer in the nightstand where he kept a few extra bucks, foraging here and there trying to discover if anything was missing: The iPod and iPad. His watch. A couple of cell phones. Credit cards stashed in a metal box in the dresser.

Nothing appeared disturbed.

At the sound of a distant yip, Jay raced back down the stairs and through the back door, where he found Danny bending and petting the two dogs.

"Look," Danny said, jutting his chin toward the branches of the eucalyptus tree above their heads. Jay followed Danny's gaze and spotted Lucy sitting in the crook of a branch staring down at them. As soon as she knew their eyes were on her, she gave a plaintive yowl and began climbing down to join them. Cupping Carly's face in his hands, Jay coaxed, "The bad guy, girl. Where'd he go? Is he still here?"

Carly just stared back at him, then stretched her neck out and licked his face.

"Guess you're not Lassie, huh?" Jay drawled. Rising, he turned to Danny. "I didn't see anything missing. Did you notice anything down here?"

"I don't think so. No sign of Desi, though. I looked everywhere."

Jay shrugged. "He'll show up. He's probably just scared." He stepped back into the house with Danny at his heels. "But why would anyone break in and not steal anything?"

Jay stared at the hook and eye and the splinters on the floor, then at the ragged spot on the doorjamb where the latch had been. Suddenly, Jay understood. The only way the objects could have ended up where they were was if the door had been pushed in from the other side.

"They must have come in through the trapdoor to the basement. They kicked the kitchen door in to gain access to the house, and when they left, they went out through the back, leaving that door wide open behind them."

He took off down the stairs, and sure enough, he saw a bar of light stabbing across the basement floor. The burglar, or whatever the hell he was, had left the trapdoor at the back of the house open. Jay checked it out and saw a crowbar that had previously been in the unlocked shed out back lying in the dirt next to the hasp, which had been violently pried from the wooden door. The end board comprising the trapdoor had been splintered to kindling in the act.

"It was half-rotten anyway," Jay said, worried but not overly so. "I've been meaning to replace it."

Danny had never spent much time in the basement because of what Jay had told him about George. Danny wasn't a big fan of snakes. He gazed around now as if he thought maybe George was just waiting for a chance to bury a couple of fangs in his ankle, but no snake appeared. No rattles rattled.

He looked around. The basement was a mess, with crap strewn everywhere. "Did the burglar do this?" he asked.

Jay laughed. "Afraid not. It's always like this. Actually I'm surprised he didn't trip over something and break his neck."

Danny smiled. "Would have simplified matters, I guess."

They heard Lucy crying at the top of the stairs. Carly and Jingles took off first; then Jay and Danny followed. Lucy was standing atop the refrigerator in the kitchen, back arched, teeth bared, wailing like a banshee.

Jay scooped her off the fridge and into his arms. She immediately squirmed away, leapt to the floor, then hopped onto the stove. From there, one graceful leap carried her back to the top of the fridge, where she recommenced crying.

"Are you sure nothing's missing?" Danny asked.

"Pretty sure. The computer's still there. My money's in the nightstand, what little I had."

"There really isn't a lot to steal."

Jay gave a sardonic grin. "That hurt."

Danny laughed. With Lucy still wailing in the background, Jay followed Danny around the house as Danny checked off his own list of assets. It didn't take Jay long to realize Danny had been right. There really *wasn't* a lot to steal. Nothing any self-respecting burglar would be interested in, except maybe the computer and the flat-screen TV, and those were still sitting where they always did.

"Maybe it was some homeless guy," Danny said. "Maybe he was looking for food."

They headed back to the kitchen, both dogs at their heels. Through the kitchen door, they checked the pantry on the service porch, where all the canned stuff was stored. The upright freezer, an ancient relic that weighed a ton, stood by the basement door. Again, nothing seemed to be missing. In the kitchen, Lucy had ratcheted her wailing up a notch, sending icy chills down Jay's back. Jesus, that sound was awful!

Danny checked the cupboards where other foodstuffs were stored. Everything looked like it always did.

The sound of clawing interrupted their search, and they gaped up at Lucy, who was now trying to tear her way through the top of the fridge using her claws like a can opener. Her razor-sharp nails screeched across the metal, making Jay and Danny both clench their teeth.

Finally, Jay snatched her into his arms again and held her while she fought against him.

"What is it, girl?" Jay cooed. "What's wrong?"

Danny stepped forward and pulled the refrigerator door open. His back stiffened. "Oh God."

Still clutching Lucy, Jay stepped up beside him and stared into the refrigerator's lighted interior. On the bottom shelf lay Desi. He sprawled there unmoving, his little tongue hanging out, his eyes squeezed shut. A loaf of bread, which had been on the shelf in the door in front of him, was shredded to bits, the crumbs scattered everywhere.

Danny dropped to his knees in front of the poor beast and lifted the still body, cradling it in his arms. Desi's hair was cold, the body limp. "Poor thing," Danny murmured, pressing his face to Desi's frigid coat. He stared at the shredded loaf of bread. "He tried to claw his way out."

With another yowl, which scared the bejesus out of Jay and Danny both, Lucy leapt from Jay's arms and stretched her long legs over Danny's arm, brushing her pads across her mate's still body.

"Come away," Jay whispered, and pulling her into his arms again, he snuggled his face against Lucy's neck, making gentle cooing noises to quiet her. Finally, her crying ceased.

At that moment, Danny said, "Wait...."

There was hope in his voice. Jay could hear it. He stared over Danny's shoulder, dumbfounded, as Danny began massaging Desi's chest, stroking him, not quite gently, his fingers digging deep trenches through the frigid coat. As he stroked him, Danny blew warm breath over Desi's face. Jay's heart gave a lurch when he saw one of Desi's feet twitch. Then another. His tail flicked. The tongue hanging from Desi's mouth retreated, and to Jay's utter astonishment, Desi's eyes peeled open.

"He's alive!" Jay cried. "Holy shit, he's really alive!" He dropped to his knees beside Danny and slid a hand under Desi's head. With his thumb, he gently stroked the cat's forehead.

"He's breathing!" Jay gasped. "He really is! I can feel it on my skin!"

Beyond all hope, he heard a purr erupt. While Lucy squirmed in Jay's lap, determined to be let loose, Desi lifted his head and peered around. A plaintive meow erupted from his throat. A moment later he sprang from Danny's arms, startling Jay and Danny both. He and Lucy took off running and raced up the stairs leading to the bedroom on the second floor.

When they were gone, Jay and Danny stared at each other. Jay still couldn't believe it.

"If we'd have been gone any longer...," Danny muttered.

Jay mindlessly nodded. His eyes rose to the ceiling where he imagined Lucy and Desi entrenched under the bed, railing to each other about all that had just happened. Jay lowered his eyes to Danny's face, then back to the open fridge.

"What he must have endured in there," Jay said. "How scared he must have been."

Danny nodded, his eyes still wide with a mixture of fear and relief. In the ensuing silence, he and Jay remained kneeling side by side on the kitchen floor. Because he needed his lover's touch more than anything else right then, Jay reached out to take Danny's hand.

"Could—could it have been an accident?" Danny quietly asked. "Did he crawl in there the last time we opened it, and we didn't notice?"

"No," Jay answered, his voice as cold as Desi's body had been. "At least I don't think so. Someone must have closed him in there."

"But why? Who would do such a thing?"

With that question hovering over them like the reek of something foul on the air, Jay and Danny slowly turned to each other.

"No," Danny said. "Joshua wouldn't do this. He *wouldn't*. It must have been a random thing. A spur-of-the-moment act of cruelty perpetrated by whoever the hell it was who broke into the house."

"Are you sure?" Jay asked. "Are you really sure?"

Danny stared down at Jay's hand in his. "N-no. I'm not sure." Only then did Danny begin to cry.

JAY CAREFULLY hung up the phone. It was the landline. As soon as the whine of a broken connection went silent, he sat there staring into space.

"What'd they say?" Danny asked. Jay had heard exactly what he expected to hear. "They said unless we have proof that it was Joshua who broke into the house, we would be making a big mistake to accuse him. And since nothing was stolen, they informed us we didn't have much to accuse him of anyway."

Danny couldn't believe it. "What about the cat?"

Jay was exhausted. He needed a nap and he needed it now, but he made an effort to answer for Danny's sake. "They said pretty much the same thing we said. There's no proof the cat didn't sneak into the fridge while someone had the door open, which would make it an accident, not a crime. Then he suggested we take better care of our pets."

"I can't believe they'd say that," Danny said, fury lighting his eyes.

"As soon as they found out it was my lover's ex-boyfriend we suspected, they sort of lost interest. I'm pretty sure I even heard a chuckle or two. Maybe homophobia isn't quite as dead in this city as we thought. At least not in the hallowed halls of the San Diego Police Department. The fuckers."

"But they're the police! They're supposed to help *everybody*!"

Jay shrugged. "I'm sorry, Danny, but they're not coming. You said yourself you didn't think it was Josh anyway."

"I know, but still—"

Jay bent over him, kissing Danny's forehead. "Calm down, baby. It's over now. Desi's okay. You saved his life, you know. You should be happy about that."

Danny laid his hand on Jay's arm. Tears stood in his eyes again. "I'm not happy at all. This is my fault. It's because of me this happened."

Jay pulled Danny into his arms. "Danny, you said yourself you didn't think Joshua would do something like this, and I agree with you. This is beyond the pale, even for him. What rings truer to me is what you said earlier, about it being a homeless person looking for food, maybe, or kids causing trouble—or hell, it could be anyone. Besides, I still don't think Joshua knows where you're living."

He suddenly remembered what Ernie had said about Joshua coming into the bar. He drank one drink, chatted with the bartender, and left, Ernie had said. Jay wondered which bartender it was. He tried to think back to the night in question. Who was tending bar that night? What night had Ernie been talking about? He couldn't remember. More importantly, what had the two talked about? Hell, even if Jay figured out who the bartender was that night, that bartender probably wouldn't remember one customer out of hundreds, let alone be able to recall what they had talked about.

He shook away his doubts, his suspicions. It didn't matter. Danny was wrong. Joshua wouldn't have done this. Danny's ex, as cruel as he was, wasn't that fucking crazy. The guy was a CPA, for Christ's sake. A glorified bookkeeper. A bully. Nothing more. He wouldn't jeopardize his own freedom by coming after them like this. Danny had been out of his life for months. Joshua must know Danny was lost to him by now. He must have accepted the fact that Danny was never coming back and that nothing Joshua did could ever change that.

"Don't worry, Danny. This isn't your fault. It wasn't Joshua. I know it wasn't."

Jay pressed a kiss to the top of Danny's head. A moment later, Danny stepped from his arms, wiping his eyes.

"I hope you're right," he said softly.

THE NIGHTMARE yanked Jay awake with a start. He blinked himself into awareness. It was still the middle of the night. No stars were visible through his bedroom window, probably because another rainstorm was on the way; at least one had been promised by the local weatherman. Obviously, the clouds were rolling in already.

Jay gathered up a fistful of sheet and wiped the sweat from his face. Jesus. What a dream! He had no idea what it had been about. The memory of it had already left him. Still it had been frightening enough to leave him trembling and more than a little sick to his stomach. An indeterminate dread filled his thoughts. There was a horror here, lurking in this dark room, in this silent house. But what the hell was it?

He twisted his head, and in the shadows he saw Danny's face resting against his shoulder. Danny's hand lay on Jay's chest, his fingers twined in the patch of hair between Jay's pecs. Unmoving.

Danny lay so still. As still as—

Jay's heart gave a lurch. The boy was *too* still! Dear God, not again!

Jay flung himself up from the pillow, dragging Danny up with him and shaking him hard. Danny cried out, trying to jerk away. A curse spilled from his lips.

Jay roared with relief. Snatching Danny into his arms, he enfolded the warm body in a tight embrace until Danny started squirming to be set free. "Thank Christ," Jay sobbed. "Thank Christ!"

"What the hell are you doing?" Danny wailed, still fighting, still trying to pull away, likely as frightened as Jay now that he'd been torn from sleep so quickly he didn't know what the hell was going on. "What's wrong? Why did you wake me? Jesus, Jay, are you crying? Why are you crying? What's *wrong*?"

Jay shook his head, his face still buried in Danny's sleep-tousled hair. Danny's reassuring heat coursed over him, through him. He wrapped his arms more tightly around Danny's smooth back and held him so tightly he could feel Danny's chest expand when he breathed. Danny wasn't fighting anymore. He was giving himself to Jay. No longer angry, probably just concerned. Confused. Rattled.

"I thought…. I thought—" But Jay couldn't finish. He couldn't explain. Not yet. It all came rushing back. That morning. That morning over a year ago when he woke to find another still body lying beside him, a cooling hand on his chest, a breathless mouth resting against his shoulder.

MY DRAGON, MY KNIGHT

He cupped Danny's face in his hands and rained kisses everywhere he could reach. Danny managed to offer a couple of kisses back before he finally tore himself free and held Jay at arm's length.

"Tell me," Danny insisted, his voice ragged with sleep. "What's wrong? What did you think happened? Did you hear someone in the house? Did you think the prowler was back?"

"No, Danny. No. I thought…." Jay sucked in a deep breath, trying to calm himself. Again the memory of that morning rushed through him, chilling his heart, burying him in fear.

"The night Simon died, Danny. The morning I woke up to find him—gone. He was still in my arms. His life—his life had bled away while he slept. You were so still against me. I thought—"

"Oh God," Danny groaned. He pulled Jay into his arms, cupping the back of his head, resting his cheek against Jay's, stroking Jay's chest comfortingly, whispering in his ear. "It's okay, Jay. I'm okay. We both are. It was just a nightmare. I'll—I'll try to snore from now on like you do so you'll know I'm still alive. I'll lift the covers. I'll flutter the fucking curtains. I promise."

Jay expelled a shuddery breath and tried to smile against Danny's cheek "I don't snore," he said.

"Yeah, right."

Danny switched on the lamp by the bed. He eased Jay down onto his pillow and loomed over him, gazing down. His eyes were filled with such love and concern it took Jay's breath away. But Jay had yet to banish the fear that had possessed him. Danny brushed his lips over each of Jay's eyelids as if trying to kiss the fear away.

"I'm okay, baby. I'm still here. It was just a nightmare."

Jay jerked his head in a little nod, his eyes never leaving Danny's face.

"I can't lose you too," Jay said. "I'd never survive it."

"No," Danny cooed. "Neither would I. But don't worry. We're mated for life. Like swans. Or wolves."

Jay grinned. "Or termites."

"Say what?"

"Termites. They mate for life too."

"No shit? That's not very romantic."

"It is for the termites." Jay grew serious again and reached up to stroke Danny's cheek. "Tell me again," he said. "Tell me again you're still here."

"I'm still here, baby. I'm right in front of you."

"You promise?"

Danny smiled. He reached down to brush Jay's bangs out of his face. His fingers lingered there in Jay's hair, his thumb stroking Jay's temple. He laid a gentle kiss to Jay's mouth. Then another.

"I promise," Danny said, their lips still touching. His warm breath flowed over Jay, blending and melding with his own, fragrant with sleep. "I promise," Danny said again.

And with those two simple words, Jay finally closed his eyes. His heartache began to abate. That horrible, torturing dread began to release him from its grip.

"It was poor Desi, I guess." Jay's eyes slid open. He stared up at Danny. "He came so close to dying." Jay tried to blink away the memory. It hurt too much to think about it. "Maybe that's what the nightmare was about. I don't know. But when I woke and you were lying there so still in my arms, I freaked. I just—*freaked*." He closed his eyes again and let Danny's warm, caressing fingers calm him.

"You're okay now, Jay. I'm here. We're together. Nothing can hurt us. Desi's okay too. Try to go back to sleep, okay? Try not to think about it anymore."

Jay nodded. "Okay." With a tiny grunt, he lifted his head from the pillow and gave Danny a kiss. Just a little one. Then, wearied to the bone, he dropped his head again. Danny slid his hands along Jay's ribs and laid his head on Jay's chest, and Jay held him close.

"Leave the light on," Jay whispered, sleep already reclaiming him.

Danny kissed Jay's chest, a nipple, the flurry of hair across Jay's pecs that he never seemed to tire of. "I will, baby. Just sleep now."

SLOWLY THE silence of the long night returned. No more nightmares came to tear it away. When they woke, the interlude was almost forgotten… lost in the terrors that followed.

CHAPTER TEN

THE WEATHERMAN said the storm was still a day away. The sky above the cabin was black and brooding, yet the hovering darkness had not reached the horizon quite yet. The waning sun still cast red rays through the stained-glass window, the dragon and the knight splashing streaks of color on the garret walls where Jay sat at his computer, working on the payroll for his employees at the bar.

Bored downstairs by himself, Danny had joined him. He lay sprawled on the old leather couch that had been relegated to the garret after too many teeth-and-claw marks from a houseful of pets had rendered it unfit for the living room downstairs. Although it looked like hell, it was still comfortable, and Jay hadn't been able to part with it, so he stuck it in his garret office.

Jay turned from the computer and stared at Danny, flat on his back on the ratty sofa, reading a book. Funny thing, but the couch looked pretty darn good with Danny stretched out on it. Sort of in the same way a Jaguar XKE makes a tumbledown shack look better just by being parked in its driveway.

"You're increasing that couch's property value," Jay said.

Danny set his book aside and tilted his head to stare at Jay still sitting at his desk. "It's sort of a gift. I do that wherever I go."

Jay laughed. Leaving the spreadsheet on the computer screen, Jay propelled himself with a push and rolled his desk chair to Danny's side. Danny snagged his leg and pulled him even closer.

"It's a pretty big couch," Danny said. "There's room for two."

Jay slid his hand over Danny's shirtfront and slipped a finger in between the buttons to stroke the warm skin beneath. "You think?"

"Well, maybe not if we're fully dressed." Danny smiled. "Clothes are so bulky."

"That can be fixed."

Jay stood and kicked the rolling chair away. Standing at Danny's side, he starting peeling his clothes off. Danny watched him for a few seconds before he started shedding his clothes too. In a moment, they were both naked.

Jay stared down at him. "Look at you," he said. "Look at the colors on your skin. The sunset's hitting the stained-glass window just right." He trailed his fingers along Danny's stomach. "Here"—he gently prodded Danny's belly button—"I can make out the knight." And gazing up at Danny's face, he breathed words as if in prayer. "And here, Danny. The colors of the dragon on your throat and face. You're beautiful. It's like you're rendered in watercolor."

Danny lifted his hand and moved it around, smiling at the play of pigments on his skin.

Jay stooped to kiss Danny's hand, then slipped down onto the couch beside him and pulled Danny into his arms. He purred. "Mmm."

Jay's cock, already filled with blood, lay hard and hot against Danny's thigh. Since Danny was still flat on his back, his own cock stood erect in the empty air until Jay wrapped his fingers around it and made it his own.

"That feels good," Danny groaned, lifting his hips.

"I can tell."

Jay slid his lips over Danny's chest and began foraging downward over his warm stomach, the play of colors a palette of delight. While he tilted Danny's dick straight up into the air with his fingers to give him space to work, Jay pushed his mouth into the bristly blond pubic hair at the base of it.

"Mmm," he said again.

"Sit on my chest," Danny murmured.

Jay stopped what he was doing and gazed up. "What?"

Danny's voice was husky. "You heard me. Sit on my chest. Put your cock in my face."

Jay narrowed his eyes. "Well, if you insist."

Before leaving Danny's crotch, he imparted a parting shot by sliding his mouth over Danny's dick all the way down to his nuts. Danny laughed and gasped and jerked around like a fish on a hook. As soon as Jay was certain Danny was good and turned-on, he released him and did as he was asked.

MY DRAGON, MY KNIGHT

Folding his legs around Danny's chest to comfortably straddle him, Jay eased his ass down over Danny's sternum, resting his nuts squarely on the boy's chin. His dick stood straight up in front of Danny's nose like a light pole, and his warm thighs hugged Danny's ears.

"How am I supposed to suck that?" Danny asked with a laugh. "It's like putting my mouth over a fencepost while I'm lying flat on the ground."

"Oh, let me help."

Lifting his ass and resting himself on his knees with his hand on the sofa arm for support, Jay positioned himself to where the head of his cock lay directly atop Danny's lips, which opened happily to accept it into that heavenly well of moisture and heat.

Jay trembled. "Oh my. That *is* better."

Danny rolled his eyes and mumbled something. Since he had a humongous dick in his mouth when he mumbled it, Jay had no idea what he'd said. And he didn't much care.

"Your cock needs attention," Jay said. "I'm going to do a U-ey."

Danny slipped Jay's cock from between his lips, all the while running his hands over Jay's torso, obviously reluctant to let him go.

"This should be interesting," Danny grinned. "Sure you're not too old to manage it?"

"Fuck you," Jay said with a snarl.

"Only if you ask nicely."

Awkwardly, Jay twisted around on his knees until he faced the other way. With his balls now resting on Danny's stomach and his hands on Danny's thighs to brace himself, he bent to take Danny's cock into his mouth yet again, just like he'd planned.

"I'm beginning to see the upside of this," Danny muttered.

Before Jay could respond, Danny buried his nose between Jay's buttcheeks and laid his lips to Jay's opening. Jay let out a whoop and tried to pull away. Laughing, Danny grabbed his hips and pulled him back. This time he explored Jay's opening with his tongue instead, and a tremor reminiscent of the earthquake that flattened San Francisco in 1906 passed through Jay's body.

"I think you like that," Danny mumbled.

Jay answered by reaching around, taking a fistful of Danny's hair, and holding him right where he was, as if afraid Danny would try to pull away. Like that was going to happen. Danny rewarded him by swiping his tongue once again over Jay's puckered hole, this time lingering just long enough to *really* drive Jay crazy.

"Oh Jesus." Jay writhed around over Danny's mouth. The kid was good.

"Don't call me kid," Danny growled, his mouth never leaving Jay's ass.

"I didn't!"

"You were thinking it!"

Jay gave his head a shake and decided, *fuck it*. Bending down, exposing his ass even more than it already was, if that was even empirically possible, he once again sucked Danny's cock down his throat as far as it would go.

Danny's tongue did a magical dance over Jay's hole, and apparently that turned Danny on so much, Jay found himself suddenly the recipient of a surprise orgasm. And an explosive one at that. Danny's come sprayed the roof of Jay's mouth, drenching Jay's tonsils, firing volleys everywhere it aimed. As happy as he had ever been in his life, Jay clamped his lips around Danny's dick so he wouldn't lose a precious drop. As his ejaculation dwindled, Danny reached a trembling hand between Jay's legs and began stroking Jay's cock. Jay gave a grunt, and with his ass still covering Danny's face like a Halloween mask, he bellowed once and shot his come all over Danny's belly.

While Danny held Jay in place until both of their convulsions ceased, Jay huddled close, heart pounding, relishing Danny's heat. His touch.

Danny shook with silent laughter. "You sounded like a camel."

"Oh, hush," Jay muttered, and turning himself around with a groan, he sprawled out next to Danny on the narrow sofa. Danny accepted him there while with his free hand, he scooped Jay's come from his belly with his fingertips and carried it to his mouth, where he sucked it away while Jay watched.

"That's fattening," Jay said.

"Leave me alone. I'm eating."

Jay laughed. Dragging Danny's face toward his, he buried that beautiful come-smeared mouth beneath his own. When Danny twisted around to face him, his come-soaked stomach pressed against Jay's, smearing Jay's seed all over both of them. Their legs entwined, their cocks snuggling together, softening side by side down below.

Danny pushed his face into Jay's throat, kissing the stubble over Jay's Adam's apple, dipping his tongue into the little triangular indentation at the base of Jay's neck. Danny's heart beat in rhythm with Jay's. A perfect duet.

Danny breathed warm words over Jay's skin. "I love your ass."

Jay pulled him closer. "Good to know."

Danny opened his mouth to respond but was cut off by a loud crash downstairs. Jay tensed, Danny's body going rigid against him at the same time. "What the hell was that?" Danny cried, nearly whispering. He pried himself from Jay's arms. His eyes were wide, his jaw slack with startled fear. The fractured splashes of color from the stained-glass window still lay on Danny's face, brighter and shinier in the smears of Jay's come. "What the *hell* was that?" In unison, both of them hauled themselves off the couch and, still naked, stomped down the stairs. The sudden barking of both dogs added wings to Jay's feet, and by the time he reached the first floor, he was practically flying, Danny right on his heels.

Just before they leapt from the bottom step into the living room below, Jay reached out and pulled Danny roughly to a stop.

"No!"

Danny regained his balance in Jay's arms and stood shivering on the last step. They both stared out at the living room. At the horrific mess it was in.

The floor was covered with broken glass. Jay glanced at Danny, whose eyes were as big as dinner plates, and then turned toward the picture window overlooking the front porch. A cold wind was tearing through the large, jagged hole in the glass, whipping the drapes, rattling the blinds. The wind was so strong, it tipped over pictures on the mantle. Lucy and Desi were nowhere in sight. Jingles was cowering in the kitchen doorway, staring out, back bristled, teeth bared. Danny shivered, and Jay pulled him into a protective embrace.

"It's okay, baby," Jay whispered, suddenly shivering in the cold.

Danny burrowed into Jay's arms but shook his head. "How is this even remotely 'okay'? What happened? Was it… Josh?"

Jay cooed in Danny's ear, shushing him, trying to calm him. "I don't see a rock on the floor anywhere. Nobody heaved a brick inside. It could be an accident."

"What do you mean an accident? You mean like—like a bird flying into the window?"

"Maybe," Jay said. "Or maybe just the wind."

Danny gave him an incredulous look. "Really?"

Jay didn't believe it at all, but he wasn't about to tell Danny that. "Let's go upstairs and get dressed and get some shoes on. Then we'll come down and clean up the mess. You go ahead, Danny. I'll be right there."

"If you're sure," Danny said, looking unconvinced.

"I'm sure. Go ahead." Jay gave him a gentle nudge, and Danny went, slowly climbing the stairs, casting backward glances at Jay the whole time.

When he was gone, Jay stood at the base of the stairs, his own come crisping on his belly, staring through the shattered picture window at their two cars parked out front, at the brooding clouds skimming past overhead.

As he watched, the setting sun dipped below the horizon, leaving the mountaintop in dusk.

Jay clenched his fists, suddenly angry, suddenly *furious*. Despite the fact that he was naked and smeared with come, despite the cold and the broken glass, Jay raced across the living room floor and flung himself through the front door. With trembling hands, he gripped the porch railing and stared out at the grounds. There was no one there, of course. He knew there wouldn't be.

He glanced down at Jingles. He had followed him out and stood there now, cowering at his feet. The dog, too, was staring along the slope of the mountain, over the rutted lane, past the boulders and the chaparral and the sloping miles of cactus. Jingles's ears perked up, and off in the distance, Jay heard a car roaring to life. Jay heard Carly, frenzied, somewhere down the lane out of sight, barking and howling like the fucking hound of the Baskervilles, totally unlike the pussycat Jay knew her to be. Something had pissed her off.

Jay shivered in the raw air and folded his arms across his bare chest, his cock still dripping, still half-hard. He could still taste Danny's juices. He could still feel Danny's golden skin on the palms of his hands, Danny's mouth on him, savoring.

He pushed those thoughts away. Immediately, anger came rushing in to fill the void. With a hiss, he reached down and plucked a shard of glass from his heel.

"Josh, you fucker," he growled under his breath.

JAY AND Danny stood side by side, staring at the shattered picture window, sealed now from the coming storm by some old wood paneling Jay had retrieved from the basement, left over from when he remodeled the garret. After sweeping up the glass, they had nailed the sheets of paneling over the exposed window, closing out the cold and wind but shutting out the light too. In broad daylight, the living room had never seemed so dark and gloomy. Until they hired a glass company to come out and replace the window, it would have to suffice.

As soon as the hammering and racket was over, Lucy and Desi made an appearance, acting nonchalant, as if they had been simply off chasing finches, not hiding from insane, window-smashing criminals. Jay gave them each a long chin rub, welcoming them back, relieved they were safe.

While they worked on the window, Danny apparently decided to face the truth Jay had already become convinced of. At least Danny was willing to voice the thought now.

"It's Josh," Danny said, tossing a hammer to the floor. "I know it is."

Jay nodded, no longer angry, just weary and sad. "I know it is too. But without proof the cops won't do anything."

"That's stupid."

Jay shrugged, trying to give the impression that it all meant very little to him, which was about as far from the truth as one could get. "It's the way it is. Maybe I should talk to him."

Danny jumped. "No! Please, Jay. Let me. I'll call him. Maybe he still doesn't know we're together. You'll just make him crazier."

Jay had to smile at that. He rested a comforting hand on Danny's shoulder, giving it a gentle squeeze. "Danny, he already knows we're together. If not as lovers, then at least living together. Why else do you think he's pulling this shit here? At my house? I didn't tell you this, but he was in the bar one night. Ernie told me he came in for a drink, and while he was there, he talked to the bartender. He could have asked about you, Danny. All the bartenders know we're together now. Not knowing who Joshua was, they wouldn't have thought twice about telling them about us. They're always kidding me about having a new twink. They might even have told Joshua where we lived. If the guy asked the right questions and acted innocent enough, it wouldn't even look suspicious."

"Jesus," Danny breathed.

Jay cupped Danny's chin between his thumb and forefinger, giving his head a little shake to get his attention. "I don't want you to talk to him. Even on the phone. I don't want you to have any contact with him at all. All right? I want you to promise me."

"All right. I promise."

Jay offered what he hoped was a bracing smile. "The guy isn't an idiot, Danny. He'll get tired of harassing us sooner or later."

Danny didn't look like he was buying it. "What if he doesn't? What if he just gets madder? And how much damage are you willing to accept to your house until he *does* get tired of being a prick?"

Jay considered that. "Then I'll talk to him myself."

"No."

"Danny, sooner or later, the cops will *have* to see we're not making it all up. Maybe they'll at least talk to the guy for us. Scare him. Put the fear of God into him."

"Jay, when Joshua gets like this, I don't think he knows what fear is."

Jay's jaw tensed. He narrowed his eyes. "Then I'll *show* him what it is. I'll do what I once told you I'd do. I'll knock him into next week." As if considering the matter closed, Jay glanced at the clock. "You have to get to work."

Danny didn't budge. A gentler fire suddenly burned in his eyes. A teasing fire. "So I'm your new twink, am I? Just how many twinks have you had?"

Jay made a perfect O with his mouth, but he didn't quite manage to look appalled before a grin appeared. "I didn't call you a twink. They did. Honest. And you're the first. I swear." He crossed his heart like a good Boy Scout. "Now go to work."

"Just because I'm smaller and decades younger than you, it doesn't make me a twink."

Jay chewed on a grin. "Ouch. That hurt."

"We'll discuss this twink business later."

"I thought we might. Can we do it naked?"

"Absolutely."

"With lubricant?"

Danny rubbed his ass while his eyes lit up. "God, yes."

"Good. Now go to work."

Danny's eyes grew serious again. "Should I call him?"

"No," Jay said, his own smile gone now as the muscles in his cheek knotted. "Let's wait."

"If you say so. I don't know what I'd say to him any—" Danny rose up on tiptoe and peered over Jay's shoulder. "Thank God!"

Jay whirled to see what Danny was talking about, and there, padding up the lane, came Carly. She appeared deeply satisfied with herself, as if she had chased their vandal all the way to kingdom come.

"The troops are home from the war," Jay mumbled, smiling briefly.

Danny laughed, gave one final sad glance at the boarded-up window, and headed off to dress for work.

"DANNY? COME with me, please."

Danny had just clocked in and was in the process of storing his jacket in his locker when his boss at the store, Miss Turner, hooked her finger at him, beckoning him to follow.

Miss Turner was fiftyish, pinched, never smiled at anyone but customers, and wore really ugly shoes. Everyone hated her, except quite possibly management, for she had been in charge of the Macy's Men's Department for years. She laid down the law like a third-world dictator, brooked no opposition, accepted no excuses if her edicts were not carried out to the letter, and always, *always*, ate lunch alone at her desk in the back room.

Uneasy, Danny followed her into the back, where she plopped herself down at her desk and pointed to a chair in front of it for Danny to occupy.

She got right down to business.

"You've been working here almost a year, Danny. I've had reservations about you from the beginning, not least of all because of the injuries you seem to continually sustain falling off bikes and tumbling down stairs. It's disconcerting for customers to deal with clerks who look like they just climbed out of a cage match."

Danny was surprised Miss Turner knew what a cage match was. "I'm more careful now," he said. "I haven't had an injury since—"

"Unfortunately, your injuries aren't the reason I called you in here."

Danny squirmed around on his seat. He needed this job. He tried to do it to the best of his abilities and couldn't understand what the hell Miss Turner was driving at. "Have I done something to displease you?" he asked carefully. "If you'll tell me what it is I can—"

Miss Turner sat up straighter, as if someone had just rammed a broom handle up her ass. "You've done nothing to displease me. Your work has been acceptable."

Danny was getting a little impatient. "Then what's the problem?"

"This," Miss Turner said, sliding a sheet of paper across the desk, but before Danny could lift it and read it, Miss Turner snatched it back.

"What is it?" Danny asked.

Miss Turner allowed herself the slightest glimmer of humanity by sighing sadly. "It's a letter from the head office in La Jolla. There's been a complaint filed against you."

"Filed by whom?" Danny asked. A trickle of cold sweat slid down his rib cage. He refused to look away as Miss Turner nailed him with a stare that pretended to show concern but in actuality showed nothing but dislike. That stare made Danny ache inside. He had had no idea she hated him so much.

"It was filed by a customer." She tapped an unpolished fingernail to the paper in question. "It's a very disturbing accusation, Danny. You gay boys. I don't understand how you can do the things you do. Or why you insist on thinking everybody else shares your predisposition to—"

"To what?"

One word spilled from her lips, as accusatory as the paper she held in her fist. She spoke the word softly, as if the mere sound of it scared her to death. "Sin."

Danny went from upset to angry in two seconds flat. "What sin exactly has this *gay boy* been accused of committing?"

Miss Turner lifted the lid from a candy jar on her desk and extracted an M&M. A red one. She popped it into her mouth, then held the jar out to Danny. He didn't even glance at it but continued to coldly eye the woman in front of him instead.

"Well?"

She tucked the M&M in her cheek like a squirrel and replaced the lid, setting the candy jar aside. "It says here that you accosted a customer in the fitting room."

"What do you mean 'accosted'?"

Miss Turner leaned forward with her scrawny arms folded in front of her. She looked disgusted, as if someone had just taken a dump on her desk. "The customer claims you made overtures of a sexual nature. He says you helped him pick out trousers, and while you were measuring his inseam, you—oh dear—you cupped his genitals and tried to open his zipper to extract his penis."

Miss Turner finished her accusation at a gallop, her bloodless cheeks for once infused with blood. It almost made her pretty. Almost.

Danny laughed. "That's ridiculous."

Her eyes narrowed. "Is it?"

It was Danny's turn to lean forward. He left his hands clenched in his lap, afraid of what he'd do with them if he didn't. "I've never once been inside a fitting room with a customer. I've never once even measured a customer's inseam. I show them how to do it and let them take it from there. And just because I'm gay doesn't mean I want to have sex with every dumbass customer who walks through the fucking door!"

"Don't curse at me, young man."

Danny waved her words away, as if her sensibilities meant very little to him, which they did. "I demand to know who filed this complaint." He reached out to grab the accusing memo off the desk, but she got to it first, yanking it away and stuffing it in her desk drawer as if she thought he'd try to wrench it out of her hand.

"I'm sorry, Danny. I have to terminate your employment immediately. If you go to the fifth floor, they will print up your final paycheck."

"You can't do this. Don't I get a chance to defend myself? How can I prove I didn't do it if you won't tell me who lied about me to begin with?"

"I'm sorry. Please close out your locker. I wish you all the best in your new endeavors elsewhere. I'm sure you'll understand if I tell you there will be no stellar references to future employers from either myself or this company."

"I'll sue."

"That is, of course, your prerogative."

Danny knew as well as she did, he didn't have the money to take the company to court.

"Just give me the name of the man who said this. Please. I'll talk to him. Prove to him he's accusing the wrong person."

"No. Our customer has suffered enough. Now please clear out your locker as I suggested. You are, of course, always welcome back as a customer."

At that, Danny finally barked out a laugh. "Well, thank heavens for that. I was scared to death that if I wasn't working here, accosting customers left and right and watching you clomping around like Idi Amin in your fucking ugly shoes, you might not take my money anymore."

Her pinched face got even pinchier. She stood and pointed to the door. "Go before I call security."

Danny opened his mouth to call her every name in the book, then just as quickly decided he wouldn't.

Fighting back tears, he rose and turned his back on Miss Turner for the very last time.

"I didn't do it," he said softly.

Not waiting for a response, he walked out the door.

JAY PARKED in his usual spot, several blocks from the bar on a residential street, where he never had to pay exorbitant fees for monthly parking. He heard sirens in the distance but thought little about it. San Diego was the eighth largest city in the country. There were sirens screaming on one street or another every day of the year. He was barely two blocks from the Jeep when his cell phone rang. It was Ernie, and he sounded upset.

"Jay, you'd better get down here. There's been a fire."

Jay stopped in his tracks. Listening closer, he realized the sirens were stopping nearby. By the sound of it, right about where The Clubhouse was located. Still holding the phone to his ear, he took off running.

"Is it the bar?" he asked, already knowing the answer.

"Yeah, boss, I'm afraid it is."

Jay's heart sank. "I heard the sirens. Have they put it out?"

"They're working on it."

"I'm only a couple of minutes away, Ernie. Hang on."

"I'm in the alley out back," Ernie slipped into the conversation just before Jay disconnected.

In the alley. Shit. Jay stuffed the phone in his pocket and ran even faster.

Rounding the last corner, out of breath, he stumbled to a stop. There were police cars everywhere. Two fire trucks were parked in the front, along with a News 8 van with an obligatory overcoiffed female reporter being a pain in the ass, interrupting the firemen while they were trying to work.

Aside from the fact that the front door had been sledgehammered open, the bar looked okay. One fire hose snaked through the door, but it didn't look like it was pumping water. Two firemen simply stood there holding it. Another fireman, obviously the commander, was on his cell phone, possibly to the people in the back actually fighting the fire.

This entire end of the block was black with smoke.

Jay didn't bother speaking to anyone but simply jogged down the side street to enter the alley. It was there he found all the action. Fire hoses were shooting torrents of water through the billowing smoke that blanketed the backside of the bar. Jay couldn't see or hear any flames, but he could tell already there was extensive damage. The entire back wall was charred and crumbling in the rushing spray. Firemen yelled orders back and forth, nobody paying any attention to Jay at all.

Ernie, on the other hand, spotted him immediately and came running up, his baseball cap on sideways, a smear of soot on his cheek. Considering all the mess and the stink and the smoke, Jay was surprised to see Ernie looking relieved.

"They've knocked it out, Jay. Outside of some smoke damage inside, and this back wall being rotisseried into a charcoaled fucking mess, the rest of the bar should be fine."

The smoke was beginning to clear. Jay could see the damage more clearly now. Ernie was right. The back wall of the bar was one bigass charcoal briquette.

"Where'd it start? Do they know?"

Ernie pointed to one of three dumpsters that always sat lined up by the back door.

"There. In a dumpster. The cops don't know if it was started on purpose or not. Maybe somebody just tossed a cigarette inside and poof! I'm sorry, Jay. I think you're going to be closed for a while."

Jay nodded. "You may be right." As an afterthought, Jay realized it could have been a lot worse. He pulled Ernie's mountainous body into a hug and slapped him on the back. "You okay? Was anybody hurt?"

Ernie blushed. "No, boss. I'm fine. Nobody was hurt. I'm hoping you've got insurance."

Jay couldn't quite dredge up a smile, but he tried. "Yeah, I do. Don't worry."

The two men stood side by side, well out of the way, watching the firemen still poking at the ruins with their firehoses. They had set their nozzles to a wider spray now, the narrow, high-powered stream of water no longer necessary to punch down the flames. Jay cringed when a fireman with an ax gave the back wall a whack and a ten-foot section of wall collapsed under the blow. No flames shot out, only a black, reeking cloud of smoke. Jay turned away.

At that moment, his cell phone rang again. Jay slapped it to his ear, not in the mood for idle conversation.

"I'm busy," he said. "What is it?"

There was a momentary hush on the line. Then Danny spoke. "It's me. Are you all right? I just heard about the fire on the car radio."

In the midst of what was turning out to be one of the worse days of his life, Jay drew cheer from the voice on the line. "Danny! Yeah, I'm fine. What are you doing in the car? Aren't you working?"

Danny hesitated for a moment, then said, "I got off early. I was headed home. What about the bar? Can you open?"

Jay sighed. "No. We'll be shut down for a while. Maybe even a few months. But all isn't lost. It can be repaired. As soon as I finish here, I'll come home, baby, and you can tell me about your day. I have a feeling it isn't much better than mine."

Danny sighed audibly. "You got that right. But I won't bother you with it now. Come home when you can. I'll be waiting for you."

"Okay, baby. Don't worry. Whatever's going on at work, we'll take care of it."

"Yeah. I'll see you when I see you."

"I love you," Jay said, torn between the mess he had in front of him and the unhappiness he could hear in Danny's voice. "Don't worry. Everything will be all right."

"Okay, Jay. I love you back." And with that he broke the connection.

WHEN DANNY turned off the freeway onto the county road leading to the lane up to the house, he suddenly swerved onto the shoulder and slammed on the brakes. His brain was racing. He was so mad his knuckles were white on the steering wheel.

You got me fired, you son of a bitch. You got me fired and you burned down Jay's fucking bar.

Danny punched in Joshua's phone number. After a brief delay, a canned voice came on the line and said, "The number you've called is no longer in service. There is no new number. Please check your listings and try again."

Danny flung the phone to the floorboard and stomped the gas pedal, tearing back onto the road, flinging gravel up behind him. He forced himself to calm down, and by the time he pulled into the lane he was almost back to his normal self, except for worrying about not having a job. And the fact that his lover's business had just burned down. And there was a big hole in the front of their house.

By the time he walked through the door, greeted by Lucy and Desi and the two dogs, Danny's jaws ached from clenching his teeth so tightly. He had never been so mad in his life.

He dropped into a chair at the kitchen table, still dressed in his coat and scarf, and just sat there while the storm clouds rolled in overhead, burying Jay's mountain in gloom.

Danny dropped his head onto his arm and closed his eyes. Before he knew it, the day's stress caught up with him and he fell into an uneasy sleep.

IT WAS almost dusk when the front door squeaked open and the clatter of doggy toenails rat-a-tatted across the living room floor. In the midst of making dinner, Danny lowered the flame under the canned spaghetti sauce and ran to meet Jay at the door. The spaghetti itself was sitting in a strainer in the sink waiting for some hot water to bring it back to life. Before Jay got the door closed, Danny was in his arms.

He pressed his face to Jay's coat front and smelled the smoke. Jay's hands were cold on the back of his neck. He had dark circles under his eyes. His hair was damp. It had started to rain.

"How bad was it?" Danny asked.

Jay grunted. He had never looked so tired since Danny had known him. In a dull tone, Jay described his day—staying with the firemen through the long ordeal of checking for hot spots, overseeing the placement of plywood sheets over the back of the bar to prevent anyone waltzing in, stealing all the liquor, and walking off with the pool table, waiting for a locksmith to repair the damage to the lock on the front door after the firemen battered it open with their trusty sledgehammer.

"We can probably reopen in a couple of months," Jay said finally. "It looks worse than it is. Nothing inside was damaged, thank God, except for being marinated in smoke and drenched with water. The carpet will have to be replaced, and the back wall, and that's about it. My insurance should cover it."

Danny rose on tiptoe and kissed Jay's cheek. "I'm sorry, baby. Are we okay financially?"

Jay smiled down at him. "Hey, I'm loaded. We've got nothing to worry about at all. Why? You wanting to dump me if you learn I'm suddenly destitute?"

Danny couldn't smile back. "No. I just—lost my job today."

"Why? What happened?"

Danny heaved a sigh and pulled the zipper down on Jay's jacket. "I'll tell you later. Here, you get out of these stinking clothes and take a shower. I made dinner. Spaghetti."

"Goody," Jay said. "I'm famished."

"I thought you might be. Go clean up. I'll tell you everything over dinner."

Jay shrugged out of his coat and kicked off his filthy shoes. "I won't be a minute."

"Take your time," Danny said.

But after Jay gave him a kiss on the forehead and stepped away to head toward the stairs, Danny reached out and snagged his sleeve. "Jay?"

Jay turned to face him. "Hmm?"

Danny swallowed hard. "It was Joshua. My job, the bar, the broken window. Everything. It's been him from the start."

Jay nodded. "I know. I came to that conclusion myself a while back."

"I tried to call him, but his phone's been disconnected. I think maybe the worst isn't over yet."

Jay stepped forward and once again pulled Danny into his arms. He buried his lips in Danny's hair.

"That's another conclusion I came to, about three hours ago standing in back of my burned-out bar. I don't think he's ever going to give up. He's never going to leave us alone."

"No," Danny sighed. "Never."

Jay gripped his arms and gave him a gentle shake, smiling down. "Don't worry, Danny. Tomorrow we go to the police. I'm not doing it over the phone. We're going in person. I'll get somebody to help us one way or another. This has gone on long enough. The fucker has to be stopped."

A flash of lightning lit the sky, and less than a heartbeat later, a horrendous boom of thunder made them both jump. The dogs cowered at their feet, and both cats flew underneath the couch.

"The storm's starting," Danny said.

Jay nodded. "I'd better close up the chickens."

Danny laid a hand to his cheek. "No. You go shower. I'll get the chickens in. Then I'll feed my lover dinner. Tonight we'll act like none of this ever happened."

Jay grinned. "Save it for tomorrow, huh?"

"Yes. Save it for tomorrow. Go shower. You stink."

"Nag."

Hours later, both Danny and Jay were sound asleep, wrapped as always in each other's arms. The house was darkly silent, but for the storm raging outside. It was a testament to how weary the two men were that they could sleep through the lightning and thunder.

While the wind thrashed the branches of the eucalyptus tree out back and the thunder rattled the sky above their heads, it may seem odd that it was actually the smallest sound that pulled both men awake.

It was almost as if they'd both been waiting for it.

The dogs heard it too. They were asleep, curled at the foot of the bed, huddled close together just as their masters were. When Danny and Jay sat up, all ears, squinting through the dark, jarred awake as if they'd been poked with a pin, the two dogs whimpered and turned their heads toward the closed bedroom door.

The sound they all heard was the click of a door latch. Downstairs.

"It's the front door," Jay whispered. "Someone's in the house. It's Joshua. It has to be. This time he's gone too far."

Before Danny could answer, they heard another sound. It sounded like the gentle scrape of a drawer, maybe in the kitchen.

The dogs heard this sound too, and it threw them into battle mode. Jingles and Carly flew off the bed, howling like demons, then stood tap-dancing in front of the bedroom door, clawing and growling and scratching to get out.

Jay tossed the covers aside and hurled himself out of bed, while Danny did the same on the other side. Each pulled on the shirt and jeans they had dropped at the side of the bed when they'd retired the night before.

Still barefoot, Jay raced toward the bedroom door to release the dogs. Danny grabbed his arm and pulled him to a stop.

"No," Danny pleaded, standing wide-eyed in a sudden strobe of lightning slashing through the bedroom window. "Don't go down there, Jay. He—he owns a gun."

"What?"

"I never told you, but Josh owns a gun. A revolver. He bought it for protection, he said. About a month before I left him."

Jay stared at Danny, then back to the dogs growling at the door.

"Call the cops," Danny urged. "Please, Jay. Don't go down there. Call the cops. If we tell them there's someone in the house, they'll have to come."

"All right," Jay hissed. "We've had enough shitty luck for one day. We don't need bullet holes too."

He reached for the landline on the nightstand and keyed in 9-1-1. Nothing happened. He pushed down the receiver and tried again. Nothing. The line was dead.

Jay turned back to Danny. "The phone's out. Maybe it's the storm."

Danny didn't look convinced. "Maybe he cut the wire."

"Whatever," Jay said. "Where's your cell phone? Mine's downstairs."

Danny's face fell. "So is mine." He stepped closer, and Jay's arm automatically slid around him, holding him close. From the slight shaking in his body, it was obvious Danny was truly frightened.

Jay hesitated, then said, "Fuck it," and reached out and swung the bedroom door open, releasing the dogs, who took off baying and banging their way down the stairs like a herd of water buffalo. A crash came from downstairs, then heavy footsteps racing through the house, with the howling dogs obviously in pursuit. The front door slammed shut, sealing the dogs inside, still snarling and howling and hurling their bodies at the closed door, trying to get out, dying to sink a few teeth into the intruder.

Jay's fingers tightened on Danny's arm. "He's gone. Stay close to me. We'll go downstairs and grab one of the cell phones. You call the cops while I secure the front door."

Danny nodded, eyes as big as Frisbees. "All right. Don't go outside."

"I won't. Come on."

They stepped through the bedroom door. Danny reached out to turn on the hallway light. He flipped the switch. Again, nothing happened. The power was off. Danny turned to him with frightened eyes.

Jay cursed, but despite his anger, he took a moment to brush calming fingertips along Danny's arm.

Hand in hand, with intermittent flashes of lightning illuminating their path down the pitch-dark hallway, they headed for the stairs.

Before they descended the first step, Danny pulled Jay to a stop and gazed up into his face with soulful, frightened eyes. "You're my hero, Jay. You're my knight. You'll protect us from the dragon. I know you will."

Jay bent and tasted Danny's trembling lips. "I love you, Danny. I'll protect us both from anything that tries to tear us apart. Just stay close to me, baby."

Danny nodded, squaring his shoulders. Together they squinted down the dark stairwell.

Without another word, they began their descent.

Dear Reader,

By now, your cock must be HORNY. I wish I were with you to suck your cock.

How big is your cock? 7" – 8" – 10"?

Are you circumcised? I am not.

John Inman

CHAPTER ELEVEN

"Hurry," Jay whispered.

"It isn't here," Danny hissed back, his voice rising, desperate.

They were standing in the living room. Danny's backpack was on the floor by the unlit fireplace, right where he'd left it. He dropped to his knees. Since it was too dark to see anything, he shuffled through the backpack with trembling hands, checking every compartment by feel. His cell phone wasn't inside. All he found was a bunch of worthless papers and junk.

Danny tossed the backpack aside. "I don't understand. It's always in there. Oh, crap. Maybe I left the phone in the car. We'll have to use yours."

Jay reached across the baying hounds to twist the dead bolt on the front door, locking them inside. He rushed over to Danny and clutched his hand, tugged him to his feet. "Mine's in the kitchen. Come on. Stay away from the windows in case Asshole decides to take a potshot at us through the glass."

"Oh, man."

On bare feet, they padded across the room, through the dining room, and into the kitchen. The dogs were still growling and snarling at the front door. The blinds were up on all the windows, except for the one boarded up with plywood. Intermittent flashes of lightning strobed through the house. Every time a lightning bolt flared, it took Danny's eyes a second to readjust to the dark.

"Damn storm," Danny muttered.

Another flash of lightning illuminated Jay groping across the countertop. "Fuck," he hissed. "I know I left it here to recharge. The charger's still here, but the phone's gone."

The kitchen contained another landline, a wall phone. Hoping beyond hope, Danny lifted the receiver. No dial tone. It was as dead and still as the phone upstairs. Fuck.

"He's taken the cell phones, Danny," Jay said. "Christ, how long was he inside the house?"

"How are we going to call the cops?"

Jay snapped his fingers. "The computer! Surely he wasn't able to sneak past our bedroom door and climb up to the garret without the dogs hearing him. Come on. We can contact 9-1-1 on the Internet."

"Can you do that?"

"Hell if I know. If we can't, maybe I can e-mail somebody and have *them* do it."

"Assuming they answer their e-mail." They both glanced at the wall clock on the kitchen wall. It was three o'clock in the morning.

"Shit. You're right."

They stood staring at each other in the lightning bursts. The thunder rolled and grumbled over their heads like a truckload of barrels tumbling down a hill. Between the dogs and the storm and his heart pounding in his ears, Danny could barely hear his own voice, let alone Jay's.

Jay grabbed a fistful of Danny's shirtfront and coaxed him back toward the stairs. "Come on! We have to try, at least. Up to the garret."

With the dogs on their heels now, they raced up the stairs to Jay's office in the tiny garret on the third floor. Crashing through the door, they stopped short when a flash of lightning sprayed the garret walls in garish colors from the stained-glass window. Unfortunately, garish colors weren't the only thing to be seen.

The computer was trashed. The connections were mangled and ripped out, not only unplugged but cut in two, obviously with the pair of scissors that were still there, standing on end, poking out of the keyboard where someone had stabbed it with such force that the keyboard was split almost in two.

Someone my ass, Danny thought. *Joshua.*

Jay and Danny stood staring. Danny shook his head. "He must have been in and out of the house a dozen times lately. How else would he have known where everything was? He had this planned, Jay. I told you he was nuts."

Jay chewed on his lip, holding a dead Logitech mouse in his hand. "Yes, you did. More than once. I guess maybe I should have listened."

Danny edged up close and slipped a hand in Jay's back pocket. He could feel his own knees shaking. Jay seemed merely pensive. Not even furious. Just trying to work things out in his mind. Like it was a puzzle he was trying to solve. Danny had never been so impressed by the man he loved than he was at that moment.

"What are you thinking?" he asked quietly. "What do we do now?"

Another slash of lightning exploded across the sky. The image of a dragon in full-blown Technicolor was momentarily tattooed on the wall in front of their faces in excruciating detail. Danny almost cried out, it startled him so.

When his thumping heart quieted, he mumbled to himself, "I hate that stained-glass window."

"We need a weapon," Jay announced, ignoring the dragon and tossing the broken mouse into the wastebasket by the desk.

Danny decided a little sarcasm couldn't hurt. "I don't suppose you own an UZI."

"It's in the shop for a tune-up."

"Well, that's a pity."

Jay smiled. "Don't give up. I have not yet begun to fight."

"Jesus. Now you're John Paul Jones?"

As incongruous as anything else that had happened tonight, Jay coughed up a laugh. "Listen. We have knives in the kitchen. There's a nail gun in the basement. Not sure how effective that would be. The cast-iron fireplace poker would put a pretty good dent in his head if we got close enough."

Danny couldn't make jokes anymore. He just couldn't. "If you get close enough to use a knife, a nail gun, or a poker, he'll simply shoot you with his *real* gun."

Jay grunted. "Yeah. That's a drawback."

Danny clutched his shirtsleeve. "We could just sneak out the back under cover of the storm. Take off down one of the trails. Try to get to the highway. Flag somebody down." In the strobe of another lightning flash, a jigsaw pattern of colors splashed across his vision. He reached into his jeans pocket and pulled out a set of keys. "Or we can take one of the cars and get the hell out of Dodge!"

JAY SHOOK his head. "And leave him here to do what? Burn down the house? And what about the animals? I'm not going to leave them to the mercy of a madman. No, we just have to take Joshua out ourselves. I'm tired of running from this fucker. I'm tired of *you* running from this fucker. And I'm *really* tired of him fucking up our lives. Getting you fired. Burning down my bar." Jay narrowed his eyes, fury flaring. "Trying to kill my poor cat."

Still grumbling, Jay dragged the desk chair under the window and stood on the seat. Flipping a latch, he quietly pushed the stained-glass window open. Hinged in the middle, the top tilted in and the bottom tilted out, giving a view of the front lawn below. A cold wind immediately chilled the room. Jay had to wait for a flash of lightning to really see anything, and even then his vision was impaired by the rain. Still, he thought he caught a glimpse of something moving behind the Jeep. It had to be Joshua. What the hell was he doing now?

Danny tugged at Jay's pant leg. "Get down from there!" he whispered. "What if he sees you and takes a shot at your head?"

Jay stepped down and folded Danny in his arms. "Hush, baby. I've got a plan."

"You do?"

"Well, no. I guess not."

"I didn't think so."

"But I think I should get that nail gun. And while we're down in the basement, I can see if he tripped the breakers. We need to get the power on. I'm not sure what for, but I'd feel better if we had electricity. Maybe we can electrocute the bastard or something."

"Good idea," Danny said. "Basement it is. We haven't climbed the stairs *enough* tonight."

Jay dragged him close, lips to nose. "You making fun of me?"

"Who, me?" Danny batted long pale lashes. Jay could see them in the staccato flashes of light that poured through the dragon's belly in the window, although he really didn't need to see them at all. He had Danny's eyelashes memorized. Along with every other square inch of his body.

Even through Danny's efforts to joke, Jay saw the fear in his eyes. The fear he had every right in the world to be feeling. Hell, Jay was feeling it too. He wasn't dumb enough to think getting out of this mess would be a cakewalk. They were in some serious shit here.

Jay turned solemn. "I *will* protect you, Danny. I told you I would never let him hurt you again, and I meant it. I hope you believe me."

In a flash of lightning, which sizzled overhead like a slashing sword, bright as steel and razor sharp, Danny nodded, even while he shivered. "I do. I told you. You're my knight. I trust you completely."

Jay smiled softly. "Good. Then let's go." He clutched Danny's hand, pulling him toward the stairs. Still barefoot, they padded their way downstairs as quietly as they could.

On the service porch behind the kitchen, they discovered how Joshua had entered the house. He'd entered it tonight the same way he had entered it before, by breaking through the poorly repaired trapdoor in the back, then simply climbing the rickety basement stairs to the main house and walking through the door to the service porch, which Jay hadn't had the chance to repair at all since the *last* time the fucker broke in.

"I've got to get this house burglar-proofed," Jay growled to himself, standing in the open doorway staring down into the unwelcoming black abyss that on any other day of the year was simply a basement. Today it looked like the gaping maw of hell.

"It's a little late to burglar-proof the house. The horse is already out of the barn," Danny muttered under his breath. "Or in it."

"Hush," Jay said, then bumped Danny with his hip.

Out of sheer habit, Jay flipped the light switch that ordinarily illuminated the stairs. Of course it didn't work. No surprise there.

"Be careful," Jay whispered. "Stay right behind me. There's crap everywhere down here. It's hard enough to walk around in broad daylight, let alone in the dark."

"Maybe we need to clean house."

"No shit."

This time Joshua must have closed the trapdoor behind him when he entered through the back of the house. The basement was as black as pitch. Even the lightning flashes didn't relieve the darkness.

Danny stayed one step behind Jay all the way, his hand on Jay's shoulder. Jay stubbed his bare toe on something and spit out a curse. "Watch it," he hissed, warning Danny not to do the same.

They were across the basement floor, weaving their way through piles of junk, when Jay located the workbench by the wall and began rummaging around, groping through all manner of tools, trying to find the nail gun. Instead, his hand landed on a familiar cylinder. He'd found a flashlight. Hoping the batteries weren't dead, Jay thumbed the switch, and a sudden sharp beam of light pierced the shadows.

With light to navigate by, Jay headed for the circuit box in the corner with Danny at his side. Jay wasn't sure which switches illuminated what, so he flipped them all. He rushed back to the workbench and pulled the string that operated a light bulb hanging overhead. Nothing happened.

Jay switched off the flashlight. "He cut the wires. The bastard cut the wires."

"Find the nail gun," Danny urged.

At that moment Jay heard a strange noise. It seemed to be only a few feet away. It sounded like a bag of dried pinto beans being shaken and squeezed in somebody's hand. A *schkkk*ing sound.

Danny stiffened beside Jay. "What is that? I've never heard anything like that before!"

Jay had. "Oh, Christ. Now the motherfucker shows up."

Danny eased still closer. "Which motherfucker is that?" he squeaked.

"George."

"I was afraid you'd say that."

Jay switched on the flashlight and aimed it at the floor in the direction of the sound, which hadn't let up even one iota since it had started.

Schkkk. Schkkk. Scchhhhkkkkk.

Jay's flashlight beam hit a bull's-eye on the very first try. There, not three feet away from their bare feet, lay George, and he was looking fairly annoyed. Curled into a fat coil, his triangular, mottled head hovered a foot off the floor, his golden reptilian eyes aimed directly at them. His tail, with four inches of husked shells *schkkk*ing up a storm, rattling so fast it was merely a blur, stood straight up in the middle of the coil like a really pissed-off exclamation mark. The snake's broad mouth opened periodically, and his forked tongue flicked out as if tasting the air. As his jaws gaped wide, fangs sprang out, readying for an attack. In the beam of the flashlight, glimmers of venom gleamed at the tip of each fang. George's head swiveled first to Jay, then to Danny, then back again, as if he was deciding which to go for first.

"Well, this is a revolting development," Danny said, rather conversationally under the circumstances. His sarcasm was belied by the glazed look in his eyes when Jay glanced at him.

"Ssshh," Jay ordered. "Don't move."

Danny's voice crept up an octave. "Not moving, Jay. This is me not moving."

Still aiming the flashlight at the snake's cold eyes, Jay groped around on the workbench as quietly as he could, searching for something to throw. The best he could come up with was a pint paint can. It was about half-full, so it had some heft to it. He clutched it in his hand, gave it a gentle toss straight up into the air like a pitcher gauging the feel of a baseball just before the pitch, then let loose and hurled it as hard as he could right at the rattlesnake's head.

He missed. The lid flew off. Black paint splattered everywhere. It was enough of a distraction to at least snag George's attention. The minute he snapped his triangular head around to see what had flown past him before exploding, Jay grabbed Danny and took off for the stairs. They tore up them as fast as they could and slammed the door shut behind them the second they flew through it.

Gasping for air, they stood in the middle of the service porch, trying to calm down. Jay switched off the flashlight. Once again, darkness was probably their best friend. The less Joshua knew of their whereabouts, the safer Jay figured they were.

"Shit," Jay said.

"What?"

"I didn't get the nail gun."

The dogs were howling at the front door again. Jay sent up a silent prayer of appreciation, thanking God the dogs had not followed them down to the basement and tangled with George.

"Danny, I'm going to see if I can find Lucy and Desi. They're probably under the couch. Since I've got your car blocked, we're going to make a run for the Jeep. You're right. It's all we can do. The dogs will follow us, I think. We can carry the cats."

Danny breathed in short little gasps. "Are you crazy?"

"Hey, this was your idea. Remember? But don't worry. It'll work. It has to. We can sneak out the back door like you said and be at the Jeep before he knows we're—"

"Oh, no!"

"Jeez, Danny, we have to try *something*!"

"It isn't that," Danny hissed. "Look!"

Danny gripped Jay's shoulders and twisted him around until he faced the other way.

"Look at the walls," Danny whispered. "Look at the walls in the living room."

Jay took a step forward. Then another. "Wh-what is that?" he stammered.

Danny had left his side and was now creeping up on the one unboarded window looking out on the front porch. The blinds were closed, but through the slats, bright orange streaks of light appeared.

Just like the orange glow painting the living room wall.

Then they both heard it. Even above the roaring storm. The sound of snapping flames. It sounded almost like George's rattles clattering below. A sudden *whoosh* and the crunch of broken glass made them jump. Carly whimpered.

The cars!

Jay raced to Danny's side, and together they swept the blinds aside and peered outside. The Jeep and Danny's Toyota were both ablaze. The fire was eating at the interior of both cars, the seats consumed in flame. As they watched, another Jeep window shattered and exploded outward from the heat. Then another. This time in the Toyota. Black smoke billowed, illuminated by the lightning, which was almost constant now, tearing across the sky in sizzling flashes that seemed to rip the sky asunder. The storm was at its peak, the thunder a continuous rolling *boom*. The rain battered down, turning the yard to mush. The screaming wind pummeled the tree in the yard, tossing its limbs around like the flailing arms of a madman.

Off to the side, in the light of the burning cars and those horrific explosions of lightning—stood Joshua. The *real* madman. He held his arms high and wide, as if he alone had summoned the storm that surrounded them. In one hand, he held a gun. At his feet, lying on its side, was a red gas can, obviously empty. It's what he'd used to set the cars afire.

He was laughing.

At that moment, the Jeep exploded. A mushroom of flame lifted it three feet off the ground. When it came back down, the bumper fell off, a door swung open, ripped from the hinges, and glass shot out in every direction, some of it tearing through the burning cab of the Toyota parked in front.

Before either Danny or Jay could say a word, the Toyota exploded too. Compared to the Jeep's explosion, it was small potatoes.

"I was almost out of gas," Danny sadly explained. It was almost an apology.

Even in the face of everything that was happening, Jay had to bite back a snicker.

"Lucky you. Naturally, I had a full tank. Full tanks explode *so* much better."

The two balls of flame were contained by the downpour. At intervals, tires exploded with muffled pops, and more glass windows cracked, snapped, and expanded, then exploded out into the yard in glittering fragments. Still, the rain prevented the flames from spreading, and that, at least, was a good thing.

Sometime during the course of the cars blowing up, Joshua disappeared. He was no longer standing where he had been. Only the empty gas can remained, lying on its side in the mud.

Danny grabbed Jay's arm. "Look!"

"I know," Jay said. "He's not there anymore. I didn't see which way he went. Did you?"

Danny's grip tightened. "Not that. Look! Down the lane."

Jay's gaze followed where Danny pointed. Suddenly his eyes grew wider.

"My God! Is that—"

"Yes!" Danny cried. Jubilant. "It's headlights. Someone's coming."

CHAPTER TWELVE

GLASS SHATTERED above their heads as a bullet tore through the window, then exploded a globed ceiling light that, on kinder nights than this, lit the room from above. Danny and Jay threw themselves to the floor and frantically crawled away from the window, crunching over the broken glass, cutting their palms and knees, slithering back toward the kitchen where they had a little more protection and where their feet wouldn't be sliced to ribbons when they stood up.

While they crawled, another shot removed the remaining shards of windowpane and took out the TV in the corner with a shattering crash. Cold, wet wind tore through the room. The raging storm bellowed through the broken window. Danny tried to crawl and hold his hands over his ears at the same time, while Jay sputtered an ongoing string of profanity as they scrambled from one room to the next.

In the kitchen they tucked themselves into the space between the refrigerator and the stove, where it would be harder for a bullet to find them.

After they shook the glass off their clothes, Danny tugged at Jay's sleeve. "Who would be driving here at this hour? It's after three in the morning."

"Maybe someone on the main road saw the flames after all. I didn't think they'd be able to. Whoever it is, when they pull up, we have to yell at them and let them know they're in danger."

"You think he'll shoot them?"

Jay growled. "I can't imagine he'd be too happy about seeing a witness show up, would you? Or somebody to interrupt his fun?"

Staying close to the wall, they crept to the window over the kitchen sink, easing the blinds apart to peer outside. The window afforded a perfect view in the direction of the lane leading up to the house. While the lane itself was hidden from view by twists in the rutted path and boulders as big as semis, they should still be able to see the glow from the stranger's headlights approaching.

But they couldn't. The distant glow of headlights was gone.

"The lights aren't there anymore," Danny whispered. "Where's the car? Did we imagine it?"

They watched for two minutes. Three. Jay strained to see, desperate to learn what had happened to what might very well be their only chance for escape. Hell, maybe it was even a cop. Now, *that* would make Jay reassess his contempt for the San Diego Police Department.

Torn between worrying about the stranger's safety and seeing their one chance for assistance disappear in front of their eyes, Jay spat in fury. "No, dammit! We both saw a car coming! Where the hell did it go?"

Danny pointed to a spot illuminated by the flames, the flames that were now corralled inside what was left of the two vehicles by the wind and pounding rain. "Someone's there!" he cried. "I saw him moving among the bushes."

Jay looked but didn't see anything. "Was it Joshua? Could you tell?"

"I'm not sure. I only caught a glimpse through the damn rain. Maybe it was just the wind blowing stuff around, but I don't think so. It looked like a person."

A flurry of gunshots erupted, followed by a bellowing cry of anger and also one of fear.

"What the hell?" Jay cried, pressing his face to the window, trying to see what was going on outside.

A sudden clamor of footsteps on the back porch made them both whirl around and stare at the back door leading off the service porch.

"It's Josh!" Danny wailed.

Fists hammered at the door. A desperate voice, clearly *not* Joshua's, boomed out above the storm. "Let me in! Jay, open the fucking door."

"Holy shit!" Jay barked. He raced to the door, slid the dead bolt aside, and yanked it open. A mountain rolled through the open door at the same moment the dogs tore outside.

"Dammit," Jay cursed, but in spite of the dogs, he immediately slammed the door shut behind them as his unexpected guest collapsed, exhausted, to the floor.

Jay slid the dead bolt back in place quickly before he dropped to his knees beside the man on the floor. Once there he promptly hugged him and pounded on his back, laughing.

When Jay turned his face up to Danny, he was standing there staring down at them, his mouth hanging open like a mailbox. He looked like he was about to faint.

"Holy shit!" Danny said. "Is that *Ernie?*"

ERNIE'S CLOTHES were smeared with mud, and his dripping hair had soggy twigs sticking out of it like some weirdass geisha where he must have crawled through a patch of brambles.

His eyes burned into Danny's like two live coals. "The bastard that shot at me. It's your ex-boyfriend, ain't it?" His smiled slipped away. The line of his jaw grew tense and angry.

Danny could only nod.

It was Jay who spoke. "But why are you here? What made you drive all the way out here in the middle of the night? And how the hell did you get past him?"

Jay pulled Danny to the floor, and the three of them hunkered down, their backs to the door, trying to stay out of sight.

Ernie squeegeed the rainwater off his face. His smile was back. Or at least most of it.

"I was sitting at home thinking about the fire at the bar. How it might have started. Then I got to thinking about the jerk we rescued Danny from, and I started putting two and two together." He turned away from Danny and trained wily eyes on Jay. "I didn't know if you'd figured it out yet or not, so I decided to call and tell you."

"When was this?" Jay asked.

"I don't know. Maybe midnight. But you wouldn't answer your phone. You *always* answer your phone, Jay. *Always*. So I got worried. And since I couldn't sleep anyway, I decided I'd just drive out here and make sure everything was okay. That's when I saw the flames. I was coming up your lane, which by the way sucks like a two-dollar whore what with those axle-deep potholes every three feet, and damned if I didn't hear gunshots! I didn't figure it was safe to drive up any closer, so I parked and took off through the bushes, trying to get to the house without getting aerated by any bullets. Aerated was the word for today on my word calendar. See how it comes in handy all the time?" His eyes grew serious, even a little mean, as he trained them back on Danny. "Your ex-boyfriend is a fucking asshole. Anybody ever tell you that?"

"We pretty well worked our way up to the same conclusion," Jay said, while Danny sat there nodding, still amazed that Ernie was actually sitting in front of them.

Ernie shivered. It was cold outside. The rain was maybe five degrees away from turning to sleet.

"Can we get to your car?" Danny asked.

"I don't know," Ernie said. "It's risky. We could try to...."

They heard a sharp crack of wood behind Ernie's head. Ernie's words peeled away, as if he'd lost his train of thought. His eyes opened wide. A moment later, a rivulet of blood leaked from his ear and dribbled down into his collar. Like a ventriloquist's dummy, he doubled over at the waist and slid to the floor.

Behind him a momentary flicker of light from the storm's pyrotechnics pierced the door through a tiny hole.

A bullet hole.

JAY GRABBED Ernie's arms as Danny wailed in horror, then jumped in to help. Grunting and groaning, they dragged Ernie away from the door. Jay cried out against the weight of the man before he finally succeeded in flipping Ernie over onto his back.

Bending over him, Jay caressed Ernie's cheek, patting him gently, trying to get a reaction, while a steady stream of blood continued to ooze from Ernie's ear.

"Ernie! Ernie, talk to me! Don't die, dammit. We'll get you out of here, I promise. Just hang in there."

To Jay's utter amazement, Ernie's lashes fluttered and he opened his eyes. Danny gasped behind him. Ernie's gaze bore into Jay hovering above him, not quite focused, but almost. A gentle smile softened his mouth. "Don't worry," he said, his voice breathy, the cadence of his words oddly altered. "It doesn't hurt. Am—am I bleeding?"

A tear leaked onto Jay's cheek. He slipped his hand under Ernie's head to cradle it, the warmth of blood spilling over his fingers. "A little,

Ernie. Yeah," he whispered. "But that's okay. You'll be all right. We'll get you out of here. Just hang in there."

"I'm making a mess on your floor."

"Hush now. Try to lie quiet."

"You got a mop?"

Jay tried to smile, but his face was as unbending as tile. "Yeah, I got a mop, Ernie. Don't worry about it."

Ernie's eyes closed. Only one of them reopened. "Danny and I share a secret, Jay," he breathed. "Danny knows what it is. You don't, but Danny does."

Jay leaned closer. "What secret is that, Ernie? What is it Danny knows?"

Ernie reached up and brushed his fingertips over Jay's cheek, but his strength gave out and his hand banged against the floor. He swallowed hard and his body shuddered, out of his control perhaps for the first time in his life. He tried to focus on Jay's face. Jay could see the concentration it took for him to do it, to stay awake. Ernie found his voice. It was altered again. Weaker. It sounded like a stranger's voice. A stranger's words. "Danny knows I love you, Jay. I always have." He reached out blindly, groping for a hand. Danny's hand. "Didn't you, Danny? Didn't you know it?"

Danny slipped both his hands around Ernie's gigantic paw. He edged in close, speaking low. He managed a smile, when Jay had not. "That's right, Ernie. I knew it the first time I met you. I told Jay, but he didn't believe me."

"What's happening?" Ernie gasped. "My eyes. I can't see."

Jay was weeping now, his own eyes filled with tears. "Just relax, Ernie. We're going to get you help. Just lie still. Try not to talk."

Ernie shook his head. "No. I have to tell him. I have to tell him."

Jay leaned in even closer, speaking directly into Ernie's ear now. Ignoring the blood. Ignoring the clamoring of his own heart. "What do you want to say, Ernie? Who do you want to say it to?"

"Danny. I have to tell Danny."

Danny clutched Ernie's hand more tightly. He leaned in like Jay, his mouth to Ernie's other ear.

"I'm right here, Ernie. What is it? What do you want to tell me?"

Ernie managed to smile, but it only bent one side of his mouth. Lopsided as it was, it looked almost cocky. Like a real wise guy's smile.

Or a stroke victim's. He twisted his head toward Danny's voice, his eyes unseeing, unfocused.

"Love him," Ernie said. "Make him happy. He loves you so."

Visibly fighting tears, Danny said, "I know, Ernie. I love Jay too. You know I do. I'll—I'll make him happy. For me and you both. I promise. I'll make him happy."

A tiny stream of blood leaked from Ernie's mouth, painting a thin, dark line down his cheek to the side of his neck. "You're a good boy," he whispered as his breath drained from his lungs for the very last time, forming a bloody bubble on his lips. His fingers relaxed in Danny's grip. His eyes slid shut, and his head fell back in Jay's supporting hand. The bubble of blood popped.

His great heavy body lay unmoving between them, as still as the mountain on which they knelt.

Jay dropped his forehead to the vast unmoving chest and wept, but even through his tears he could discern Danny stroking Ernie's wet hair, caressing him, soothing him, whispering a prayer for one more movement, one more heartbeat.

His prayer was met by only stillness. As always, God failed to answer.

Danny's voice trembled. "I'll love him for you, Ernie. I swear I will."

Jay sought Danny's hand where his fingers lay twisted in Ernie's hair. Their eyes met through flowing tears. Even in his grief, Jay was overwhelmed with hate.

"I'll kill him for this," he rasped, spittle flying from his mouth. "I mean it, Danny. Joshua's a fucking dead man."

Danny dropped his head to Jay's shoulder, his hand still resting on Ernie's unmoving chest. Then he looked up at Jay, eyes wide. He reached beneath Ernie's coat and pulled something out. It was an iPhone.

"Holy crap," Jay breathed, staring at it.

Jay plucked the phone from Danny's hand and tried to activate the screen. Nothing happened.

"Crap."

Jay punched the screen again. Still nothing happened. He gave it a shake. Nothing.

"Fuck," he yelled. "The battery's dead! We're back where we started."

Jay flew to his feet when a window over the kitchen sink smashed open and a blazing chunk of firewood from the stack at the back of the house came flying inside, ripping the blinds from the wall and scattering sparks everywhere. The tablecloth on the kitchen table caught fire, and while Jay grabbed the burning chunk of firewood with his bare hands and tossed it in the sink, Danny ripped the burning tablecloth off the table and stomped out the flames with his bare feet.

When the fire was out, Jay stood there staring at Danny, who was staring back at him, panting and trembling. Jay was shaking just as hard. His hands hurt, and he knew Danny's feet must be hurting too. Before Jay could do anything for either of them, the back door crashed open.

The storm raged in, and on the wings of the storm came Joshua.

He stood in the doorway, legs apart, backlit by a flash of lightning.

Then he lifted his gun and aimed it directly at Jay's head. Jay heard the noise when Joshua fired, but to his surprise, he felt nothing as darkness took him.

WHEN JOSHUA fired, the muzzle flash startled Danny. He stumbled backward, hitting the floor hard.

Jay simply collapsed in a heap.

Joshua laughed, his eyes burning with madness. He was drenched to the bone. There was a burn on his cheek. He had the gun now pointed squarely between Danny's eyes.

"I told you, kid. I don't share what's mine."

Danny's horrified gaze was welded to where Jay lay unmoving on the floor. Scrambling sideways like a crab, he frantically crawled to him and laid a quivering hand to the back of Jay's neck. Jay's skin was warm and sticky with blood. He didn't move beneath Danny's touch, and Danny's heart writhed in his chest. An ache strummed through him. An anguish, a *fear*, such as he had never felt before tore at him. The pain was so intense he actually paled in the throes of it.

The sob Danny had been fighting all night finally broke through. Tears welled in his eyes. Jay lay crumpled over, folded in on himself. As still as stone. Danny dropped his head to that still, still shoulder. He stroked Jay's unmoving hand. Massaging the fingers one by one, pulling at them, trying to squeeze life into them. Trying to pluck a heartbeat from the silent body.

He lifted his eyes to Joshua, stricken, anguish a ball of fire inside his chest. "You've killed him."

Joshua sneered in Danny's face. "Yeah, well. I told you not to fuck with me, Danny. I told you not to break my heart."

Anger swelled in Danny—an anger of such intensity his eyes grew hot and the boyish spirit that had sustained him through so much twisted inside him into something hateful, something murderous. "Heart? *Heart*? You don't have a heart!"

Joshua clucked his tongue. An impatient teacher facing the dumbest kid in the class. "Let's not get maudlin."

Joshua gazed around the house, studying the broken window with the storm screaming through, rain pooling on the floor beneath it. Eyeing the two bodies on the floor, one as dead as the other. Then staring at Danny, a smirk of triumph on his evil face.

"So here we are," he said. "Alone at last. What'll it be? Popcorn and a movie? A round of Monopoly? Maybe a stiff cock up your hungry young ass, huh? Would you like that? Did you miss being fucked the way you really like it? Huh, Danny? Did you miss it rough?"

Danny closed his eyes for a second before slowly opening them again to face his tormentor. "You'll never touch me again."

Joshua smirked, staring down at the gun in his hand, then back at the window, at the storm raging outside. The dogs were howling and scratching at the back-porch door, trying to get in. Joshua smirked at that too.

As Danny watched, Josh's body rocked with a tremor, either from the cold or some internal struggle with shattered sanity. He had obviously dived headlong over the edge. His eyes were red in the lightning flashes, his skin pale. Danny had never seen him look so ill. Or so possessed by his own demons. There was a disconnect in his eyes. A disconnect that scared Danny more than anything he had endured from the man before. Madness. Madness was written on Josh's face now. Danny was sure of it. A deadly, menacing fury.

Danny knew the time for reasoning had passed. He had nothing to lose. Nothing.

"You've thrown your future away," Danny said, his voice low, emotionless, accusing. "You're a murderer now, Josh. A murderer and a coward. Your life is over. You'll spend the rest of your days in prison. I'll make it a point to hang around long enough to see you die behind bars. Locked away where you can't hurt anybody else. I'll be out here waiting, Josh. Waiting for you to fall down dead in some cockroach-infested cell. Praying for it every day. Every single fucking day."

Joshua threw his head back and brayed out a laugh. He laughed so hard it took him a moment to regain his composure and wipe the happy tears from his eyes. Those eyes went from disbelieving to mean to *insane* in a heartbeat. "You always had a sweet ass, but you never were very smart. You'll not be waiting for anything, Danny. You're going to die in this house tonight. Haven't you figured that out? Haven't you grasped the big picture yet?" He glanced down at the gun in his hand, then back to Danny. "Cuddle your dead boyfriend for a minute. I'll be right back. Don't run off now." He grinned. "We have unfinished business to attend to."

Ignoring Danny as if he knew he had nothing to fear from him, Joshua stepped across the two bodies on the floor. He headed through the kitchen to the living room, where he stood at the bullet-shattered window gazing out at the burning cars. He stood in the light from the fires and reloaded his gun with cartridges he pulled from a trouser pocket. Fear, anger, and Jay's stillness beneath his hand finally sapped Danny's last ounce of defiance. Suddenly there was nothing left but grief. The thought of running never crossed his mind. He was too tired, too heartsore, to run. And he couldn't leave Jay. He wouldn't.

He bent over Jay's huddled body, rocking him, cooing soft words, waiting for the gun in Joshua's hand to point at him again and fire. That would be the end of it, he supposed. Then he'd be free of it all. The fear, the grief, the madness.

With his arms wrapped tightly around Jay's still body, he began to weep. He gave up then, from sheer hopelessness as much as anything else. He buried his face in the crook of Jay's blood-soaked neck, and there, against his cheek, he felt it. Beyond all hope, beyond all imagining.

A pulse.

Danny's eyes flew open when Jay's body stirred in his arms. Jay turned his head toward him a fraction of an inch, just enough for Danny to almost cry out in relief. But before he could do that, Jay gripped Danny's hand and whispered in his ear. "The stairs," Jay said, his voice as soft as the spilling of air. "The basement stairs."

"Y-you're alive," Danny whispered, tears of joy streaming down his face.

"Do it," Jay insisted, still so softly the words did not carry to Joshua's ears in the other room over the roar of the storm. "Push him. Do it."

Danny nodded. "All right. I—I'll try. Can you move? Can we run?"

"I think so," Jay said. "The bullet grazed the side of my head. It must have knocked me out for a minute, but I think I'll live. I've got a hard head."

Danny burst into tear-filled laughter, then just as quickly began weeping again. "Jesus, Jay, I thought it was over. I didn't care anymore what happened. Now you're back and I'm scared all over again. Stay with me this time. Don't get shot anymore."

"I won't," Jay whispered through a smile. "Be strong, Danny. This battle isn't over yet." Then he tightened his grip on Danny's hand. "He's coming!"

Danny froze as determined footsteps approached. It was time to do what Jay had told him to do. He had to try, anyway. He had to at least *try*.

He released Jay from his embrace, pulled himself to his feet, and quickly opened the basement door, then moved away, hoping Josh wouldn't notice the change. His jaw was set, the muscles in his cheeks clenched. A fresh flurry of hatred pooled in his chest. He planted his feet firmly and straightened his spine.

Joshua walked around him, as if thinking Danny was about to make a run for the back door. It was exactly what he had *hoped* Josh would do.

Behind Josh, Danny could see the open basement door. *Closer*, he pleaded silently. *Closer.*

But Joshua wasn't moving. He had anchored himself in place on the service porch floor, facing Danny now, the gun held out in front of him and aimed squarely at Danny's chest.

Josh was employing the same hurt look he had used back when they were together, every time he thought Danny had slighted him. Or disobeyed him. Or took him for granted. "You shouldn't have done it, Danny. I was good to you. I loved you."

Danny clenched his fists and took a threatening step forward. When he did, Josh stepped backward but raised the gun higher.

"Why would you throw your life away over me?" Danny asked. He tilted his head, as if he were really trying to understand. "And if you loved me this much and if you want me back this badly, then why did you treat me the way you did when we were together?"

Danny took another step forward. His shoulders were squared now. He wasn't afraid. He was even less afraid when, once again, Joshua moved a step back to keep some distance between them. Josh wasn't ready to shoot yet, Danny knew. He wanted to talk. He wanted to drag the misery out, just like he always did.

That played into Danny's hands too, so Danny kept talking, all the while moving forward, one lazy, threatening step at a time.

"Jay's been kind to me. Jay understands what love is. It isn't ownership, Josh. It isn't bullying and demanding more than a person is willing to offer. It's acceptance and understanding."

Joshua's mouth twisted in a sneer. "You should work for Hallmark."

Danny ignored him but took another step forward. "It's giving and taking. It's thinking of the other person first. It's listening, not talking. It's sharing, not using."

Josh was ten feet from the basement door. Danny rose onto the balls of his feet, ready to make his rush. Before he could move, Jay cried out behind him and stumbled his way to his feet. He ran past Danny, barreling straight for Josh, his arms held in front of him, a large shard of window glass clenched in his fist like a knife.

Joshua froze for a split second, astonishment on his face, then swung the gun from Danny to Jay. He fired and missed. Before he could fire again, Danny and Jay both plowed into him, pushing him backward through the basement door, where he swayed for a moment at the top of the stairs, eyes wide. He tried to bring his gun around to point it at them once again, but his balance was already lost. He hurtled backward into the darkness, tumbling down the wooden stairs with a fierce roar of anger.

Jay slammed the basement door closed. "Help me," he pleaded with Danny, and together he and Danny manhandled the upright freezer standing in the corner across the floor, then tipped it over onto its side. It toppled with a horrendous crash, neatly blocking the basement door. If Joshua tried to get back inside the house, he wouldn't be coming in this way.

Jay grabbed Danny's shirt and pulled him away from the door. Danny remembered that Ernie had died from a bullet fired through a wooden door. Jay obviously wasn't about to let it happen to Danny too. Blood was now pouring from the side of Jay's head where the bullet had sliced his scalp, likely stirred by his exertions. His ear was bloodied and mangled, as if it had taken the brunt of the shot. Jay looked pale. He swayed on his feet.

Danny peeled his shirt over his head and pressed it to Jay's wounds, trying to staunch the flow of blood.

Only then did they turn to stare at the basement door.

Danny wrapped an arm around Jay's waist, and with Jay leaning heavily on him, they turned to go—to run through the back door and down onto the trails they knew so well. Danny was certain they could lose Joshua there if he followed them down the mountain. But before he could move, before they could take a single step toward freedom, they heard a scream from below, deep behind the basement door. A scream and a curse. Then *bam, bam, bam,* three shots echoed through the house. Both Danny and Jay hunkered low, but the bullets never passed through the walls.

"Fuck!" They heard Joshua cry out, his words suddenly indistinguishable. A moment later, the trapdoor at the back of the house creaked open, then slammed shut again with a bang.

The dogs outside roared. *Bam.* Another shot tore through the night, and Danny heard the dogs retreating. Still howling, still pissed, but fleeing the gunshots. They weren't stupid. They knew when to run and when to stay. And with bullets flying around, now was the time to run.

That's what we should be doing, Danny thought.

But before he could act on that thought, a figure illuminated by another flash of lightning passed outside the kitchen window. It was Joshua, stumbling, silent, running around the corner of the house. He was clutching at his throat, the gun no longer in his hand.

Danny cried out, "The back door isn't locked!"

But it was too late. In a flash of lightning and a boom of angry thunder crashing over the roof like a ton of collapsing bricks, the back door swung open. Joshua stood there, silhouetted against the lightning-slashed sky yet again, his hands still at his throat, his mouth agape, his eyes wide and panicked. Danny stumbled back a step, dragging Jay with him, but Josh didn't come after them. He simply stood there in the doorway staring in. Trembling.

In another strobe of lightning, Danny saw the reason. Joshua's neck was swollen, puffed up like a balloon, the skin turning black already. Two small rivulets of blood dribbled from his throat where George's fangs had inserted the venom. He must have landed on the snake when he tumbled down the stairs!

The venom was shutting off Joshua's air, closing his throat like another trapdoor, sealing the oxygen outside and Josh's thundering heartbeat in.

As lightning seared across the sky yet again, Danny glimpsed wide, frightened eyes and the tip of a swollen black tongue protruding from lips so puffed with poison they had ripped open. Joshua's chest heaved as he fought for breath. He clawed at his throat, a whimper of terror erupting from somewhere inside that horrible bag of blood and venom that circled his neck, tightening, strangling.

Unable to even gasp, Joshua reached out once to Danny. Pleading. But in horror, Danny stepped away, pulling Jay back with him. And in that final understanding, Joshua reeled, then fell. His back arched in a tortuous spasm as he clawed one last time at his throat for air. But it was hopeless. Perhaps even Joshua knew it.

Slowly, as if his life was simply drifting away one airless second at a time, as indeed it was, Joshua's arched spine relaxed. His grasping fingers ceased to dig at his throat, and the eyes, so filled with panic and terror before, grew suddenly empty of all emotion, all fear. All life.

Danny turned away, pressing his face into Jay's chest. Jay's arms came up and held him close. He whispered soft sounds into Danny's ear. Words of love. Words of comfort.

Outside the cabin walls, the storm raged on.

EPILOGUE

THE POTHOLES in the lane had dried out long ago. Danny was once again able to navigate his way along the twisted lane leading up the side of Mount Miguelito, only now he did it in a cute little Ford pickup Jay had bought him, with a matching one for Jay himself, since the Jeep and the old Toyota had gone up in flames on a stormy night a couple of months earlier. It was a night neither of them spoke of very often, and when they did, only in hushed, solemn voices.

But their new life together wasn't always solemn.

Danny and Jay had spent their first Christmas together, shutting down the phones, turning off the TVs and computers, and hunkering down with Carly and Jingles and Lucy and Desi, and even the chickens. They ate themselves into a stupor and made love when the mood took them, which was often.

Jay's wounds from that stormy long-ago night had healed. The scar at the side of his head lay hidden beneath his hair, and his bullet-mangled ear would be hidden as well, just as soon as his hair grew a little longer.

After resolving Danny and Jay's issues with an insane Joshua Stone by biting him in the throat on the night none of the participants would ever forget, poor George the rattlesnake met his own demise from the gun of a startled policeman not twenty minutes after the cop's arrival at the crime scene. Jay couldn't honestly say he was sorry to see the snake go, no matter how much of a help he'd been on the night in question. Danny often said afterward, and always with a grin, that it showed just how unappreciative some people can be.

Danny was working part-time at a Jack in the Box flipping burgers because he didn't want Jay to think he was a slug. When the bar reopened, he would be claiming his new position as bartender, keeping the business in the family, as it were. He had been in training for weeks at home, learning the tricks of the trade and memorizing the recipe for every cocktail under the sun. The cocktails needed to be drunk once they were mixed, so he and Jay had consumed more alcohol than was probably good for them during the last few weeks, but since they were having fun doing it, neither of them worried too much about it.

Danny and Jay continued their long daily hikes up and down the mountain, accompanied by Carly and Jingles, and occasionally the cats too. Desi, as always, rode on Danny's shoulders, perched up there like a crusty old sea captain balanced on the foremast, directing the fleet, while Lucy prissily followed along behind, hating to get her feet dirty.

After the fire, repairs at the bar had moved along nicely. The grand reopening was scheduled for the first of February, and now, a week into the new year, the workers had finally come to place the new neon sign atop the structure.

So there they were, Danny and Jay, on a cool morning in January, standing in the alley while the sign was lifted from the back of a truck by a small crane and positioned atop the bar.

Danny was a little perplexed by the whole operation. The old Clubhouse sign, rendered in ancient neon, had not been damaged in the fire at all.

"I still don't understand," he said for the hundredth time. "What's the point of a new sign?"

And this time, for the very *first* time, his question was answered.

"I decided to change the name of the bar. Ergo, we needed a new sign."

"Ergo your ass. So you changed the *name*?"

"Yes."

"But why? The Clubhouse was a perfectly good name."

Jay's smile could best be described as secretive. "Tough patooties," he said.

Danny blinked. "Tough patooties? What the hell does that mean?"

"Figure it out for yourself."

Danny slipped a hand in Jay's back pocket and squeezed his ass. He lowered his voice to a sultry croon. "I could make you tell me if we were alone."

MY DRAGON, MY KNIGHT

Jay laughed. "Don't I know it! The last time we were alone, you ended up with a new truck!"

Danny smacked his arm. "The truck was your idea. Don't blame it on me. Come on. Tell me. What did you name the bar?"

Jay took his hand. "Come around front and I'll show you."

Shaking his head, Danny let himself be steered to the end of the alley and around the corner of the block to Broadway. There they waited for the light to change before crossing the street.

As soon as they were standing on the opposite sidewalk and were no longer in danger of getting run over by downtown traffic, Jay said, "I love you."

Danny smiled and squeezed Jay's hand. "I love you too. What did you name the bar?"

"Close your eyes."

"What are we, twelve?"

"Close your eyes," Jay said again. So Danny did.

Jay led him by the hand to a spot in the middle of the block directly across the street from the bar. He gripped Danny's shoulders and twisted him around to wherever it was Jay wanted him to be looking.

"You ready?" Jay asked softly.

Danny nodded.

Jay gently rested his hand on the back of Danny's neck and pulled him in close. Breathing his warm breath over Danny's ear, he whispered softly, "Open your eyes."

Danny squinted against the sudden explosion of sunlight beaming down on the city street. The first thing he saw were pigeons wheeling overhead. Somewhere in the distance, a car horn blared. When his vision adjusted to the light, he trained his eyes to the rooftop over the bar. An electrician was still up there working on the new sign, which was hanging in midair just above his head, held aloft by the crane and four steel cables.

When the sign twisted to the proper angle so Danny could read it, he sucked in his breath in surprise. He read the sign again. Then a third time. On the final reading, his eyes misted over.

He clutched Jay's hand, staring wide-eyed at the sparkling new sign. Stepping backward into Jay's arms, which quickly enfolded him, he fought to find his voice. Finally he nodded, and when he did, a tear slid down his cheek.

"It's perfect," he said, his voice ragged with emotion. He swallowed and tried again. "It's absolutely perfect."

The sign read ERNIE'S.

JOHN INMAN has been writing fiction since he was old enough to hold a pencil. He and his partner live in beautiful San Diego, California. Together, they share a passion for theater, books, hiking and biking along the trails and canyons of San Diego or, if the mood strikes, simply kicking back with a beer and a movie. John's advice for anyone who wishes to be a writer? "Set time aside to write every day and do it. Don't be afraid to share what you've written. Feedback is important. When a rejection slip comes in, just tear it up and try again. Keep mailing stuff out. Keep writing and rewriting and then rewrite one more time. Every minute of the struggle is worth it in the end, so don't give up. Ever. Remember that publishers are a lot like lovers. Sometimes you have to look a long time to find the one that's right for you."

E-mail: john492@att.net
Facebook: www.facebook.com/john.inman.79
Website: www.johninmanauthor.com

ACTING UP
JOHN INMAN

It's not easy breaking into show biz. Especially when you aren't exactly loaded with talent. But Malcolm Fox won't let a little thing like that hold him back.

Actually, it isn't the show-business part of his life that bothers him as much as the romantic part—or the lack thereof. At twenty-six, Malcolm has never been in love. He lives in San Diego with his roommate, Beth, another struggling actor, and each of them is just as unsuccessful as the other. While Malcolm toddles off to this audition and that, he ponders the lack of excitement in his life. The lack of purpose. The lack of a man.

Then Beth's brother moves in.

Freshly imported from Missouri of all places, Cory Williams is a towering hunk of muscles and innocence, and Malcolm is gobsmacked by the sexiness of his new roomie from the start. When infatuation enters the picture, Malcolm knows he's *really* in trouble. After all, Cory is *straight*!

At least, that's the general consensus.

www.dreamspinnerpress.com

MY BUSBOY

JOHN INMAN

Robert Johnny just turned thirty, and his life is pretty much in the toilet. His writing career is on the skids. His love life is nonexistent. A stalker is driving him crazy. And his cat is a pain in the ass.

Then Robert orders a chimichanga platter at a neighborhood restaurant, and his life changes—just like that.

Dario Martinez isn't having such a great existence either. He needs money for college. His shoes are falling apart. His boyfriend's a dick. And he has a crap job as a busboy.

Then a stranger orders a chimichanga platter, and suddenly life isn't quite as depressing.

But it's the book in the busboy's back pocket that really gets the ball rolling. For both our heroes. That and the black eye and the forgotten bowl of guacamole. Who knew true love could be so easily ignited or that the flames would spread so quickly?

But when Robert's stalker gets dangerous, our two heroes find a lot more to occupy their time than falling in love. Staying alive might become the new game plan.

www.dreamspinnerpress.com

SCRUDGE & BARLEY, INC.

JOHN INMAN

A classic tale takes off in sexy new directions! Poor Mr. Dickens must be twirling in his grave.

When E.B. Scrudge, putz extraordinaire and all-around numbnuts, is visited by his dead ex on Christmas Eve, he can't imagine how his life could sink any lower. But the three ghostly spirits that come along after are even worse! Good lord, a dyke, a drag queen, and rounding out the trio, a big, hunky bear with nipple rings and a butt plug! What's next?

What's next is a good deal of soul-searching and some hard lessons learned with a dash of redemption thrown in for good measure.

And love too, believe it or not. Love that had been simmering all along at the heart of Scrudge's miserable existence, although he was too selfish to see it—until a trio of holiday beasties pointed his sorry ass in the right direction.

www.dreamspinnerpress.com

JOHN INMAN
SUNSET LAKE

Reverend Brian Lucas has a secret his congregation in the Nine Mile Methodist Church knows nothing about, and he'd really like to keep it that way. But even his earth-shattering secret takes a backseat to what else is happening in his tiny hometown.

Murders usually do that.

Brian's "close friend," Sam, is urging a resolution to their little problem, but Brian's brother, Boyd, the County Sheriff, is more caught up in chasing down a homicidal maniac who is slaughtering little old ladies.

When Brian's secret and Boyd's mystery run into each other head on, and Boyd's fifteen-year-old son, Jesse, gets involved, all hell breaks loose. Then a fourth death comes to terrify the town, and it is Brian who begins to see what is taking place in their little corner of the Corn Belt. But even for a Methodist minister, it will take more than prayer to set it right.

www.dreamspinnerpress.com

JOHN INMAN

TWO PET DICKS

Old friends and business partners, Maitland Carter and Lenny Fritz, may not be the two sharpest pickle forks in the picnic basket, but they have big hearts. And they are just now coming around to the fact that maybe their hearts are caught in a bit of turmoil.

Diving headfirst into a whirlwind of animal mayhem, these two self-proclaimed pet detectives strive to earn a living, reunite a few poor lost creatures with their lonely owners, and hopefully not make complete twits of themselves in the process.

When they stumble onto a confusing crime involving venomous reptiles, which is rather unnerving since they're more accustomed to dealing with misplaced puppy dogs and puddy tats, they take the plunge into becoming real-life crime stoppers.

While they're plunging into that, they're also plunging into love. They just haven't admitted it to each other yet.

www.dreamspinnerpress.com

FOR **MORE** OF THE **BEST GAY ROMANCE**

Dreamspinner Press
dreamspinnerpress.com